AT THE GARDEN'S EDGE, ANNA GLIMPSED JEREMY, WITH A GIRL IN WHITE . . .

She strolled into the garden.

"Oh, Jeremy!" she said with a small cry. "I thought you were sleepwalking."

Jeremy said nothing. The girl said nothing.

Moonlight cast a spell over the blossoms, gray in the darkness like otherworldly blooms. The rich perfume of summer hung in the motionless air. Waves lapped distantly.

Jeremy and the girl walked around the flowerbeds. Her skin was completely pale, framed by long raven hair and set with large, sorrowing eyes that seemed to see nothing and everything.

Anna glanced again at the girl, as if to reassure herself that she had weight, that her body was real. It was Catherine.

Anna backed away, her chest rising and falling jaggedly. She stumbled back, back, out of the garden . . .

Suddenly, a voice spoke in the night.

"Go, GO, get on! Go back to your own bed! Can't you see they shouldn't be disturbed? Can't you see they're in love?"

DEVOTION

DANIEL WESTERLY

PUBLISHED BY POCKET BOOKS NEW YORK

This novel is a work of fiction. Names, characters, places and incidents are either the product of the author's imagination or are used fictitiously. Any resemblance to actual events or locales or persons, living or dead, is entirely coincidental.

Another *Original* publication of POCKET BOOKS

POCKET BOOKS, a division of Simon & Schuster, Inc.
1230 Avenue of the Americas, New York, N.Y. 10020

ISBN 0-671-63175-6

First Pocket Books printing March 1987

10 9 8 7 6 5 4 3 2 1

POCKET and colophon are registered trademarks
of Simon & Schuster, Inc.

Printed in the U.S.A.

For P.A.J.

PART ONE

❧ one ❧

See Catherine in the battered schoolyard, thin and small in the cheap cotton smock, ankle socks down over her heels, fists clenched in fury at her sides, bodiless hair blowing in the breeze that cuts across the brown playing field. A few yards off, a yelping terrier escapes a circle of tormenting boys and races away toward the street and the dilapidated houses.

The boys turned to face Catherine, cheated of their sport by her "You stop that!" cried with such authority that, for an instant, they unquestioningly obeyed. But the command had only come from the *new* girl in school.

Catherine's heart sank: later her father would tell her the terrier could probably have taken care of itself. But to Catherine Dancer all animals were an extension of her own dolls and stuffed toys. They needed care; somebody had to stand up for them. So she squared her shoulders and put on the mantle of her mother's strength, even as the boys began to advance threateningly, brandishing weapons and asking her, "Who do you think you are?"

All action in the schoolyard froze. Other children began to draw closer.

"You can't hit me with those sticks," Catherine said. "It's illegal."

The lead boy considered this, then threw down his branch. "We don't need any sticks," he piped.

3

"You do too, to beat up on helpless puppies!" Catherine cried, anguished anew by the horror of their sadism.

A savage glitter came into the eyes of the boys. The onlookers fell silent as other branches clattered to the packed earth. But just then, from different parts of the crowd of assembled children, sprang two girls of Catherine's age. They took up positions to her left and right.

"You get away, Ned!" one of them cried to the lead boy.

Catherine Dancer stood fierce and spiritual in the center of the circle.

The scene was repeated in kind in the many schools Catherine attended while in tow to the wandering fortunes of her parents. Never staying long enough in one place to make friends, she nevertheless found willing defenders, small squads of children, who, almost spontaneously, would see in her something that must be protected from harm. Brought up traveling, and herself an only child, Catherine never learned the rituals of friendship. Early on, she had tried the straightforward tactic of declaring "Let's be best friends!" to some surprised companion. It was a heartfelt proposal, born of desperation strong enough to overcome the shyness of a little girl forever consigned to be a newcomer—but it failed to have the magic effect Catherine hoped for. And as one outcome of her perpetual condition, Catherine grew to regard friendship as an ideal state; never having possessed any but a shallow measure of it, she dreamed that true friendship would be self-sacrificing, grand, and eternal. As a result, even those who liked her found her unapproachable and difficult, and more than once a brief camaraderie that might have grown into attachment was shattered by some minor infraction of the chivalric rules Catherine swore by. Catherine would weep, and like a jealous lover she would accuse. The first offhand public cruelty would set her off and wreck the delicate structure—she would fail those first tests of resiliency and character which children apply to their peers, in the form of taunts and insults and petty betrayals.

But at night, as she lay on her parents' bed listening to their radio, with her stuffed animals seated in a semicircle at her feet, Catherine would still dream, to the falsetto strains of popular love music, of secret clubs devoted to horses and dogs and nothing else—except maybe spider monkeys, which she admired intensely. She assembled intricate hierarchies of friends, and these in turn, as the music droned on, dissolved into misty visions of simple nobility and vague high deeds. She grew more attached to the disembodied voices of disc jockeys than to any real people in her daily life—mother and father excepted. One especially, a Detroit deejay who conducted humorous conversations with a bear between sets, became her guiding light, and one of the first horrors of Catherine's young life was trying intently to keep his voice clear on the radio of the family wagon during the inevitable migration from Michigan—only to have it crumble into static forever, even as the bear was commenting on the nature and meaning of the Beatles.

This child, like most, had no concept of her parents as personalities, especially as she lacked the discourse with others her age that would have permitted her to make comparisons. What she knew about herself was: I am shy, I am good with numbers, I like animals. What she knew about her family was: we're poor (this especially was hammered into her by the children: her clothes were inferior, she lived in a rented apartment instead of a house, she owned almost no furniture and had a bad old black-and-white TV set), we travel around a lot, there's just the three of us. What she knew about her parents came directly from how they themselves characterized each other.

The other things—private sorrows and doubts—she

could sense. Alice Dancer once had been rather beautiful, and one night Catherine, in the cramped quarters of the motel her parents were temporarily managing, watched her mother let down her hair in front of an old pink vanity. The long, chestnut tresses were already streaked with gray, and as Mom examined her face, a look of near despair came over her. She cast a glance at her husband asleep in a chair. A great stillness, like a heavy suit of invisible armor, weighted her limbs. Catherine felt the lost hope in her mother, and it stabbed her coldly.

In the family photo album, a book Catherine often opened in her lap because it reassured her of continuity through all the changes of scene, young Mark Dancer was well dressed, with sharp glinting eyes and an open smile. A graduate of Colgate, he had begun with a large packaged-goods firm in what is now called marketing but was then known bluntly as "sales." Possessed of a simple, clean personality that quickly won the trust of strangers, and featuring a quick wit and strong memory for faces, phone numbers, and above all jokes, he raked in good and growing commissions until the onset of depressive episodes soon after Catherine's birth. Inexplicably, the sharp eyes became dotlike and empty; the golden smile became weak and apologetic, and the forthright bearing wilted into a half shamble. There was no drinking, nor—as Alice had at first feared—any other woman. And there was also absolutely nothing Alice could do. The very bones of Mark Dancer became melancholic. Once, in their favorite restaurant, toward the end of the time when they could afford such places, Alice watched Mark lift a napkin from the table and open it on his lap. He performed the simple act with such drained and dreamlike ennui that she ran to the powder room and sobbed.

There was no question of Mark's keeping his job. His performance ratings plummeted. Even when the depression was not upon him—and these periods grew increasingly rare—he was not the same man. The memory had weakened, and the will to please, to get across, to close the deal, which is the essence of the will to sell, failed him. For a while he was taken out of the field and given a desk job. But the office gave him terrors: the coldly furnished rooms and the breezy, perfunctory smiles of his coworkers confused him. He had become odd, and he was let go with great regret by the superiors who had once so cheerfully lunched with him.

Alice herself was trapped in the condition of wordly incompetence that once held many women. She had her beauty, and that beauty had won her the affection of a promising young man. Her own family were lower-middle class, her father working as a shipping supervisor in an industrial, upstate New York town not far from Mark's college. Given enough time, Alice would no doubt have learned secretarial skills and made her way in the world. But instead she met Mark Dancer, was courted by him, and languished hopefully at home until the magic moment when he slipped the diamond ring upon her finger and her future was sealed.

Before, the variability and continual growth of Mark's income had combined to discourage the learning of money management. Now the stark facts of no money, and a husband too depressed to interview successfully, began to have their impact. At last, Alice was forced to sell the house, in which they had but small equity, and try to find work for herself. She hated, however, the idea of leaving her baby daughter at home with Mark. And she almost as badly disliked the very idea of her husband dragging around the house without the stimulation and effort that were necessary, so the doctors said, if Mark were to forestall deterioration. So when she chanced upon a Help Wanted ad seeking a couple to manage a motel, she inquired.

The responsibility for the motel devolved completely on Alice, and the truth was that she began to become hardened. They were let go the first time, and the second job, also at a motel, lasted only nine months before business dwindled to the shut-down point. The family moved five times in six years, and with every year Alice grew tougher. When the work and the stress and the struggling to make the finances work out overcame her, she saw her husband's condition as mere laziness. She resented the medical expenses and the costly drugs Mark required, and there were arguments.

When these broke out, Catherine would subside into terror and then muster the courage to intervene, weeping torrentially and begging her parents to make peace. Even hard words and looks wounded Catherine, and one side effect was that it became extremely difficult to discipline her. One day when Catherine was nine, she committed a major infraction: pilfering her mother's wedding china, she served dinner to her stuffed animals. It was a frenzy of disobedience: there was a baking spree which produced a slaglike "cake," an attack on the liquor cabinet for cocktails, and the appropriation of jewelry as party favors. But though she may have been motivated in part by willful naughtiness, Catherine was mainly caught up in the qualities of the perfect hostess, possessed by genuine anxieties that the event go well. All the while, her brain stored plans of returning everything to its proper place, but in the end, when the bears, monkeys, and other creatures had been luxuriously feted on the sacred plate and crystal, Catherine tumbled into childish exhaustion and was found amid the debris of her multiple transgressions.

The parents went into conference.

"She has to be spanked," Alice declared to her husband. "And you have to do it."

Once upon a time, Alice Dancer would never have dared such direct orders. But necessity had made them a habit. The veil that covered Mark Dancer's eyes parted and he registered pain. Alice steeled herself and poured forth persuasion, cajoling, and threats.

Adversity had beat her into a harridan. And for another truth, the real Alice Dancer, very much a woman of another generation, would gladly have given the fingers of both hands to be anything else—to cook and do for the dashing, grinning young man she had married; to raise his children and defer to his judgment; to be loved and cared for and submissive in an agreeable and decorous fashion. But that was over for good.

She talked him into it.

Catherine was awakened from her après-party stupor by two horrible stern faces, and her fate was announced in condemning tones that would have wrenched the heart of any girl. The oversensitive Catherine nearly swooned.

Then came the long march from her bedroom, the scene of the crime, to the small living room. Alice, in a gesture of confidence—and also because, for all her demands for discipline, she held her daughter more precious, more full of hope, than anything in her now-bleak world—retired to the only other compartment, the bedroom she shared with her husband.

From beyond the door came piteous, imploring sounds, and then the inevitable whacks. Each made Alice wince. Sympathetic tears crawled into her eyes.

At last the door opened, and the evildoer trudged in to say "I'm sorry." After her came Mark. Both were haggard and pale, almost in shock.

The aftermath was appalling. Catherine cried for nights on end and could not eat. Normally a physically robust and energetic child, albeit given to long stretches of odd contemplative silence, she was now afflicted with listlessness. Mark could barely look at her, and seemed tormented with a ridiculously profound guilt. The next time Catherine did wrong—letting the bathtub overflow, mesmerized by the rising water and then falling into it in a last-ditch attempt to prevent the flood—Alice could not bring herself to suggest spanking.

So Alice beat Catherine's animals. So strong was the little girl's empathy that this hurt her intensely. She shrieked for mercy for her stuffed toys, her high-pitched voice charged with anguish and even outrage. For *she* had committed the crime; neither the bear nor the monkey had let the tub run or fallen in. As for Alice, she felt the strange justice of these protests and at the same time realized that these Gestapo hostage techniques were all that remained if her daughter were to grow up straight, proud, and well behaved.

For the entire duration of her brief life, Catherine would retain her literal interpretation of the imaginative, the figurative, the symbolic. One of her most acute disappointments came out of a dream in which a terrible dragon had been rampaging through the countryside, stamping out the cars that roared nightly down the highway that streamed past the motel. At first Catherine, like everyone else, had simply run around in circles shrieking. But Catherine, it turned out, had been chosen by a man from Mars to save the day. The Martian presented her with a ray gun of incalculable power, and with it Catherine zapped the dragon like swatting a fly. At the conclusion of the dream, she took her well-deserved rest, setting the ray gun on her night table and sinking into sleep.

Upon wakening into the real world, she reached at once for her powerful gift. It was gone. A bitter, bitter disappointment.

And much earlier, at the age of six or seven, Catherine had been sent off to see a summer play for children at a nearby high school. During the play she was given instructions on whistling, which she mastered. But the play itself concerned a ballerina who, at the climax of the drama, was awarded a pair of red toe shoes imbued with magic powers. Accepting them with radiant joy, the ballerina cast off the slippers she had worn through the earlier part of the story. These were multicolored satin, a motley of cunning patchwork to suggest genteel poverty, and the ballerina flung them offstage in a broad gesture.

Catherine thought: *Those are nice shoes! I'll take them! Don't throw them away!*

The conclusion of the play was lost on her. She hungered for the patchwork shoes, despised by everyone but really very fine to her. While the audience dispersed, Catherine clung to the walls and, when the hall was empty, crept to the stage. Her heart thumping, she delved behind the curtains stage right and searched for the beautiful slippers.

She never found them, and finally decided that some equally discerning but more clever scavenger had struck first.

For all the confusion, loss, and loneliness of Catherine's childhood, she came to look back on those early years as a time of peace and contentment. During the three years of junior high, she attended two schools in two towns and managed to remain as friendless as it was possible for a beautiful young girl to be.

And Catherine had become beautiful. Her hair was long and black, her complexion translucent and miraculously clear, as if her body were free of the grosser matter that caused her coevals to break out in pimples. Her breasts were her principal agony: they refused to grow; and although at first Catherine panicked at the early budding on her chest, she panicked in a different way when later the budding failed to bloom. She developed only the mild but distinct curves, both of bust and hip, that in a mature woman are regarded as elegant—but which in post-grade-school culture were simply inadequate to win attention.

There was also the problem of height. Although Catherine would finish sprouting in the first year of high school, ending her growth as a young woman of considerably less than normal height, she took up much of that growth early. In brief, she was tall and skinny and shy, a figure of fun—all the more so because she was so easy to get a rise out of. See Catherine as she was: a remote, doe-eyed girl, tall and thin, standing alone at the edge of the chattering crowds that waited for the bus to take them home at the end of the day, touchy to the point that no one cared to bother with her except those who needed to score points for themselves by mocking her poor clothes and awkward motions. Beneath the touchiness dwelt a strain of intensely proud resolve. Catherine would not, could not, enter the world of taunts and abuses. Would not give back what she got, or defend herself in any way other than the adoption of a martyred expression not unmixed with a holy contempt for the baseness of her schoolmates.

The world seemed hopelessly *coarse* to Catherine Dancer. Boys leered at breasts and flipped skirts; girls compared their bodies and whispered dank secrets of the flesh, or dwelt endlessly on clothes and pop musicians. It was all very revolting to Catherine.

Yet she had no other entertainments to fill the place of this low-class socializing. Her mother and father, anxious about her isolation—and blaming themselves —encouraged her to read, hoping to be spared the sight of their daughter staring out the window at the highway or moping lifelessly around the motel.

Catherine tried to read, but novels drove her mad, with their accounts of young-adult embarrassments and tawdry successes. What history books had to tell her seemed nothing more than a rehearsal of endless cruelties, wars and seizures of power. Biographies were an exception, especially the inspirational type designed to build young characters by the presentation of noble examples. As for television, it made her recoil, especially the brutality of cartoons.

She was, to see her in the negative light of her peers, holier-than-thou and next door to simpering. The only influence that saved her from really being as she was perceived was that of her mother. Alice Dancer's resiliency—it could not be called genuine strength of character any more than a suit of armor could be called strength of body—had bred in Catherine an an inner staying power. This power in Catherine showed itself as a hatred of injustice, of which the childhood scene of outrage and pity for the terrier was an early example.

Despite her rejection of the coarseness of the fledgling humans she was forced to mingle with in school, Catherine was subject to overwhelming attacks of identification when one of these classmates was being needlessly hounded. Unable to stoop to her own defense, she would flare into righteous anger at the corridor spectacle of a younger boy being pushed around by tougher specimens. Then Catherine Dancer's heart burst forward in anger, and she became a figure of pure accusation, trembling with rage in the hallway, pointing her finger—and creating a moment of still awe for the young onlookers. This earned for her a measure of respect that saved her from sinking to the very lowest levels of the eighth-grade social order.

Always, as Catherine lay in bed, in a room not so different from the rooms for rent in the rest of the motel, there was the sound of the highway. She fell asleep to the roar of vehicles approaching, reaching a crescendo, and then fading into nothing. In the dead of night or in the off-season, the cars and trucks would come infrequently, and the sound of each was exquisitely solitary.

When Catherine was in her junior year of high school, Alice and Mark Dancer tried a new form of employment. The family had made its way across the Midwest to New Hampshire and down the coast to a motel in Long Island. There, from one of the black maids who came in every two weeks to help with the heavy cleaning, Catherine's mother learned of an open position with a wealthy family. Domestic help, it seemed, had become increasingly difficult to obtain, and in this case the need was for a couple to act as cook and groundskeeper on an estate on the North Shore.

If someone had suggested to Alice Dancer, in better days, that she would one day apply for work as a servant, she would no doubt have laughed. But it had come to a point where she was thoroughly disgusted with a life of tending to identical, numbered rooms and the revolting couples who used them, often only for a few hours at a go. The latest motel, in particular, nestled on a stretch of road dotted with bars and dance spots, was little more than a do-it-yourself brothel. Alice would come in to make up beds in the morning and find signs of dope and heavy drinking, mirrors pulled from walls and arranged next to stained mattresses. Everything was suggestive of the dreariest carnality.

It is time to tell of the effect this kind of thing had on Catherine. That Catherine was still in possession of her virginity was no oddity. But what usually comes to every girl—dreams of embraces and of passion—came to Catherine in a different way. Throughout her youth she was surrounded by the nocturnal, and midafternoon, bustlings of fornicators.

As a little girl she merely knew that *something* was up. Many guests, signing in two by two, had about them a sly and furtive aspect that any child instantly recognizes as the badge of imminent wrongdoing. In the parking lot, whispered conferences. In the lobby, hushed agreements about names. And even in the absence of these precautions, a certain lush and tipsy abandon seasoned with guilt. No luggage. A double bed they asked for, always. The register, which Catherine would often examine on the sleepless nights when she wandered in her stocking feet, was always aswarm with improbably common Anglo-Saxon names.

Above all, the noises. There were nights when

Catherine felt hemmed all around by banshees, coyotes, men at hard labor, and dying women. Even for the experienced, it requires a great act of the imagination to credit pleasure, much less any spiritual soaring, to the grunts and wails of the act of darkness. To Catherine these were the sounds of torture, and it amazed her that otherwise seemingly normal families would *ever* check into a motel: didn't they know it was a madhouse?

So to Catherine's mind the places where she lived had two starkly polar uses: as homes-away-from-home for pleasant or irritable, but always tired, wayfarers; and as hideaways for the utterly demented and sadistic.

One day at school she sat blearily at a table in the cafeteria. A lull in the conversation led to the yawning question: "Why *do* you look so awful today, Cathy?"

"I couldn't sleep last night," she answered. "The motel was jammed. They make so much *noise.*"

This comment won a big round of laughs, and Catherine, knowing instinctively now what type of laughter it was, blushed to the roots, setting off another wave of howling.

In this way Catherine Dancer came to know that the screamers and grunters who filled the night were engaged in the very activities that were the subjects of her classmates' dank secrets—this was what the ogling of breasts and the flipping of skirts presaged: shrieks and moans in close impersonal rooms whose soullessness Catherine knew only too well.

All children have heard, from time immemorial, the sounds of their parents making love. These noises—the squeaking of jointed furniture, the twanging of springs—are without doubt the primitive origin of the creaking boards and clanging chains that are the stock-in-trade of ghostly literature. But to Catherine these sounds had been multiplied, all the nights of her conscious life, a dozenfold. And to apprehend in one awful moment that this was the end and consummation of the relation of boy and girl was, to her, a sudden horror.

All the more so because Catherine's early dreams of idyllic friendship, of a roundtable of perfect and heroic amity, had naturally matured into a vision of perfect love between the sexes. She saw a pure ideal—and not just for a moment. It was no mere glimpse, not a fleeting image, but a steady, true, and burning flame within the now-somewhat-less-flat breast of Catherine Dancer.

For a while, because it was close to one half of her nature—that withdrawn, all-negating side that came from her father—she had flirted with the poignancy of eternal aloneness. Having been forced into the bad deal of boredom and friendlessness by her nature and circumstances, she made a solipsistic stab at erecting a cathedral out of her misfortune.

That paled quickly enough. Increasingly, from just offscreen, a boy began to intrude upon Catherine's fantasy scenes. He began as a lost animal character desperately in need of help. But by stages he was transformed into a young man of haughty but sympathetic bearing, more saving than saved.

Can anyone describe this imagined young man? He had grown high in spirit, not through lucky breaks and a snappy personality, but in the crucible of suffering, as Catherine believed all good human beings must. She had read wondrous, awful things about the plagues of the Middle Ages in a book, and her dreamboat had, she told herself, lost everything—family, lands, friends—in the confusion of that epidemic. He was not an errant knight, but an erring one: he had sunk to banditry. Why, he was scarcely better than a criminal in the eyes of the world! Then he met Catherine. The story went sixteen ways from that point; but the main idea was that she—Catherine—brought him not merely back to the path of nice behavior, but to ever-more-astounding heights of heroism. For her sake.

The radio played and Catherine dreamed. She spun the knob of that old Zenith, snatching the rising tones wherever she could find them, and, lacking the love songs she wanted most, making do with anything, anything.

❧ two ❧

So at last the Dancers became domestics. Catherine's mother was full of trepidation; once proud and hopeful, she was still very far from voluntary obsequiousness. It happened as a result that she hit on just the right note with her prospective employers.

The Penn estate was large—"sweeping" was the word that came to Alice Dancer's mind as she and her carefully briefed husband were shown in (through the front door, thank God) to an interview with Mrs. Randall Penn.

The estate itself occupied some ten acres on the North Shore, "sweeping" down to a marshy stretch of Oyster Bay. It was all there: separate servants' house, guest house, pool and bathhouse, private pier. No yacht was moored, but Alice expected one to cruise up at any moment, bedecked with laughing, sun-ripened offspring of the privileged.

The house itself was not at all what Alice had expected. She had prepared herself for a true seignorial mansion. But from the outside the place seemed simply an overgrown, wood-sided residence of the rural, upper-middle-class sort.

And on the inside, no lavish furniture, no French Impressionists—simply airy design, a great deal of light, and a great deal of space. It would only be after months in the Penns' employ that Alice would realize that this family—though in a markedly different way from her own—was without any real home: they owned residences in Palm Beach and in Ireland, and a beach house in Southampton, as well as a yacht, the *Wayfarer*, that did quite nicely in the Mediterranean. This vast demesne, though certainly no smaller than the others, served mainly as a kind of "summer house"—and hence its studied and expensive casualness, with an almost seedy patio that just happened to offer a view of territory the annual tax on which, alone, would have easily provided for Alice's family four times over.

Alice had small idea that there was no real competition for the job. She and her husband were well spoken and sober seeming. Alice could talk food without returning overmuch to potatoes and roasts, and Mark, for a moment brightening into the salesman again, was both respectful and vibrant. When Mr. Penn happened to trundle by, Mark rose and offered his hand manfully.

Mrs. Penn had a musical voice and struck Alice as a frustrated opera singer—an image she would soon lose. And if she had known more about the physical type of the opera singer, the impression would never have formed in the first place; Elizabeth Penn was tennis-slim and taut, with a smart face weathered slightly by too much sun, tan to a fault. The brief glimpse of her husband Randall was the very picture of the grouchy but immensely easeful patrician, tall and silvering.

Mrs. Penn showed Alice the servants' house, which was located not far from the main residence, just across the car park and up a steep driveway. In the big garage were lodged a Bentley and a Jaguar, both dusty. "The sports car is our son's," Mrs. Penn explained. "He's off at school."

The screened-in porch was like that of a true summer house, a bit battered, and stacked with firewood and old magazines. Even before they had climbed the stoop, Mrs. Penn began apologizing for the state of the place; and when they finally entered, Alice understood why.

Inside, it was a shambles. The living-room walls were grimy, the carpeting filthy, the furniture sagging and worn. Alice's heart sank, but Mrs. Penn quickly assured her that everything would be fixed up. "Our previous caretakers were positive drunkards," she huffed. "Why we kept them so long, God only knows. But we finally had enough. They've only been gone a month, so we've had no chance to make the place presentable."

The bedrooms, though—the bedrooms offered views of the bay. Not of a parking lot, not of a highway, but of glistening water, wintered trees, and a shoreline broken here and there by mansions. Alice turned from the window to Mark, and he nodded.

For Catherine it was final, wrenching displacement —this time in her next-to-last year of high school. Her acquaintances had always been few, but now she would graduate with strangers. Still, she adored the peace and quiet of the setting; within a few months she had the local animals literally eating out of her hand. In this pacific neighborhood, the squirrels, rabbits, and birds knew no human predators and were disposed to trust anyone who would feed them.

At almost all times, Catherine had free run of the estate. The Penns were often at their other residences; and although Oyster Bay was purportedly their home, she came to realize that for the Penns, "home" was a sentimental concept proper only to the lower classes. Catherine found this offensive: she had always longed for a fixed place to call home—one without highway travelers, at least—and learning that this longing might be looked down upon as merely middle-class was disturbing.

But the fact was that she hardly ever saw the Penns. The house, though never really shut down, was never completely open either—except when the whole family was present. For the most part, Catherine's mother changed linens that had never been slept in, dusted furniture touched by no human hands other than her own, and vacuumed carpets trod on by no one else. When the Penns did return, it was often on short notice, as if a fit of pique had driven them from Eire or the South. The family numbered three, as did Catherine's. But instead of a daughter, the Penns boasted a son, often spoken of but never seen. His name was Jeremy, and he was off at preparatory school in New England, some hatchery of future presidents and chief executive officers. Mrs. Penn, the doting mother, suffered from the perennial afternoon ennui of the unemployed—wealthy or otherwise—and continually interrupted Alice Dancer's chores to regale her with news of her son's achievements, including weight gains and haircuts. The impressionable Alice Dancer, naively glad to be made privy to the inner life of the elite, invariably conveyed these revelations at the dinner table. Catherine dubbed Jeremy Penn "Wonder Boy" and fed her squirrels.

Spring does give way to summer, however, and though spring may engender in a young person's fancy thoughts of love, summer provides the opportunity: no school.

The Penn estate included, of course, a swimming pool, which was a rather old-fashioned affair. It was in wretched condition when the Dancers arrived, but Mark threw himself into cleaning the mechanisms and repainting. With summer came heat, and although the stony beaches of the North Shore were not far off, the pool was nearer yet. And so the Dancers began to poach upon the domain of their employers, first sitting by the pool on hot days and then sliding into it. Having put so much work into it gave the family, if not a sense of ownership, then at least one of participation. Besides, no Penn had ever been observed in the pool, and the Dancers had grown accustomed to the use of such facilities as one of the few perquisites of being motel managers.

The pool is where Jeremy met Catherine.

The girl swam her heart out, slashing through the cool blue water, enjoying the luxury of a setting in which aloneness *was* a luxury: one's *own* swimming pool. She had come, all in all, to regard herself as the proper mistress of the whole estate. The animals, to her simple way of thinking, were the true owners of the acreage. And they came to her. Who was there all the time? She, not the Penns. Who tended the flower gardens and boxwood gardens? She and her father. Who cut the hedges, down by the perpetually flowing natural fountain? Her father. They, the Dancers, were the makers and keepers. The Penns were only visitors who occupied from time to time the rather overlarge dwelling with the best view.

But even that view was Catherine's. In the spring she sat on the patio and did her homework, gazing over the bay. In the summer she lounged.

Catherine avoided the sun. Her complexion was fair, and she was vain about it. Though she did too often regard herself as an outcast, she was not blind. She was good-looking and knew it. Not "cute," for sure, but fair and dark-haired and lissome. She sometimes formed futures in which she was a model, but she knew what models had to do. *They* were sluts.

So it was in the shade that Jeremy found her. It was in the shade that she was discovered by the boy, and her first impulse was flight. She could have been famous for fleeing if she had ever stayed in one place long enough to gain renown for anything.

Remember your first dance, Catherine? Seventh grade. You set your teeth and decided to go. You made anxious preparations, brushing your hair so much you had to wash it again and start all over. All your clothes were so pitifully tacky that you broke down weeping in that motel bedroom, with your mother holding out a blouse and crying in dismay: "It's a lovely blouse, Catherine!" It *was* a lovely blouse, Catherine: you had a few good things. Alice Dancer saw to that. She remembered what it was like to be a girl: that old dread never fades; those embarrassments are never forgotten.

But you wept anyway. Your father, very worried, drove you to the school and asked, "Cathy baby, will you be all right?" And you almost stepped out without a word. At the last minute, though, you turned and gave him a kiss, because he needed you so badly and you could not bear to sting any heart.

You were ridiculously early, as if you might not be admitted if you came past the appointed hour of seven. The deejay was just finishing his setup, and he smiled down at you from his bandless bandstand which bore the call letters of his very local station. You were in awe: a living disc jockey of the sacred airwaves. Amused, he invited you up, doubly insistent when he saw how shy you were.

All those singles! The disc jockey laughed in the clear, pure tones of a voice trained for the public. But you were never good at interpreting laughter, and so excused yourself. You clicked across the gymnasium floor and hid in the girls' room, head spinning, ready to do the tears routine again. Girls began to float in, and you heard their harsh, high words outside your chosen stall. You thought they might speak of you— you knew them, popular creatures without scruples, almost lacking souls. They spoke knowingly of mascara and males, as boys talked of cars and warfare. You knew nothing. Then the music began.

Picking a moment when the tiled room was clear, you crept out. There was cigarette smoke in the air, forbidden, and that hurried your exit lest you be associated with it by the teachers who chaperoned.

The gymnasium enveloped you. They were dancing. The big room, with its basketball nets folded back, was a mass of bodies, and they were stomping their feet.

You knew the music, knew the words, but had never associated them with this primitive rite. The rhythm that had driven you upward drove these bodies wild, fueled by nothing more than soda pop and backbeat.

You, Catherine, you hung back by the deejay stand. The deejay was now deep into his act, Olympian and unapproachable, but still you felt safer in his shadow. A homeroom acquaintance lurched out of the swelling crowd and leaned against the wall beside you. She had seemed like a nice girl to you, but now she was breathing hard and grinning blankly.

"You should try it!" she said. "All you have to do is feel the music and go stomp stomp stomp! My mother sent me to dance class, but I'm telling you, Cathy, all you have to do is go stomp stomp stomp in time to the music!"

Then she plunged back into the crowd, breathless and glad. *Stomp, stomp, stomp,* you thought. The music, a galaxy louder than you had ever heard it on the radio, throbbed around you.

A boy asked you to dance. He was a rather weasely character, and if you had known anything, you would have known how hard he had worked to muster the courage to ask such a blooming wallflower to stomp along with him. You nearly said no, and then you meekly said okay, as if that moment were the sacrifice of chivalry, nobility, and eternal romance to the squalid.

You stomped your feet in time to the tunes, trampling out the vineyards where the grapes of love were stored. A sheen of sweat glistened on every half-seen face, and when the song was done you hurried off.

Off to empty hallways transformed by dimmed lights into mystery places. The lockers stretched anonymously down the corridors.

You fled.

. . . And so when Catherine was lying in the poolside shade, protecting her fair complexion under the branches of a tree restored to long life by the ministrations of her father, and Jeremy Penn made his debut into her world, her first impulse was flight. She was seventeen, but the reflexes of the twelve-year-old were still alive.

First, she had been caught in the act. Caught *stealing* the pool, because who could this self-assured young man be but Wonder Boy? Second, it *was* a boy, and the whole thing of boys and bathing suits was, if anything, worse than boys in other settings. One was so close to naked in a bathing suit. The nylon clung to the space between the legs, clung to the breasts and curves. And on the boys, it was obscene. Catherine averted her eyes, most of the time, from the anatomy so starkly outlined between the thighs of the opposite sex. Part of her could scarcely believe a civilized society permitted such obvious displays of gender. Nudity itself was just an increment more blatant, and in a way more pure.

But Wonder Boy only gave her a nod, threw his towel on a deck chair, and leaped into the turquoise with a giant splash. He churned the water professionally, without warming up, at top speed, flip-turning smoothly.

My chance to slip away, Catherine thought.

She gathered up her book and towel and rose slowly. But just then Jeremy came to a stop and said: "No, stay. Stay," and returned to his laps.

Catherine hesitated. Since moving to the big estate, she had always been uncertain of her status, wondering if she herself were part of the domestic crew the Penns had hired. Always obedient to her mother, Catherine often helped out with the chores, changing sheets and chopping vegetables in the main house's kitchen when the Penns had to be fed. But she always stayed out of sight, and thought of herself not as an employee but as her mother's helper.

Jeremy heaved out of the water and toweled his head.

"Don't feel shy about using the pool," he said. "Hell, you're here more than any of us, right?"

He put out his hand, and Catherine shook it. The hand was still damp, but warm. They exchanged introductions, and at his invitation she returned to her lounge, feeling the quick travel of his eyes over her body.

"You blush more than anyone I've ever met," he said. "That's three times now. Four times! Don't blush again, please. You'll get your circulation in an uproar. I just meant to say that it's unusual. Most people only blush when they make fools of themselves. You seem to do it like breathing."

Catherine felt another blush coming and tried to suppress it—anything to turn the conversation away from herself.

"You swam awfully well," she said.

"That? That wasn't swimming. That was floating. What're you reading there? Fantasy, huh? Does it have dragons?"

"It's mainly about dragons, actually."

"Any been vanquished yet?"

"I think the dragons are going to turn out to be good in the end. One got killed, and it was sort of sad."

"Well, if you breathe fire you're bound to be unpopular. You don't play tennis, do you?"

"I'm afraid not. Badminton."

"Don't apologize. Badminton can be fierce. Those little Pakistanis are intense."

Catherine loathed sports. Her badminton game, far from being fierce, was the dancing of a sober-faced sprite. She wondered what Pakistanis had to do with it.

She looked at Jeremy, really looked at him, for the first time. He was tall. His eyes were black and deep, driving out the whites. His hair was raven too, like hers, lank and thin. His legs were muscular and long, but around the chest he was stocky, smooth. As he sat in the deck chair, towel draped over his lap, his eyes focused far off, and he was so motionless he seemed to have been switched off.

"You'll never get a tan sitting in the shade," he said.

"I don't want a tan."

I don't play tennis, Catherine thought. *I don't want a tan. I'm a freak.*

From the pool they could look out over the bay. Sailboats. Jeremy regarded them longingly.

"Have you been down to the boat house?" he asked. "It's a total wreck."

"I know. My father wonders what the last caretaker did with his time."

"Is he going to paint it? Do you want to go down there?"

Catherine froze.

"Come on," Jeremy said, slinging his towel around his neck and springing up. He laughed.

"I've really got to—" she began.

"Bad excuse, bad excuse. Here." He held up her little rubber pool slippers. "Let's examine the ruins."

Catherine complied, and they slipped through the pool-area gate. She glanced back at her house. The kitchen window looked out across the estate, and she worried, for no particular reason, that her mother might be watching. Possibly this kind of fraternization was a no-no. Jeremy continued on ahead. He was a swimmer, but he had the uneasy grace of a boxer, and a middleweight's taut, explosive biceps. His posture was slightly stooped, and this reinforced the boxer image: as he walked he seemed almost to be wading into a fight, ready to fend off blows.

"He says—my father says it's past painting now. The boat house, I mean. The wood's all rotten."

"Let's check out the pier first."

A small cabaña with what must once have been changing or storage rooms stood at the foot of the long, narrow pier. The building was in complete decay: the bare wood had blackened and the roof gaped with big holes. The pier was in somewhat better shape, extending a hundred feet or so into the bay. The tide was out, the waves rippling four yards below.

"What's it like in Ireland?" Catherine asked.

27

"Green. Then wet for a long time. Then green again."

Jeremy slowed down, Catherine walked ahead. Then suddenly, sure he was looking at her, she spun around.

"Five times," Jeremy said.

On the way back, Catherine conversed easily. Whenever Jeremy spoke, the words poured forth with an intensity inappropriate to the subject matter, as if he were talking about death and eternity when he was actually telling of tennis and school. From time to time he glanced around, as if taking in sights and scenes half remembered. At those moments an ironic grin appeared, charged with melancholy around the eyes. Always he seemed ready to do battle; the blows, maybe for a long time, had never come, and the fighting reflex had dimmed, become modeled into this irony.

Catherine realized very little of all this. To her he seemed to act and move as if he had never encountered resistance. This was her mental picture of wealthy, prep-school boys, and by comparison she felt as if she were struggling through glue. She felt . . . older, even though she knew that Jeremy had a full year on her and was due to enroll at Yale in the fall. His face was boyish, and when he laughed, he lit up like a child, only to fall into his button-eyed stillness again.

At the parking circle they parted company, he turning left to the big house, she right and up the slope to the servants' quarters. She saw a face watching from the kitchen window as she climbed. It was her mother.

✣ three ✣

The pitiful truth: Catherine was already in love. Those twenty minutes with Jeremy were the best time she had ever had with a boy. She admired the way he leaned against things. He was polite and had a way of making fun of her without causing her to panic. She sensed that he wanted her to make fun of him too, so she tried to think of quips as she lay in bed that night.

She giggled and fell still, giggled and fell still, rehearsing her comments into her palm and then declaring aloud that she could never say *that*. The night wore on, and the stillness settled, Catherine staring up at the ceiling with wide eyes like polished gray stones, dreaming about an actual flesh-and-blood, nonfictional boy.

In Jeremy's eighteen years of life, he had encountered plenty of resistance and more than enough woe. He was the *step*son of Randall Penn, the offspring of Mrs. Penn's first marriage to an insurance agent of undoubted salesmanship, Arthur Stocker by name. Arthur Stocker had two giant flaws: he was an alcoholic and a whoremaster. He had married Elizabeth, a company stenographer, in the throes of an acute sentimentalism that proved only long-lived enough to get him down the aisle and halfway through the honeymoon. They wed in mid-October; he was goosing waitresses by Halloween. Stocker had risen quickly in the firm due to a bond of friendship between himself and the boss's eldest son, a man of no talents whatsoever, but also a whoremaster and an alcoholic. They had fun together. They disappeared for days on end. It all ended with a drunken fight—not a disagreement, but a scene of windmilling incompetent fists—and Stocker was out one job. Another acute attack of sentimentalism followed, and he vanished for an entire month, reestablishing contact only to demand a divorce.

Jeremy was eighteen months old.

Elizabeth, his mother, was a Catholic of the old school, but finally she acknowledged the increasingly hostile demands of her apostate husband and gave him his walking papers. For herself, she piously insisted she could never remarry. She was a good secretary, and her experience with Stocker gave her the practical gift of contempt for reliance on the support of others: she became coolly capable and dedicated to her work.

Jeremy grew up as what is now called a "latch-key child." After he began the second grade, no one made his breakfast, no one was home to let him in when he returned from school. For the record, home was an apartment building in a section of Queens where the local residents had had a mass of public housing foisted on them, bringing an influx of dreaded Negroes and other low-class types. The boy learned how to fight: first, make a fist with your thumb *outside,* jerk! Second, when threatened, aggress relentlessly: your opponent is most likely a coward; third, look tough and no one will mess with you in the first place. He lacked the weight, but he had the speed, and there were things he was mad about: no smirking greaser would torture *him* for the amusement of a dipshit girlfriend. The only reward was that he often made friends with the boys he vanquished. He was not a loner.

Against the grain of this savage *demimonde* was Mother and her demands on him. Jeremy took piano lessons and attended to his homework. He was blessed in a broken-down music teacher who fathomed his wants. The old Czech gave him simple, intense pieces, and Jeremy squeezed joy out of hammering on the keys, to the neighbors' grief.

Then came the big change. Randall Penn, not Elizabeth's boss, but working only one floor above at the investment firm that bore his family name, took notice of the handsome, standoffish woman who worked so well for one of the junior partners. Years of celibacy had passed for Jeremy's mother, and although she would abandon the stricter tenets of her religion to marry the millionaire, she believed firmly that her fortitude and uprightness during the long, lonely intervening years had earned her the prize.

So at the age of thirteen Jeremy was catapulted into another existence entirely. Randall Penn wanted to take advantage of his new bride, who was so actively making up for a decade of self-denial. Jeremy was packed off to boarding school. He had the glum expectation of suffering through complete ostracism at this exclusive institution, but his fate was better. A model of Colonial-style order on its sweet acres, the school possessed a classic bully. Jeremy sized the boy up in the second week. He was large, lumbering, deep-voiced, and gifted with an unnatural, bearlike strength. Jeremy had learned how to fight from swift, lean black boys. It was a story of might versus quickness, and it ended with the bully groaning on the playing field.

Besides, Jeremy had learned more than combat; he had learned camouflage. He was quick with fists, quick with language. He had mastered, perhaps with the aid of his father's salesman genes, the art of falling into a milieu and seeming to belong. He had made pals with many an adversary, and in his part of Queens, that meant familiarity with as many idioms. Prep school was just another set of codes, and he picked them up fast.

Now on vacations he went here and there, seeing places. He saw Ireland and Palm Beach as a matter of course. By and large, the *Wayfarer* was a less frequent treat, being reserved for intimate times between Mom and "Dad"; but he managed to take in fair stretches of Greek Islands, Sardinia, Majorca, and the Côte d'Azur. Like the true salesman, the traveling salesman, he was at home everywhere and nowhere.

It would be handy to say that Jeremy had inherited his father's taste in women, which had been the only catholic thing about the man. But this was not so. Wealth had accorded Jeremy a not inconsiderable status among girls, and although he had come to realize that there was just one truly all right guy for every hundred, no matter what the trust fund, he was not about to knock the instant privilege. But for him the one-in-a-hundred rule seemed only to work for the male sex: he had yet to meet even a single female he could pass two comfortable hours with.

Jeremy Penn—*né* Stocker—found a kindred spirit in Catherine. They washed the old black Jaguar, which had once been his stepfather's, and drove aimlessly around Long Island, playing the radio and wasting gas. Jeremy refurbished his Sunfish, and they went sailing. Certainly he was not in love with her, but felt a bond of friendship growing; and although Catherine's emotions were stronger, she was deeply at ease with the slow pace of things. They held hands, he kissed her on the cheek once or twice, but there were none of the embraces and grapplings, the mere thought of which threw her into a panic.

Jeremy's summer had been planned in advance, including a brief passage on the *Wayfarer*, but he proceeded to unplan it. Pressured by school chums, he left Long Island only to join them for an archeological hike in Central America. When he returned, he took more joy out of telling Catherine about it than he had from the trip itself. As they stood on the pier under the stars on the night of his homecoming, he spoke with a greater ardor, and Catherine thought: *He is beginning to love me.*

The season passed with dizzy speed, and by the end of July Jeremy realized he had fallen, and told Catherine so. He kissed her on the mouth and his embrace was fierce and Catherine did not mind.

The only smudge on her otherwise stainless happiness that summer was her mother. Mark Dancer was perhaps only a little dismayed that another man was vying for his daughter's hitherto exclusive affections. But Alice Dancer took a fierce interest in Jeremy. From the first day, when she had seen her daughter walking and talking with him from the kitchen window, she urged Catherine on, nurturing a desperate hope that she might marry the boy. She raided the family's meager savings to buy Catherine's hot-weather frocks and beachwear. She fretted over the girl's shyness and reticence, and far from worrying about her susceptibility to sexual advances, she feared her daughter might be all too robust in the defense of her virginity.

Every night she quizzed Catherine about the day's activities, and every morning sounded her out, with decreasing tact, on the previous night's adventures. It was plain to her that Catherine was infatuated with Jeremy, but the boy's physical coolness caused her anxiety: Where was the kissing? Where were the heated attempts at fondling—first base, second base, and all that?

Catherine came to hate those interrogations. They were demeaning, not only to herself, but to her love for Jeremy—and also, she thought, to her mother. The woman was tough, and had also, in this delicate matter, grown callous.

Still, Catherine was obedient by reflex. She possessed little of the rebellious spirit that so often fevers adolescence and had grown accustomed to relying on her mother's judgment. Her father was a gentle man,

and her times with him, straightforward and affection-
ate and a little sad, were good. But he was ineffectual,
and Catherine sensed as much. It was Alice who had
really ran the motels, and if not for her efforts, they
would still be living by the highway.

So Catherine told her mother everything. To the
girl, each detail was rich and fine, and she wished
devoutly for a more sensitive confidante, someone
whose eyes would not narrow shrewdly at each mention of a sign of attachment, who would not say "yes,
yes, go on. Then what?" in such a penetrating, cold
way. Someone who would not confuse her with impossible advice, and disturb her with insinuations of
abnormality. Someone who would encourage her and
give her sweet hope, rather than press her to be
forward; that was not in Catherine's nature.

The morning when Catherine told her mother that
Jeremy had said the magic words "I love you," the
mother clapped her hands in triumph. That night Alice
Dancer sat in her bedroom and got quietly drunk,
exulting and planning. It could actually *happen*. It was
possible. Elizabeth Penn herself had been nothing but
a secretary, and look at her now; *she* couldn't possibly
object to the marriage. Pouring herself shot after shot,
Alice imagined obstacles and tore them down. She
would have this for her daughter, come hell or high
water.

Her principal agony was the thought that autumn
would bring separation, with Jeremy going off to New
Haven. A *coeducational* school. The boy was still so
young, and the hope that his love for Catherine would
last four years—or grow so strong that they would wed
as undergraduates—seemed farfetched to the more
rational part of her mind.

But it was not the rational part that held sway on this
topic. It was the much larger portion of Alice Dancer's
spirit, a caldron of frustrated dreams, degrading priva-
tions, and steely resentments. That part clung with
powerful tenacity to the idea of Catherine in white and

Jeremy in morning coat. When her husband crept into bed with her at the close of her night of drunkenness, she poured out her vision to him.

"Come on, Alice," he said. "They're just kids. They've got years ahead of them. He'll go off to college and she'll go back to school, and who knows what'll happen after that?"

These were the very words Alice least wanted to hear. She reacted violently, and that night her husband made his bed on the couch.

August came and went in a mist of romance. Jeremy grew more lustful, but Catherine's love for him imbued their urges, in her own mind, with a halo of fatal passion. Thinking about sex was one thing, she discovered, but when it was really happening to you close up, it was a different thing altogether. You couldn't get around it, over it, or under it. It wasn't an activity; it was a presence. She let him undress her partially and caress her, and one night he took off all his clothes, and she held his rampant sex in her hand, amazed by it—and even more amazed when, after a few light touches, it spurted hot white jets onto her naked breasts.

Yet when September came, Catherine was still a virgin.

The Penns were in Oyster Bay so intermittently that it had been easy to hide their affair from them, which both Jeremy and Catherine had decided was wisest, for her parents' sake. But Jeremy's mother and stepfather dutifully returned from a stay in Vermont to take their son to the airport and see him off. Catherine had to say her good-byes the night before.

She would have let him take her that night, but it was all too depressing. Jeremy promised he would drive down weekends, and she made him vow to write to her constantly. She had a consuming desire to receive love letters, and even hoped for poetry.

* * *

Will it be too sad, too brutal and mean, to tell that there was no poetry, that Jeremy drove down less and less frequently, and that soon Catherine was phoning him more often than he her? It was all true, however. Jeremy became profoundly immersed in college life. Between studying and swim practice and the demands of his numerous friends—weekend parties and football games—he began to lose track of Catherine Dancer. Gradually his communications stopped referring to their summer, and grew packed with data about his new life. Phone conversations became awkward and difficult, and often, when Catherine dialed his dormitory, she got the sense that she was being given the runaround by Jeremy's roommates.

Alice Dancer literally tore her hair, thinning a patch at the back of her head with nervous plucking. As for Catherine, she began suffering chronic aches and pains that sometimes debilitated her to the point where attendance at school was a torture. As for school itself, Catherine was completely uninterested, unable to concentrate or work.

Her father was the first to suggest that Catherine might really be ill. He was worried about his daughter's loss of appetite; she had lost a shocking amount of weight and had begun to walk slowly and painfully, as if treading barefoot on broken glass.

Catherine visited a local doctor who gave her a checkup and took routine samples. But when Alice told him, briefly, the story of Jeremy, he nodded and smiled paternally. He took Catherine aside and told her about time, youth, and the future, and sternly ordered her to eat three square meals a day. The blood and urine tests would come back in a week.

In the meantime, Alice Dancer was seized by an inspiration. She dictated a letter to Catherine in which the girl wrote telling Jeremy of her illness. Three days later, Jeremy called and said he was driving down immediately. Alice set her daughter up in bed, with flowers all around, and cleaned the bedroom minutely.

It was only then, with Catherine propped up in bed, pale but happily expectant in the artfully dressed sickroom scene, that Alice realized how truly wasted the girl looked. The effect was too strong, she feared, and touched some blusher onto Catherine's cheeks.

The visit went perfectly. Catherine became radiant as Jeremy drove into the parking area. She hopped up and down at the window, and her mother had to persuade her to return to bed instead of running down to greet him. "Look sick," Alice commanded. Catherine let herself go limp, and suddenly felt overcome by authentic exhaustion after her eager wait.

Jeremy was dutiful, properly contrite, deeply concerned, even—as mother and daughter agreed later—loving. He kissed Catherine more than once and held her hand during the two solid hours they spent together. Of course, he brought flowers, and even books, magazines, and a record.

Alice hovered outside the door, in transports of pleasure. There was no helping it, though. Jeremy had to leave that night. He had a meet the next day, and needed his sleep. Catherine, truly weak, tottered to the window and watched him drive off.

On Monday the tests came back. There were more tests after that and a week at the hospital for observation, and by early December medical science had determined that Catherine Dancer was dying.

Catherine did not need medical science to tell her. She never *was* told, not in so many words. But in the house everything changed. Her father became infinitely solicitous, and her mother grew crazed. She herself could barely muster the strength, most of the time, to make it to the bathroom, and this brought, as Christmas neared, occasional humiliations.

At other times, though, Catherine's strength was boundless. Boundless, driven by pain. This was her symptom: agony that flowed from the bones and superheated the body into an inferno, choking her, mottling and flushing her complexion, picking her up and chewing on her with blunt, grinding teeth. And then casting her down again, as if losing interest.

Alice simply refused to believe that Catherine would not recover. Her contempt for doctors became a regular feature of her conversation. She laughed when she talked about doctors, and it was not a lovely laugh.

The mirrors were removed from Catherine's bedroom. Her parents told her it was because she threw herself around when the pain attacked. But she knew the real reason: she was growing ugly. Her face was thin and haggard, and her lips, dry and leathery, had pulled back from her gums. Every morning she found swatches of hair on her pillow. Her hands were like rakes, her elbows knobbed and purplish.

She wrote constantly to Jeremy except on days when she lost control of her fine-muscle coordination. But always now she wrote what her mother dictated. She had recovered from her illness, the letters said. She was enjoying school. There were intimations of other boys, to pique Jeremy's jealousy and prove Catherine's worth.

Inwardly, Catherine longed to tell Jeremy the truth, in the hope that he would come to her and sit by her bedside, smile at her and hold her hand as he had that one afternoon that now seemed so far in the past.

But when she implored her mother to end the lies, Alice only hissed: "Do you want him to see you like this?" and then begged Catherine's forgiveness, kneeling hysterically.

Alice lived in terror that Jeremy might pay an unexpected visit. It was her plan to keep Catherine out of sight until she was over this rough patch, this lingering but ultimately powerless disease that had transformed her daughter from beautiful, raven-haired child to wasted, sunken-eyed crone. So when Jeremy called to say that he would have to spend Christmas with his parents in Palm Beach, Alice was relieved. By spring vacation, Catherine would surely be well again.

Catherine had a Christmas tree in her bedroom, and there the family passed Christmas morning. Catherine had never received so many presents. The ones her mother gave were appalling: bouncy skirts and blouses that hung on her with miserable looseness—"You'll fill out again," Alice said—and a tennis racket. Catherine could not hold the tennis racket out at arm's length: it was too heavy for her. Jeremy sent a big, funny hand-puppet, a rabbit with wonderfully soft white fur that was made in Switzerland and which Alice declared must have cost fifty dollars.

Alice worked to disguise Catherine's illness from the Penns. When the Mrs. commented that she hadn't seen the girl in months, Alice asserted that Catherine was studying hard to improve her grades so she could get into a fine college.

Catherine, of course, was not studying at all. She had begun her senior year, but her days of debilitation had come more and more frequently. She developed a pattern of falling asleep in class that earned her considerable derision from her schoolmates and teachers, and finally, one afternoon, she simply collapsed in a hallway when a fight broke out near her locker.

Catherine had always had an anxious fear of falling behind in school, even when she was well. She tried to keep up while bedridden, getting homework assignments from a well-brought-up girl in her homeroom, who was received downstairs by Alice and never allowed to actually see the recipient of the papers.

Alice encouraged Catherine to study hard. She had sent for applications and filled them out herself. At the top of the stack was Yale; the others were all in the vicinity of New Haven. Proximity was the only criterion. The local high school had no provisions for administering finals to a pupil outside of the building, but Alice stormed into the principal's office and raised hell. Provisions were made, and a substitute teacher was sent to the Dancers' home to proctor the first-semester exams.

The pain came midway through European history. The teacher did not know what to do: she had never seen a teenage girl claw at her own body and grovel at baseboards; she had never heard a seventeen-year-old beg God to end her torment with merciful death.

Catherine could not, of course, even begin the second semester. She passed part of January back in the hospital, where efforts were directed, not so much at finding a cure—hers was one of the many deteriorative afflictions for which none was known—but at developing the best mix of medications for the management of Catherine's pain. To be a specialist in Catherine's disease was to be a specialist in pain.

Yet the analgesics Catherine took did not begin to touch the core of her suffering. On the contrary, it seemed to her, at times, that the drugs killed everything *but* the pain. They dulled her mind and her senses, but the agony still grinned at her with its sharp red teeth, as if to taunt: "I am invincible. You may destroy the whole world, but I will remain."

She began to think of it as *he,* and even gave him a name: the Wolf. She talked to the Wolf as he prowled around her, snarling and foaming. She pleaded silently with him—and when he attacked, she begged aloud.

It was a good thing for Alice Dancer's furtive plans that Catherine was not given to screaming. When the seizures came, they were accompanied by a constriction of the lungs and throat that crushed her pleas into a coarse whisper. Catherine's mother, ever ready, prepared a thin mattress which she judged would cover the one window in Catherine's bedroom nicely, should the girl begin at any time to emit louder noises that might reach the ears of the Penns in the main house.

It was a winter of heavy snows that cushioned all sound. From her bed, Catherine could watch the flakes fall, the drifts gather. Her room was always hot, and she lay beneath a thin, ultra-light comforter; anything heavier pressed achingly on her nerve endings. Catherine's father had purchased for her a cassette player and an assortment of cartridges. The walls were covered with gay pictures he had clipped from magazines.

With trembling hands, Catherine loaded folk songs or soft rock into her music machine.

And waited for the Wolf.

One week in late February, Jeremy phoned to say he would be coming down to visit, but Catherine never even learned of the call. Her mother told the freshman that Catherine was on a school trip, but perhaps some other time . . .

In March Catherine suffered a massive seizure in the middle of the night, starting suddenly from her shallow sleep. Her parents were awakened by an irregular, loud thudding and ran to the bedroom, where they found Catherine hurling herself against the walls, rolling on the floor, toppling chairs, and thrashing wild-eyed into her white desk. Only at dawn did the Wolf let her go and skulk back into his forest.

The next day she found she could no longer see clearly. Space began to break up into large, unsteady lozenges, the bright pictures no longer coherent, the titles on the cassettes no longer readable. Her father traveled to libraries—Alice would not permit him to use the local one for this purpose—in order to find large-type books. But soon even these became impossible for Catherine.

The Penns were at home the night of the all-night seizure, and Mrs. Penn inquired about the loud thudding noises. An animal had crept into the house, Alice Dancer briskly explained, a raccoon. Perhaps it had climbed in through the attic. In any event, the family had spent the whole night trying to corral the clever creature. "You should have seen us!" she laughed. "Me with the broom, Mark with a blanket, and Catherine yelling her head off!"

The mattress went up over the window. And Catherine's father carted in a dozen other mattresses. Except for the bed, every piece of furniture was removed from Catherine's room. Mark laid down a thick wall-to-wall carpet with triple layers of padding underneath, and then proceeded to affix the mattresses to the walls to make a kind of wainscoting. He draped and tacked padding over Catherine's headboard and wrapped the legs of the bed in rags. He installed a swivel wall lamp high above Catherine's pillows, with a switch that dangled down conveniently. Finally, he swathed the cassette player in padding and set it on end beside the bed, so that it was within reach, the cassettes heaped nearby in a soft wicker basket. The speakers he placed beneath the bed itself. The sound was oddly muffled as a result, but there was no helping it: he didn't want Catherine to get tangled up in the wires. On the floor at the other side of the bed lay a rubber kitchen mat on which rested Catherine's pills and her plastic water cup. When Mark came in to read to Catherine, as he did often now, he brought a chair with him.

It was in this dim, padded, cavelike cell that Jeremy Penn found his wasted Catherine.

❧ four ❧

Catherine's only connection with outside time was the little wristwatch she wore. At the other end of the spectrum, she knew the month, but the date and day of the week were often lost to her. She had stopped thinking in the old sense. For long hours she simply drifted, letting the same cassette play over and over again, her thin arms draped over the comforter, sitting up in bed. Meals would have broken up the monotony if she had had any appetite, but food was sawdust and mud in her mouth. Her father talked to her for whole days at a time, Saturdays and Sundays, when he told her how he was painting the pier and how the old cabañas had been torn down and how the new flower gardens around the main house would look. Other days she was at the mercy of her mother, who tried to force food down her throat and spoke incessantly of Jeremy and the stupidity of doctors. Catherine listened and nodded weakly, having lost all power to resist. "Yes," she whispered, "someday Jeremy and I will be married."

One afternoon in April the monotony ended forever.

It happened exactly as Alice Dancer had feared: Jeremy drove down from New Haven without advance notice. Alice's plotting had succeeded in a way she had never imagined. The succession of empty, carefree letters she had dictated was so devoid of Catherine's

43

simple intensity of sentiment that Jeremy began to suspect her love for him was fading. A sophisticated college man, he had been carrying that love around in his pocket: it was one of his assets. When he thought good thoughts—pure, noble, that kind of thing—they were invariably about Catherine. But he thought that way only intermittently, and like the *soi-disant* Christian who never prays, goes to church, or shows charity, his love for Catherine became a kind of basic but undemanding personal myth.

Then the tone of Catherine's letters began to change. They grew shallow and almost shrilly playful, and they did mention other boys. The clincher came when direct contact with Catherine was frustrated by her mother. "No, she'll be out of town this weekend," and even "I'm afraid she can't come to the phone."

Jeremy felt betrayed and stupid by turns. He realized that he had neglected the only thing that really mattered to him. Sure, he had gone out with other girls, and even slept with two—but he was no longer happy about those girls or proud of those conquests. Now unreachable, Catherine began to haunt his dreams again.

Catherine had become an expert in probability. Though the frequency of the Wolf's attacks increased constantly, the current average was every thirty hours or so. And although it was possible for two or three days to pass without a seizure, every minute beyond thirty hours meant that a world of blinding, obliterating pain was imminent. Three days without was a low-probability event; only one out of every ten intervals would be that long. A two-day interval had a twenty-five percent probability, and so on. Likewise, it was possible to suffer two seizures nearly back to back, although that was a rare occurrence. Sometimes Catherine wondered what the chances of a triple attack would be; she doubted she could survive that parade.

She had always been good with numbers, and now—reduced to weak, tender bones, balding and cronelike, seeing the world through a dull prism of halfblindness—she reckoned chances and constructed inaccurate tables on the visits of the Wolf.

On the day when the monotony ended, Catherine had gone fifty-two hours and counting. A cassette droned on and on. A female vocalist crooned about love forlorn, lulling her into the drowsy stupor in which she negotiated her peace with the more daily, routine pain that never went away.

Then from downstairs she heard a voice call out "Catherine!"

She sat bolt upright. She switched off the music with a flipperlike slap.

No, no, it was a dream, she thought.

Then again: "Catherine! If you won't come down to see me, I'm coming up there!"

"Jeremy!" Catherine cried in her now-reedy and childish voice.

"Shut up, Catherine!" Alice Dancer's voice commanded.

"I knew she was here," she heard Jeremy say below. "Catherine, do you want to see me or don't you!"

"Yes! Yes!"

A change of tone came over Jeremy's words: "Mrs. Dancer, what is all this? Is my mother making you do this? Why *can't* I see her?"

Catherine threw off her comforter and tottered to her feet, a thin creature in a flowered flannel nightgown. She staggered to the door—and fell, thudding almost inaudibly into the pillowy carpeting. But then she let out a wail so fraught with misery and longing and desolation that the voices downstairs fell silent.

"I'm going up, Mrs. Dancer," Jeremy said. "Don't try and stop me!"

"Mark, do something!"

"Jeremy, boy, there's a reason—"

Footsteps on the stairs. Suddenly it occurred to

Catherine with an overwhelming violence: *I'm ugly. He shouldn't see me this way. Mom was right. She's always right. He'll see me and he'll be sick.*

But there was no lock to lock the door, and no place to hide, even if Catherine had had the energy. Instead she crawled to the side of the bed and pulled the comforter down over herself and lay on the floor.

The door burst open. Jeremy stalled in midemotion, gazing with confusion around the strangely padded room. Moving slowly and dreamily, he approached the heap of comforter beside the bed and folded back the covers, which fell away quickly from Catherine's feeble grip.

Catherine hid her moist face, too exhausted even to sob, but feeling and thinking the sobs she could not express. She felt Jeremy's hands slipping under her, and she was being lifted, lifted up from the floor and lowered gently to the sheets.

She crushed a pillow to her face, but Jeremy took it from her. She shut her eyes, not wanting to see his expression. But finally, she could bear the suspense no longer. She had to look at him one last time, for memory's sake, even though she could make out his features only dimly.

There were traces of horror and dismay in Jeremy. His lips were pressed tight and pale. The cords of his neck bulged tautly. In a way, Catherine was amazed to see how unchanged he was, an emissary from a world she had forgotten existed, a world where some things actually grew better, brighter, and stronger with time.

His dark hair was cut shorter now, and brushed back. He wore a tweed sportcoat and a tie . . . and . . . a shirt . . . and his eyes were dark. . . .

His warm hands steadied her, leaned her back against the headboard.

"Catherine," he said.

"I'm dying, Jeremy," she said. "Isn't it too bad?"

* * *

It is to the eternal credit of Jeremy Penn—if in fact there is such a thing as eternal credit, and not just an account stamped "closed"—that he stayed with Catherine. Stayed, not just for the afternoon or the week, but every day as long as days remained. If he had not tried to stay even beyond that dark limit, there would be less to tell.

Jeremy did the following: he told his mother and stepfather about himself and Catherine, and of his intention not to return to Yale until the next fall—knowing, as Mark and Catherine Dancer knew, that there would be no Catherine by September. Further, he wrung from the Penns permission to install Catherine in their beach house in Southampton and "borrowed" funds to make the necessary adjustment to one room.

The work was completed quickly, with weighty overtime premiums, and Catherine moved from the dark, stuffy chamber in Oyster Bay to a place of light. The room in Southampton was padded too, but professionally, in an overall quilting of soft blue. Two large windows overlooked the ocean, protected by a few widely spaced padded bars. It was a second-floor room—the Penns' beach residence was no shack—and the view was of dunes, beach, and water. Catherine could scarcely make out the scene, except as a band of pale yellow, a band of dark blue, and a band of sky, but she woke and slept to the crashing of waves.

The pain grew nearly continuous.

As for Alice, she lived in paradise, certain that a walk down the aisle would come soon, perhaps even before Catherine was well again. If soon, then a bedside ceremony. . . .

Mark Dancer commuted the two hours from Southampton to Oyster Bay every morning and kept up the improvements on the estate. At night he slept in one of the beach-house guest rooms, convinced his wife had gone mad.

Jeremy stayed in the room next to Catherine's. But

he was not all devotion and attention, despite his extraordinary efforts. His dutifulness was composed of love but also of pity and a kind of self-punishment. He quickly divined that Catherine was agitated by the presence of her mother and assumed even the most menial tasks associated with the sickbed. Many of those were distasteful to Jeremy and embarrassing, at first, for Catherine. But she came to accept him even as she had come to accept the prospect of death, even as she had come, having no recourse, to accept the Wolf.

The pain never slunk more than a few paces off now. Intervals and probabilities meant nothing: the Wolf attacked at will, and the doctors from Southampton Hospital, having medicated Catherine to the verge of overdose, could do nothing more to allay the suffering.

Even Jeremy could have no effect there. When the Wolf leaped and began on her with his rending fangs, the world snuffed out and a tempest of agony swallowed Catherine. But when she emerged from the storm to find herself, sweat-soaked, in Jeremy's arms, she tasted helpless bliss.

No, he was not all devotion and attention. At times, he was overcome by an overwhelming boredom. He read to Catherine by day and lay awake by night, waiting for the next seizure. Dark circles formed under his eyes, and he grew haggard and shambling, as if the disease had communicated its wasting effects. He thought of his lost season at college and his new friends there, none of whom were close enough to share his troubles. It would be good, good as life itself, to sit in their favorite pub and lift a few. It would be good to break training, to laugh. But his commitment to Catherine had been forged; they were chains, and he felt their weight and drag—but they were self-made chains, and that, he told himself, meant they were no chains at all.

One compensation, likewise, was no compensation

at all: Catherine was growing more beautiful. It was not a return to her former beauty: her youth had vanished forever. But unrelenting torture had transfigured her physically. She took on a translucence, an ethereal glow that was the incandescence of a self-consuming thing. Her eyes became enormous and perpetually woeful, her smiles childishly simple. When she succumbed to her torments, she was like a saint in ecstasies—or would have been, if not for the dreadful screaming that had begun, at last, to force itself from her constricted lungs.

When the screams became never-ending, Jeremy began to break down. *"Please God, please! Kill me! Let me die!"* The screams and the sound of Catherine wandering her room, possessed by the demonic energy of her pain, convulsing on the floor, thudding dully into the padded walls.

Jeremy moved in with her. Together they spent sleepless nights—he flattened into a cardboard figure devoid of feeling or thought, she a raving animal knowing nothing.

Alice Dancer began, for the first time, to have doubts. She chewed her fingers to the bloody quick. Mark drank until he could no longer make his commute. The parents stalked the elegant beach house, blinking away the brilliant spring sunlight that poured through the glass walls. They collided into each other wordlessly, like automatons, each deep in a private world of retreat.

Upstairs, Jeremy and Catherine, in a tormented pietà. Add sound effects: the screams, the pleadings, the questions shrieked at heaven by the girl, whispered softly by the boy. Add sensations: the weightless, clammy body in his arms writhing against the jolts, bones protruding through the flannel nightgown. Add smells: the cold, high stink of death biding its time, vomit, blood from the nostrils and the corners of the eyes, sickly-sweet breath, incontinent urine.

One morning at dawn, Catherine smiled a smile of blood. Blood coated her teeth. Jeremy kissed her on the lips, and his own came away red as he told her he would have to leave for a few hours. Catherine heard the Jaguar roar away and thought: *He is never coming back.*

See the room through Catherine's eyes. It is bare and blue. The walls and the floor merge in a blue that shifts as a hundred cells of space shift and adjust. The windows are two shapeless holes carved from the walls, and the motion of the sea, white-capped in a rising wind, is barely discernible from the adjustments of the planes of space itself.

The knobless door, a simple outline, opens inward and a figure appears. It is tall and dark-haired and Catherine recognizes it as Jeremy.

"You came back," she whispers.

The figure draws closer, slowly. Jeremy is carrying a pitcher in his hand and a small red sack in the other.

"I sent your parents to the movies," he says.

"They never go to the movies," Catherine says.

"I made them. I told them they were driving us crazy. I told them we wanted to be alone for a while."

"I bet Mom loved that."

"They were off like a shot. She dragged him away."

"I guess I don't have to tell you what she wants."

Jeremy spills the red sack onto the comforter. Red spills out; he crumples the clear plastic bag and casts it aside.

"I'll marry you," he says. "This'll be it, then."

"Jeremy," Catherine says. "Come closer so I can see you."

He leans nearer. The sun is setting, and he has not turned on the lights. She read his eyes.

"What are they?" Catherine asks, touching the red pills.

"Don't worry about that."

"Will they—is it over?"

"It's over, Catherine. Is it all right? You asked a thousand times. Did you mean it?"

Catherine nods. "It isn't wrong?"

"You'll have to eat a handful. Can you do it?"

"Yes. I can eat if I have to."

"With the medication you're already on, it won't take many."

"Will you hold me?"

She sees him heft a handful to his own mouth, and before she can reach out with her feeble arm, he has washed the pills down with a cup of water poured from the pitcher.

"No, Jeremy!"

"Forget it," he says. He holds out a second handful. "Aren't you coming along, Catherine? You don't want me to go by myself, do you?"

"Jeremy, quick! Stick your finger down your throat!"

Jeremy laughs. He holds out the pills.

"Here," he says. "I'll feed them to you two at a time. That isn't too fast?"

"Jeremy," Catherine pleads. "What's happening?"

"Here," he says. "Have some. That's right. Now drink. Now some more. Now drink. Now it's my turn."

"You're not really having any, are you? You're just pretending."

"That's right. I'm just pretending." He eats another handful.

"I should leave a note. For Daddy at least, a note."

"There's nothing to write with, Catherine."

"He'll be so sad."

"I think he'll understand."

"You tell him, then, won't you? Tell him I love him, and—I can't think. You'll know. You'll tell him."

"I'll tell him."

"And Mom. Tell her too?"

"Of course, Catherine. Can you swallow some more? Now drink."

Soon all the pills are gone. Jeremy lies down next to Catherine on the bed. Almost as an afterthought, he gets in under the covers.

"Hold me, Jeremy?"

"I am."

"I can barely feel you. I can barely feel anything. Where . . . where are we going?"

❧ five ❧

The nurse valved off the IV and reached out to hold back the doubled fists of the young resident. The resident shrugged her off angrily and raised his fists high again, pounding them down on the bared, pale chest. A thud sounded through the night ER. The resident glowered from side to side, sweat streaming into his eyes.

The nurse flicked off the oxygen. She began pulling free the esophagus tube.

The resident held up his fists again with a grimace of unholy determination. Behind him they were already wheeling the other one away, silent forever under her white sheet.

A voice said, "It's all over, doctor."

The resident spun from the table with a bitten-off curse.

"Stupid, impetuous—idiot."

He sank onto a bench, glaring fixedly at the stretcher. Somebody threw him a towel and he mopped his face, loosened the top button of his tunic. The respirator and the stomach pump were carted away. The EKG was moved.

In the center of the bare room lay the body.

The orderly returned. The nurse drew the sheet over the face, first brushing the dark hair back from the brow. Lips pursed in a silent whistle, his everyday graveyard whistle, the orderly spun the stretcher and wheeled it off.

A raw silence descended over the ER, broken irritatingly by the crying of a child. The resident swallowed his defeat.

In a corner, one nurse said to another, "That boy must have loved her very much." They both thought for a moment, knowing it was not love that had triumphed that night. The girl had been doomed, with never a doubt. But the boy who had always come with her, holding her hand and telling her jokes, that boy had taken a fall. It was a greedy night for Death.

The resident stood up.

"Bring in that brat with the broken arm," he said with a smart clap of the hands. "Let's get moving."

It was a small hospital, a short push and a quick elevator drop for the orderly and his cargo. In the tiny morgue, company waited in a shadowed, clean room lined with steel sinks, cabinets, and autopsy tables. The attendant wheeled the new arrival beside the old. They made a pair: a large, husky form lying near a slim, small one, both covered with sheets, like furniture in a vacant house.

The orderly stepped out briskly. For a while his face lingered outside the pane of the morgue door as he smoked a cigarette. He peered in with a melancholy gaze.

"What a total waste," he said philosophically, loud enough to reach the unreachable ears of the girl and boy within. Giving a fingertip salute, the orderly vanished from the little square of glass, and a stillness almost as deep as the grave settled over the spare, dim room.

On one wall of the morgue, a clock ticked monotonously. A fly buzzed across the room. Underneath one of the sheets a figure stirred, faintly at first, as if dreaming a troubled dream.

Jeremy threw off his sheet.

He opened his eyes drunkenly. Sleep was still clinging to him like the mud of a white bog. Groggily, he took in his surroundings.

He was in a room filled with soft, fluorescent twilight and blurry white forms.

Jeremy sat up. He felt bad. His left side throbbed with numbness but at the same time ached. With an effort, he swung his legs over the edge of the bed.

What is this place? he wondered.

Wincing, he got to his feet, crumpling the bed-clothes absently behind him. He limped toward the doors. It seemed strange to him that they were made of stainless steel. He felt his left shoe dragging on the floor. Mechanically, he buttoned his shirt and pushed out into the unfamiliar corridor.

The hall was filled with sharp, medicinal smells. Jeremy could hear the low humming of machinery. He sighed exhaustedly.

As he turned a corner, Jeremy saw another door ahead. Through its small window he could make out lights shifting against darkness. Swaying heavily, he drew closer.

He opened the door and found himself standing on a flight of steps overlooking a floodlit parking lot.

Swallowing back the awful taste in his mouth, Jeremy blinked at the lights. Fresh air washed over him, and he sucked in lungfuls of it.

I am incredibly drunk, he decided with a crooked smile. *And I don't know* where *the hell I am.*

Just then Jeremy felt a hand on his arm. He gave a little startled jump and glanced over his shoulder with wide, bleary eyes.

A mottled face gazed back at him, stricken with awe. Jeremy felt the other man's fear surge into his own body.

He lurched away, almost losing his balance.

"Now wait a second," Jeremy said in a slurred voice. "What exactly . . . is it . . . that we . . . are afraid of?" He glanced at the other man's clothes. He was wearing a white uniform with a name tag that read CORSO. "Mr. Corso, what is it? Tell me, please."

"You're alive," the orderly rasped.

Jeremy held up a finger.

"Very perceptive, very good," he said.

Then suddenly he felt himself swimming upward toward consciousness.

Without a word, Jeremy grew rigid. His features stiffened into a mask. The corners of his mouth turned down. His eyes swiveled like a Kabuki actor's.

One floor above, in the night ER, the resident and the nurses froze. A cry seared through the room. It was a cry that would never leave their memories, not in a lifetime of hearing cries.

"Catherine!"

PART TWO

a decade later

❧ six ❧

If I sign the contract, Anna thought, I will be wealthy
. . . and doomed.

She sat dejectedly in the shifting flicker of the
crowded, candlelit room, her attention distracted by
three naked men in the pool. Beyond the french
windows and down a brief flight of marble stairs, the
lighted pool was a classic rectangle of dreamy turquoise flanked by Ionic columns and shrubbery, with a
view of moonlit Tuscan landscapes further on.

The poolside area was almost entirely deserted;
most of the partyers were too debilitated, at this late
hour, to swim. But in the bright amniotic waters, the
three men—doll-like forms from Anna's vantage—
busied themselves in a world of their own. One lay
floating on his back while the other two worked on
him, one passionately kissing his lips, the other me-
thodically sucking the length of his erect staff.

For a moment Anna thought one of the participants
might be Jean-Louis. The idea came in a wave of
dismay—the whole day had been, really, one tidal
wave of dismay—but then she chided herself. Jean was
too disciplined to make such a spectacle of himself,
and no man on earth, she suspected, was more thoroughly heterosexual. No, Jean-Louis had only two
passions: women like herself . . . and the buying and
selling of human beings.

"I buy and sell people." That was the way he had described it himself, that first evening seven months ago. They had met backstage after the final curtain of a particularly rabid but compelling production of *Othello* on Broadway—she with a little mob of bored and wealthy young friends, he there alone, paying his compliments to the Desdemona, whom she later learned had been a lover of his in the days before maturity had eroded the perfections of her figure and the radiance of her features.

The steel-gray hair, the tall stature, almost too muscular and intense to be aristocratic—she remembered her first impressions with photographic accuracy. He wore an expression of ironic nostalgia as he stepped from the room with the star on the door, but it drifted away like a mist. He smiled brilliantly, and it was that smile, profoundly self-confident, vigorous, and young, that fell upon Anna. Impossibly, this superficially aging but essentially ageless man strode directly to her and, amid the clutter of props and ropes, said:

"Dali wrote that an artist should only smoke hashish four times in his life. I think the same thing could be said for falling in love. After four times, it becomes too difficult to believe. I am right?"

Anna, twenty-three years old, told him that he was. She had become accustomed to the cavalier absurdities of actors—which included phony speeches and other bits of routine—and Jean's manner struck her as only mildly odd, tinged with unidentifiable foreign accents.

"I am Jean-Louis Colombe," he said, extending a warm, gentle handshake. "Are you with these people in any inseparable way?"

Anna had half a mind to be abrupt in the face of this smooth but shameless pickup attempt. She had, it was true, fallen in love more than four times, but she still believed, if not in the permanence of that condition, then at least in its rituals. The group of five of which she was a part had fallen respectfully still.

"I'm afraid I am," she said softly. She told Colombe
that they were waiting in the hope of being admitted
into the presence of the great black actor who had
portrayed the jealousy-maddened general. Apparently, however, he was exhausted from the exertions of
his role, and their chances were slim, despite the fact
that the father of one of them was an underwriting
angel of the production.

"As am I," Colombe said, with a glance at the door
through which he had just passed. "For Desdemona's
sake."

Surprised, Anna shifted gears rapidly, and just then
her date, a well-mannered young man, stepped forward to introduce himself to "Monsieur Colombe." It
seemed her friends were all highly aware of this man's
identity and repute. Later, after he had invited them
all to a gathering in his suite, she was told that, far
from being a mere actor, he was *Jean-Louis Colombe*
—hadn't Anna heard of him?

The gathering at the Plaza was so infinitely dull that
no quantity of champagne could enliven it, perhaps
because the host was distracted—so much so that he
and Anna left before two and found a café. Over
second-rate cappuccino they talked, and Anna asked
Jean what he did. This was often an awkward question
in her milieu: so many of her friends "did" nothing
except dabble in a bit of collage or photography, or
watch their investments and occasionally interfere with
the well-laid plans of their bankers and accountants.
But yet Anna was sure this powerful-seeming, tough-
featured older man was more than a high-class wastrel
of the usual Manhattanite variety.

"I buy and sell people," Colombe answered. Then
with a laugh and a wave of the hand, "It is always a
pleasure to shock, especially as it becomes more
difficult with every year to find those who can still *be*
shocked. But it is the truth. I am an investor. I buy
companies that have potential, and then later, I sell
them. And what I have found is that it is always best to

look first at the management, the people. These are, without question, more important than the physical assets. So I am buying these people, you see, and selling them."

"Somehow, I couldn't see you in the white slave trade," Anna said.

"Not as it is commonly understood, at any rate." Colombe smiled.

I buy and sell people. The words rang dismally in Anna's mind now as she took another champagne from the butler. This servant was hardly the stereotype domestic: a rather young, fastidious, and well-paid Argentine, he was second in Colombe's trust, after his gangling driver, Armand. He quietly but frankly asked if Mademoiselle was not ill. Anna shook her head dully, and the butler drifted on to the guests.

In due course Anna had become Colombe's mistress, and all the peculiar, faintly humiliating and exciting ramifications of that word became clear to her. She had, with other men—if they could be called men, young as they had been—thought of herself as a "girlfriend," or even, in more impassioned moments, as a "lover." But it was impossible to regard oneself, except jokingly, as the "mistress" of an excitable squash player of Princetonian stamp—even if he *was* paying the rent on the shared apartment.

The difference was one of scale and society. Colombe was so *vastly* wealthy, so decidedly older; Anna was so voluptuous, so much the raven-haired, pale-fleshed beauty—that she was invariably regarded by Colombe's acquaintances as a species of beautiful animal that Jean-Louis had trapped during a hunting expedition. Again and again, at poolside or in tennis dress, when introduced to new people, Anna would be complimented in almost stark terms. But the compliments were almost always directed, not to her, but to Colombe: "She is beautiful, Jean," a man might say.

Or after, in conversation, the man's face-lifted wife might remark, with traces of bitterness: "A rarity, Jean—such a shape is not often coupled with sense."

A rarity: a fitting companion to a man who knew himself to be remarkable. When they traveled together, Anna would have to have her wardrobe packed. But Colombe carried no luggage, except for a slim, ostrich-skin portfolio borne by Armand. At his home on Mustique, at the lodge near Gstaad, in the Manhattan suite—at each of these residences and yet others waited a full wardrobe. The only property Colombe traveled with, in brief, was the clothes on his back . . . and his mistress.

Out in the pool, the passive floater arched in the limpid waters and climaxed. Circular ripples expanded, and there was an accompanying ripple of mild applause from the few onlookers by the water. Anna looked away, more revolted by the audience response than she had been by any part of the performance. That blasé, tepid applause said volumes about the world in which she now found herself. Here, protected by wealth, passion was never truly passion, never a *dérèglement de tous les sens*. Here one spoke of passion for a lover the same way one spoke of a passion for wine.

It was this kind of connoisseurship, Anna was convinced, that generated a document like the marriage contract she had been offered that morning.

For seven months she and Colombe had played on a grand scale, and if anything, he outpaced her for sheer physical prowess in tennis, skiing, and scuba diving. For Colombe, the core of every day consisted of four hours of relentless concentration on his acquisitions—while Anna was sent off to sunbathe, sport, and go shopping. She shopped until she was dizzy, and now the size of her own wardrobe was appalling, so much so that she could not suppress a feeling of guilt every time she slid into an evening gown; she had been raised with a continual awareness of the poor of the world and knew that even one of her gowns could feed a family for . . . But such *mea culpas* were short-lived: the touch of silk against her bare flesh and the spectacle of her dazzling cleavage in the mirror reassured her that she gloried in and deserved such luxuries.

All along she had known about Colombe's previous marriages. He was no dissimulator, though he took no pleasure in dwelling on past loves. "There are too many," he once said, "and yet there is only one. This one."

In truth, he had been married eight times, and the reason for this was simple: he was a kind of faithful lover. He was, Anna now believed, faithful to her and would be so until the moment when he tired of her or found someone else who won him over. Then Jean would be faithful to that woman, divorcing Anna and marrying the replacement. Colombe could have been truly happy in no other period of history: he had no need of polygamy because the modern practice of serial monogamy suited his temperament to perfection. No, in matters of the heart, he was not unfaithful; he merely had a brief attention span.

But Anna's bitterness, as she sat gazing out upon the classical swimming hole and the rolling Tuscan landscape beyond, had nothing to do with any waning of Colombe's affections. On the contrary, his attentions to her grew stronger every day and had culminated in a heartfelt proposal of marriage offered on the shores of Lake Como.

It was the contract. The marriage contract. "You will have now to pay a visit to my attorneys," Colombe said with an air of mild disgust at the legal aspects of romance. "A few papers they will want you to sign."

As Anna had dressed for her morning appointment, she found herself selecting her most demure and conservative garments—and realized with amusement that she was anticipating her meeting with Colombe's attorneys as she might a dinner with parents. *Mom,*

Dad, I want you to meet my girl, Anna. But of course, Colombe's mother and father were long dead.

As it turned out, however, her anticipations were oddly on target. She flew to Geneva and found herself on the premises of a building that seemed more a palace than a banking establishment. Smoothly ushered into a waiting room carpeted in Aubusson and hung with grandiose paintings, she soon was led into an austere, dark-paneled conference room of almost medieval antiquity.

There sat three lawyers. Chief among them was a wizened, bespectacled old man who presided stiffly in a thronelike chair at the head of a long, black table. The bright daylight of Geneva filtered only dimly into the chamber. He gave her the politest and most frigid of greetings as she entered, begging her forgiveness for not rising. "My legs are weak," he explained, in a tone not at all apologetic.

Anna felt a chill as she took a chair, and sure enough, the old man's air—his name was Kleist—grew cutting.

"I have been in the service of the Colombe family for more than half a century," Kleist intoned, "and have been assisting in Monsieur Colombe's affairs since the day he celebrated his second birthday."

Anna was tempted to quip something about Colombe having started surprisingly young, but suppressed the urge. This was not a laughing man. He was, all in all, more odious than the most stuffy and condescending paterfamilias could ever have been; and as he presented the documents with full explanation of the privileges they bestowed and restrictions they imposed, Anna began to register the positive heat of his arid contempt.

The marriage contract expressly stipulated, first, the limitations of Anna's draw on Colombe's credit: she was not to exceed a certain (very large) sum in personal expenditures. Second, the agreement prohibited Anna from making use of Colombe's title. There was a mild shock in this paragraph, because Anna had not been aware that Colombe bore any title. She had heard an occasional reference to such things, but they were usually of a joking nature. Oh yes, Kleist assured loftily, *Monsieur* Colombe, as he preferred to be addressed, was properly *Marquis*. A faint shudder trembled through Kleist, as if this preference expressed, as it were, the worst excesses of the French Revolution. And more, Anna realized that Kleist felt Colombe was marrying "low." *I am*, Anna thought, *a commoner*. Not just a mistress, but a commoner too. In other circumstances, she might have giggled.

The third major topic was, for Anna, the worst: every detail of a divorce settlement was present, in full, within the meticulous lines of the marriage agreement. She was entitled only to such real estate and trusts as Colombe explicitly presented to her during their marriage. Her alimony payments were not to exceed such and such a sum. Certain claims could not be made. She could not carry his name after the formal separation. For a horrible moment, as the grim, practical terms were being read aloud, each stipulation like the slow tolling of a bell, Anna began to expect an advance disposition of child custody. But apparently this was outside the realm of even such an all-inclusive contract.

There were other points, myriads of them, like motes of dust churning in the shafts of weak sunlight that penetrated the grim, walnut-paneled room. But Anna lost track, and felt herself tumbling down and down. The blue waters of the Caribbean, where she and Jean-Louis had played and splashed, were an eternity away.

And she knew, with a slow, burning anger, that for the two of them those waters would never again be so blue.

Anna had planned on spending a day or more solo in Geneva, but she flew immediately back to Italy and cornered Jean, raving at him in tearful outrage.

"But—but it is very generous!" Colombe cried in self-defense.

"I don't want generosity!" Anna screamed.

"What is it then? You have my love and my generosity. What more then?"

"Don't you understand?" Anna wailed, crumpling into a chair.

"No, I do not," Colombe said, genuinely perplexed. "No one else has complained."

Then Anna did what she would later come to regard as the single most absurd act of her life. She rose, trembling with passion, to her feet, and said: "But *I* am an *American!*"

Thrills of embarrassment coursed through Anna as she morosely quaffed yet another champagne from the Argentine butler's magic tray. What she had meant to say was that—oh, what *had* she meant to say? Below, the turquoise rectangle of the pool, perfectly still, mysteriously lit, beckoned her with its calm. She thought: *I meant to say that you've got to try and believe, anyhow. I mean, every baby born in the world will someday die, but you don't go ahead and read its eulogy at the baptism, do you? If you keep trying to believe, maybe it will happen someday. Maybe love can actually be eternal, Jean.* (She was rehearsing now.) *And you have to take the risks that that involves, don't you see?*

And what she had meant to say was that the whole notion of this contract was like . . . prostitution, really. You do this for me, and I'll give you so much. And only so much. And when those perfect, stunning breasts begin to sag, I reserve the right to terminate your contract and find another pair. As for any children, my dear, keep them: they'll entertain you in your old age, while I . . .

That little French bastard, Anna seethed.

The guests, perhaps sensitive to Anna's dismal mood, had kept clear of her seat by the great glass doors. But now, good and drunk, she wore a fierce look, and a *soigné* young English couple, slim and intelligent and friends of Jean, glided toward her.

"Off with their heads!" cried the woman, whose name was Margaret.

"Battle stations! Battle stations!" boomed her husband, Whitney.

Only half aware she was being made fun of, Anna continued to glower. *This* was another example. These two—just another childless, sterile couple, darlings of the Age of Contraception. Smiling crookedly, as good and drunk as Anna, they threw themselves into nearby chairs in a swirl of perfume and masculine cologne.

"Do you have any *idea* what kind of party this has come to be?" Margaret asked. "This little zone of yours is about the only decent place left."

"It's pornographic back there!" Whitney said jubilantly, with a nod toward the interior of the house. "All conversation has ceased. The oral stage has given way to the genital, Anna." And then more seriously, leaning closer: "And where the bloody hell is Jean?"

Who cares? thought Anna.

"You know Jean," she said. "He gives a party and then retreats with those sinister banking types. Talking takeovers in the conservatory, I'll bet."

"Oh no, not in the conservatory," Margaret said. "I doubt that."

"The conservatory has been given up to debauchery," Whitney said.

"You two have a broad-ranging reputation for exaggeration," Anna said. "Where Jean is, I don't know."

"You've had a fight," Margaret announced.

"*I* had a fight. Jean couldn't bring himself to participate."

Margaret made deeper inquiries, but Anna refused to play, knowing all too well how precious such news would be to a gossip like Margaret.

"Well," the Englishwoman said, disappointed at Anna's closemouthedness, "do tell Jean that it's time for the bucket of cold water, would you? The randiness is getting out of hand in several quarters, and unless he wants his little chateau written up as a brothel, he'd better go about separating the beasts."

"You should really go watch," Whitney said with a grin.

"Did you *see* those three pansies in the pool, Anna? You must have."

"We don't call them pansies anymore, Margaret."

"*I* do, Whit. *I* call them pansies. *I* call them whatever I like."

Bloodless, Anna brooded. *Passionless.*

"I think Anna's experiencing the Great Contempt, Margaret. Perhaps we'd better sail on."

"Jean," Anna said distractedly. "Jean is off with the bankers. Jean is buying and selling."

Later, Anna got to her feet, wobbled, and thought: *Oh no, I'm sauced.* The room was nearly deserted except for a gaggle of diehard backgammon devotees in one corner, playing and kibbitzing intently in the light of three silver candelabra. Anna drifted past them and into the interior. Colombe's villa was many-roomed, with few large, open chambers. Doors stood ajar, and all Anna could see—by candlelight, everywhere—were scattered guests conversing and drinking. The Argentine wove in and out with his tray. It was God only knew what time of the early morning, and Anna was sure only the rising sun would disperse the partyers. Jean, she realized, was most probably sound asleep, preparing himself for the business of the next day.

In the library they were doing cocaine. In more innocent days, Anna despised the drug, not because of its pharmaceutical effects, but because of the furtiveness with which her acquaintances would partake of it, hiding in cliques in the bathrooms so as not to have to share the costly powder. But in Colombe's world the costliness came to nothing, and besides, Anna despised everything tonight. So when the chattering bibliophiles offered, she accepted, hoping the stimulant would diminish the champagne's effects.

The cocaine made her want to be a cat, to slink unnoticed, stretch, hop onto furniture. Soon she felt towering and splendid, sitting at the polished reading table like an idol. The four men gazed rampantly at her torso, at her face, at her hair. They were handsome, all of them, empty and beautiful as a row of fashion models, and beneath the table a brusque, warm charge swelled. Her legs felt long and supple; she flexed them and left the table.

The corridor was dim and seemed endless, light wavering on the walls here and there through open doors, like the dank glow of flambeaux burning in a castle. But at the end of the corridor there was no glow; the doors there were shut.

Anna was drawn by the darkness, remembering Whitney's words—exaggerated, no doubt exaggerated—and heated by the electric charge and the eyes of men on her superb body, the body that had won her a proposal from a certain heartless prick. Anna laughed, feeling carelessly powerful. She stopped at the second closed door.

A young man emerged from the shadows.

"I wouldn't go in there if I were you," he warned with a wry smile.

"I wouldn't want to interrupt anything," Anna said.

"Oh, you couldn't interrupt them with anything less than a nuclear warhead. Hey, you sound like an American."

"I *am* an American," Anna said. She remembered the fight with Jean. A hot flush of embarrassment shot through her, but the cocaine doused it early. The boy—after Jean, anyone younger than thirty-five seemed like a boy to her—grinned and put out his hand.

"This party has more crashers than a demolition

derby," he said. "Maybe it's movie people or something. I'm Butch Reynolds."

Anna introduced herself.

"Wow," Reynolds said, "the hostess, no less. Look what somebody chalked up here."

LASCIATE OGNO VESTIARIO, VOI CH'INTRATE was carefully lettered on the door.

"It says, 'Abandon all clothes, ye who enter here.'"

Butch Reynolds was clean and fresh, and his hair was blond and his body looked strong. Another hot flush seared through Anna, but it was not embarrassment.

"I need an escort," she said, opening the door.

It was almost totally dark inside, a scattering of candles flickering along the walls. As her eyes adjusted, Anna made out naked bodies coupling and uncoupling. In the darkness they seemed to blend into one shifting mass.

"You asked for it," Reynolds said. "Smells like Cupid's gymnasium in here, huh? Maybe if we yell 'fire' they'll stop."

A bottle of champagne lay near at hand in an ice bucket. Anna drank from the bottle, bubbles almost surging into her nose. She gave the bottle to Reynolds and he drank too, looking at her seriously.

In the center of the room a woman of showgirl proportions was straddling one man while she took the sex of another between her large breasts. The shaft pulled back and then slid into her mouth. Slowly, her lips worked forward until her nose was pushing into his dense black hair.

There was no music, no sound but soft moans and grunts and the slapping of flesh on flesh.

Anna took Butch Reynolds's hand and led him away and down the corridor and up a flight of stairs to her private sitting room. She locked the door and went to him and kissed him on the mouth. He responded and she unzipped him. Gently but rapidly she pulled out his sex. It stiffened, full of intense warm life, in her fingers.

Tomorrow, she thought. *Tomorrow I leave Jean.*

The connection to Milan was no problem, but at Linate Anna had an anxiety attack and could not board. She wandered the airport, seething with contradictory ideas. Leaving Jean was just too radical a move. She had nowhere to go but home to her parents, and that entailed so much—and so little. Outside, it was a drizzling, miserable March afternoon.

Home. In her purse she carried letters from her mother penned in a round, girlish hand. Anna had never even seen the place her parents now lived in, but the letters described it glowingly as an estate of ten acres on the North Shore of Long Island, just outside the town of Oyster Bay. Her mother's communications were full of information and description ("March came in like a lamb this year"), but the questions outweighed both, and underlying the words was a tone of mild condemnation. What was Anna doing? What kind of company was she keeping? Was she seeing any men?

Her parents, especially her mother, were impossible. Only her younger sister, Nancy, was at all a confidante, and Anna wrote her regularly, care of a friend. High-spirited, regular-girl Nancy. Nancy the envious.

Anna sat in the airport bar and sipped bad grappa. Every time a man entered, she turned to look, half hoping it would be Jean come to retrieve her. But that was more than unlikely, she knew: she had told no one of her sudden decision to flee, although Jean would fathom what had happened when she failed to appear at dinner. What would he think? *He'll think I'm a fool of the first order.* What would he do? *It isn't like him to pursue. He'll sit back smugly, simply certain that his Anna will come scampering back after she's had her little flare-up.* Or worse, he would simply find another warm body.

Anna wanted the option of return to remain open. She had come so far from home, had seen so much, and the last thing she wanted was to be trapped in the domestic scene again, having to start all over. Perhaps Jean would even realize how much he valued her. It was unlikely he would ever dispense entirely with the marriage contract, but he might be prevailed upon to modify the terms. Then: *Oh Christ! Now I'm thinking like him. Strike and renegotiate.*

There was room on an evening flight to New York, and she took it.

It was a clear, warm evening when she arrived— *Mother was right about the weather,* Anna thought— and the cab drove eastward from Kennedy until it branched off the main routes and delved into the winding, wooded roads of four-acre-and-up zoning. The driver soon became confused, and Anna's own familiarity with the area was minimal, formed during late excursions to parties at the homes of friends.

Darkness had fallen completely by the time the cab finally rolled to a halt at an entrance gate bearing the name "Penn," set in an old, ivy-covered brick wall. The wrought-iron gate itself was shut, and Anna was about to pay off the cabbie and climb out when a girl in white appeared and let them through. Anna turned to wave at the girl as the taxi crunched along the curving drive, but she had vanished.

The driver stopped in front of a large though unprepossessing house sided in pale wood. But with a sigh composed of embarrassment and depression, Anna told him to keep going. The cab continued along the driveway, past the house and parking area, and up a steep slope to the servants' quarters by the garages.

"Is this it?" the driver asked, his eyes flickering in the rearview.

DEVOTION

As Anna Ravine got out of the cab, two stout figures trundled out into the battered, screened-in porch. There was general excitement, and even before the driver had removed Anna's luggage, she was in the arms of her mother and father, with Nancy hanging back and giving forth soft hosannas.

❧ seven ❧

Big Bill Ravine, Anna's father, opened a bottle of Bordeaux, a leftover from a dinner party at the big house, a dinner Mary Ravine had cooked and served. The family gathered around the kitchen table for a celebration. Nothing was said about Anna's unannounced arrival.

"This wine must've cost twenty dollars!" Big Bill called out, sipping and wrinkling his nose. He was a huge man with a nearly hairless, bullet-shaped head and small, piercing eyes. His grin was enormous, like that of a friendly dinosaur. His wife Mary nodded and smiled, saying very little except to chime in with someone else. Her eyes sparkled in a deeply wrinkled face, framed by stiff gray hair.

The celebration was brief: Big Bill and Mary rarely rose later than six A.M., and the hour was already late. Anna kissed them both again and they packed themselves off to bed, their footsteps heavy on the stairs.

Anna and Nancy finished the bottle. Nancy turned on the radio and they opened up a pint of Scotch.

"What do you think of the new pit?" Nancy asked, indicating the kitchen and the living room beyond. "The last people left the place a mess. The Penns haven't had steady help since their Ukrainian couple left to start a restaurant two years ago."

"We've seen worse," Anna said. "The kitchen

seems so small compared to the club. Can't be much society here for Mom and Dad."

Nancy cleared the heaps of cheese and leftovers Mary had put out. "I think they like it. There isn't much work for them here. The Penns are off on some monster world tour. *Mrs.* Penn has been after *Mr.* Penn to do it for years, Mom says. No dinner parties for Mom until Christmas. Even before, they were just about never around. No more cooking lunch for thirty old geezers like at the club."

It was good to sit in a kitchen, Anna thought. She remembered where she had been the night before— and what she had done. A blush rose to her face. She poured herself another drink. Good just to sit in a kitchen and get high. The label on the bottle had a name scrawled on it in Magic Marker: "Wagner."

"What is this?" Anna asked. "Dead-man whiskey?"

"We cleaned out the dead members' lockers before we left. It was my idea. Why not, right? I mean, Wagner's been dead for eight years. It's just that nobody touches the lockers. They've got no new members coming in, so it was all just sitting there. Now it's ours. We've got a closetful."

"Dead-man whiskey," Anna said. She had grown up at the Bird and Gun, and her first drink had been on booze like this, raided from a deceased club member's long-untouched stock.

"What happened, Nancy? Why'd you have to leave the club?"

"We didn't *have* to. Big Bill got sick of hassling with Bobby—you remember, the gamekeeper? After Bobby married June—"

"*Bobby* married *June?*"

"Yeah, well," Nancy said, "there was some difference in height."

"*June* was *six-foot-two! Bobby* was a *shrimp!*"

Nancy shrugged. "Bobby carried a gun, though. Guess that made up for it in his mind. I don't care about short or tall myself. He was a fool, that's the main thing. Well, after he married June, Bobby got real imperialistic—wanted the whole place under his exclusive control. Saw himself and June living in the club instead of that gamekeeper's cabin, with June doing Mom's job. So began the battle."

"And Dad's no diplomat," Anna said.

"I don't know. I think the membership just decided to tone the place up. They decided they wanted a real restaurant kind of setting, and somebody brought in this extremely flitty kind of chef who sold them on the idea. So they just closed the kitchen entirely and started renovating. It was great for me. I got a job in the city, Anna."

"You're kidding."

"Nope. I'm a legal assistant. I'm an office drone."

"And you're still living *here?*"

Nancy seemed stung. "I mean," Anna said hurriedly, "why don't you get an apartment in the city?"

"I'm looking, I'm looking. They want small fortunes for studios with the bathtub in the goddamn kitchen, Anna. The whole rental scene has gone berserk. Besides, it isn't so bad here."

Anna cast a glance around.

"Yeah, yeah, I know," Nancy continued. "Anna the adventurer. World-traveled Anna."

Anna put a hand on her sister's arm. Nancy was pretty, the very model of the word, with a pert nose, a slim body, and an exuberant spirit. Chestnut-haired, brown-eyed Nancy. "Got a boyfriend yet?" Anna asked.

Nancy shook her head. "How about you? You've got that worldly-wise disillusioned look. What, did you break up with your bezillionaire?"

Anna told the story, briefly. She left out the vilest parts.

"Jesus Christ, Anna! Why didn't you say *yes!*"

* * *

The two of them stayed up until dawn. Anna did most of the talking, conveying details her letters could not contain.

The next day, Saturday, brought the Homecoming Dinner. Swathed in pungent smoke, Big Bill manned the barbecue, calling out: "We got seven hot dogs and four hamburgers!" He sang his navy songs, cutting a jig now and then as he beat time with his spatula. The servants' house featured a parcel of yard, and all the nearby relations showed up to gather around the two picnic tables. Mary shuttled back and forth from the kitchen, ferrying huge bowls of chili and potato salad, smiling interminably—a smile Anna had come to associate, not with happiness, but with a certain habitual desire to please.

There was a horde of lively, dull children, aunts who seemed far more battered and bruised by life than did Mary, an uncle by marriage who was Albanian and could only gargle the English language, and another—a redemption for the family, Anna thought—who looked and talked like Humphrey Bogart, a lineman for the phone company. One girl cousin, sallow and lank-haired, listlessly dandled a baby in her lap—with no husband in sight.

The succeeding days, all wildly bright and sunny, brought increasing boredom for Anna. And more, a sexual itch.

It was a period that caused her to realize how accustomed she had become to the most direct kind of sensuality: a man's hard body on top of her, a man's hard sex driving in and out of her. Big Bill cleaned and filled the pool, said: "Go ahead, use it! The richies are in Siberia!" and Anna spent long hours lolling in the sun. The momentum of Europe and Jean Colombe helped carry her through the tedium. She never seriously entertained the notion that she was, after all, doing nothing with her life. The charge of emotion was still strong, the rest and silence healing. She heard Nancy get up at absurdly early hours to put on her tacky office gear, only to return for a late dinner, exhausted from a day of document handling and commuting. It was sad, Anna thought. Even inaction was better than that kind of servitude.

So she lolled, rested . . . and seethed. She imagined Jean-Louis shrugging Gallically and taking another "girl," another student in sensuality, perhaps one a little blanker, a little less likely to balk when offered a small fortune for her services.

She realized she had made a terrible mistake in not providing Jean a means of contacting her. He knew nothing of her parents, and neither did any of his intimates.

In fact, Anna already longed to be called back to her magical life. There was nothing for her here.

A small fortune. It had dawned fully on Anna how large, compared to the economic scale of mortals such as her family, that small fortune really was. It was her parents' annual income many times over. Several lifetimes over. What Nancy brought home every two weeks, Jean had thoughtlessly and often paid out for an intimate dinner.

It dawned on her, in sum, how lost she had become in her good luck. She had been drawn by stages into a dreamworld, without fully realizing that the dream was not truly *hers*. She had been a character in Jean's dream, because he had the power to dream in the world at large, the power to make fantasy into reality.

As she lay by the pool, Anna could imagine the Penn estate was hers, but when Nancy came back from the city, wearing her grimly determined smile, Anna knew—amid the passing of potatoes and overboiled vegetables—that her own dreams were hollow outside of Jean Colombe's.

Anna Ravine's early childhood was spent in a desolate place. After World War II, her then-childless parents set themselves to making a fortune at chicken farming, an ambition common to many veterans like

Big Bill. In later years, all that remained of this
ambition was a bad-tasting regret. Big Bill would gaze
on a roast bird at dinner and say, "Them chickens,
Mary, them chickens," shaking his head disconsolately
until Mary roused him from his stupor with a sharp
word.

After the failed chicken ranch came a trip westward:
the Ravines went "down the road," in Big Bill's
phrase. The road ended in California, and a town—
pop. 87—located on a sparsely traveled route between
a city and a wilderness. There Big Bill and Mary
operated a combination gas station and general store,
selling fishing equipment, camping supplies, and canned goods, along with fuel.

Outside town lay the desert. But the town was not
big enough to exclude the desert: tumbleweed jammed
into the alley between gas station and store and caught
on trailers in the trailer park. In broad daylight the
citizens were dazed by sun and heat. The town—gas
station, store, diner, trailer park, highway-patrol office
—reeled in the heat.

There Anna was born and partly raised. As a tot,
she toddled from her trailer home to the edge of the
wasteland. There she would stop, because she could
see all there was to see: mesquite, cactus, a nothingness peopled only by lizards and bugs.

Anna's memories of that time coalesced around a
few sensations: the parching heat, the dust on her
body, the wooden floor of the general store, the lines
of canned goods on the shelves, the highway patrol-
men's shiny boots, the reek of gasoline, the worried
faces of children who came and went from the trailer
park, TV shows on the one station that came in—
clowns lost in video snow.

Next came here and there. Anna had no recollection
of what Big Bill did for a living in these intermediate
years, but time and his own farm upbringing brought
him to a groundskeeper's job at a university in New
England. Big Bill wore a green uniform and had a way

with the vegetation, and a trustee of the university sent him to an interview at his shooting club, when that old and stodgy institution found itself in need of a caretaker couple.

The Ravines established themselves at the Bird and Gun Club. The club was situated inland, on eastern Long Island, away from the broad white beaches of the Hamptons. It recalled days when people of worth simply did not disport themselves in the vulgar waves. The club's habitués were nearly all men. Old men. And far from being elegant, the club featured, in its semicircle of dark-wood-and-white-fretwork buildings, a kind of minimalist quaintness. A few of the cottages were private, but by and large the members put up in small, powder-blue rooms with old shooting prints on the walls and gathered in an almost ramshackle bar walled with musty photos and lined with booze lockers that held the members' private stocks.

The grounds embraced a trout-stocked pond which was rarely used, and included a nine-hole golf course of the fourth caliber. Across the road lay the shooting turf, where the old men's main sport consisted in blasting farm-raised "game" birds as the fowl were hurled from a tower by the glum-faced Bobby and that gamekeeper's part-time assistants. In essence, the hunt consisted of the obliteration of live clay pigeons, and after a day's shoot the base of the execution tower would be littered with duck crates and feathers—silent reminders of the massacre.

The old men were millionaires. Occasionally some of the members brought their doddering wives, who sat in the big clubroom just outside the bar and watched television. To little Anna they never looked like millionaires' wives; they looked like old women.

Big Bill wore a white uniform of faintly naval air and oversaw the entire operation. Mary cooked, often for forty at a time, laboring over the enormous institutional stove while her temporary help—neighborhood girls—cut and chopped and served.

Rolls-Royces, Cadillacs, and Mercedes were often parked in the dirt lot outside the kitchen windows, and one home-from-college summer Anna peered through the curtains to witness the arrival of a former president of the United States, whose lawyer son-in-law was one of the few young men who had been persuaded to join.

The club was a giant playground for Anna and Nancy, with its acres to roam, its pond, and even a little village with a candy store a half mile through the woodlot. The Ravines had always been big on food, and when the little girls first arrived, they were chubby from their sedentary years in the desert and town. But six months of space and greenery melted the excess, and soon Nancy emerged from her roundness as a pretty, mischievous sprite.

As for Anna . . . Anna stood revealed as beautiful.

At nine, Anna's hair cascaded in sweeps of black from a perfect oval face set with eyes that were green and lively. Her mouth was bow-shaped, with a hint of childish pout. It was impossible that her body should have exhibited curves at such an early age, but it did, and the overall effect was disconcertingly that of a perfect, slim, little woman. Her mind was active and questioning, and she was possessed of a spontaneity the quieter Nancy rarely showed.

The old men took to Anna quickly, barely acknowledging, even to themselves, what they felt when they sat beside her on the antique leather sofas of the bar. Yet Anna was sweet enough, and schooled so deeply in innocence by her mother that it never even occurred to the wives to object. As Anna became more and more the favorite, Nancy withdrew into a private world where she was comforted by her parents.

"Mary," one of the most senior members announced one day as he wandered into the kitchen for a snack, "your Anna has *character*." And later: "Character. What character requires is *development*." Character was an important byword to these old men—though most by far had only so much as inherited riches could confer—and before long it became a topic of universal agreement, this character of Anna's which needed developing.

At eleven, Anna was—why mince words? At eleven, Anna had serious breasts. At eleven, Anna was disturbingly . . . voluptuous.

What had once been play—the old men and the little girl—began to take on an unseemly aspect, at least in the eyes of the matrons, and the wives originated a plan that struck them as wonderful. It was a plan both beneficent and crafty: Anna was to be sponsored, her character to be developed at great length. Anna was to attend private school.

Mary was jubilant. Big Bill scowled and pulled his jaw. Rich people were many things, he had discovered, but they were rarely generous. Big Bill sat himself down and thought. Nancy settled in his lap, miserable, and he stroked her brown hair absently. He put two and two together, watching his young—but *Jesus, stacked*—daughter. He figured out what the old ladies were after—they liked Anna but wanted her gone—and said fine, she could go.

The matrons had a field day in Manhattan, escorting Anna from one junior-miss department to another, outfitting her in outlandish garb of the sort they dimly recalled as appropriate.

For the young creatures of the Waverly School for Girls, Connecticut, the clothes were just the thing: enough to target this enviably lovely and prematurely developed newcomer as a thorough laughingstock. From the day Anna arrived at the pseudo-Colonial Founder's Hall—with her stiff new luggage and her embarrassing parents (whom the headmistress took, quite correctly, to be domestics and assumed, quite wrongly, were in lieu of relatives)—Anna began a descent into the most numbing and tortured loneliness she would ever know.

Anna was not one for hiding things. She wrote agonized letters to her mother. She dragged around the absurdly lovely grounds, trudging from building to building in an aura that began wounded and ended up fiery and hostile.

At home, at the club, Mary said, "She'll get used to the place." Big Bill shook his head. At Thanksgiving Anna came home and begged not to be sent back. And then, oddly, it was Big Bill who said no.

"Anna, you've got to have guts," he told her. "You've got to fight this out. Nobody is better than you, understand? Nobody."

Mary, finally seeing in the flesh her daughter's pain, sided with retreat. But Big Bill prevailed, and Anna left her slice of turkey untouched.

Late that night, Anna had a nightmare and Big Bill came to the rescue.

"I dreamed," she whispered, "that I was back at school."

The next day Big Bill rounded up the matrons—Thanksgiving was a big shooting weekend—and herded them into the kitchen. Anna listened from the stairs.

"They're making fun of my girl," Big Bill told the women. "She's dressed like a freak, she says. What I want to know is, ain't you ladies got any daughters? The kid needs advice. They're beating the life out of her over to that school."

Daughters were brought in for consultation. Arriving in limousines, they sat Anna down and quizzed her at length. Even the daughters were middle-aged, but not yet batty, with eyes still undimmed in their well-groomed and artfully made-up faces. The daughters made phone calls, and the daughters of the daughters were in turn consulted. The general response of these teenagers, when presented with the problem in full, was: "Oh Mummy! What a totally senile experiment!"

But stores were named and written down, specific

styles invoked to mothers who read the fashion rags and knew each reference well enough to proceed. Another clothes-buying jaunt ensued, with the matrons along as clucking observers while the matrons-in-the-making took the helm. Finally, Anna was made presentable as a specimen of the late-twentieth-century subspecies, a preparatory-school girl.

Of course the damage had already been done, and though Anna now dressed to code, she did so more as camouflage than from breeding. Her sartorial transformation saved her from the most open mockeries, but she was still lonely.

Then boys. There existed within the social sphere of Waverly two institutions for boys. Hence dances. Hence anxiety, insanity, frenzied preparations, feigned indifference, dull music, chaperons. And boys who wanted, down to the last short, fat, and ugly half man, to have something physical to do with Anna Ravine.

Anna, in brief, did *it* with boys at a shockingly early age. She began innocent, but her innocence was coupled with an innate sensuality that had bloomed as early as her torso.

Summers brought Anna back to the club, and every season brought startling advances in her physical beauty. Each autumn sent her back to school and the clean, wholesome, self-confident boys who found secret places to enjoy her charms. She was often in love, often desperately in love, and years later when Jean-Louis Colombe was to speak to her, backstage, about loving too many times, the twenty-three-year-old Anna could agree without pretending a knowledge she did not have.

To Anna's senses, which for long months had been overwhelmed by new sights and experiences, the return to the only place she could call home was like a return to the desert of her childhood. Ennui and nothingness held her in poolside spell. The rectangle of blue glimmered, like a swatch of the greater blue beyond, Oyster Bay, where white sails caught the wind.

The sexual itch became an obsession, driving Anna to such tacky extremes as the area's better singles spots, where she docked at the bar, watched, and froze out men in leisure suits. Men with white-walled smiles and jewelry who reminded her that she would rather come by her own hand rather than let one of these louts have a taste.

"Anna, you ought to think about getting a job," Nancy said one evening as the two of them sat on the screened-in porch.

The spring night was unnaturally hot, and Anna wore shorts, sandals, a Hawaiian shirt, and a pearl necklace.

"But Nancy," she said, "what can I do? I can't type, I can't file—"

"Anybody can *file*."

"I've never worked nine-to-five in my life. Nancy, I've never even seen the inside of an office—not the kind you're talking about."

"Anna, I hate to get stark, but you'd be hired. Don't worry about that."

"Right. As a receptionist. Big tits out front. Christ, Nan, when I think how I've been surviving, how I've been making my living all these years . . . I've been in the flesh trade, that's all. Offering a small line of specialty goods. Me."

"If you really believe that," Nancy said, "you ought to go back and take that Frenchman's deal. You'll never cut a better one."

Anna fell silent.

At night she had Nancy to talk to, but daytime was like a front-row seat at the presentation of a featureless wall. Anna had never really learned to enjoy reading. Her attention span was too short, and for her a book was merely something one held in one's lap like a tiny dog. If cash had not been short, she would have gone shopping, but all she possessed was in the form of jewelry, and to hock any of it would be, she felt, like running up the white flag.

So Anna lolled by the pool and, so much the worse for her, thought. Thinking was bad for Anna. When the sun was truly warm and her parents were gone for the day, the thoughts burned away like a haze. She took off her bikini top, as she had learned to do in less inhibited climes, and felt the lazy rays on her breasts.

It was in just such a state that a stranger surprised her one afternoon in late May.

Anna lurched from her doze and clutched a towel to her chest, blushing vividly. When she directed her flustered attention at the stranger, she was taken by surprise all over again.

The stranger was a tall, badly shaven young man with long black hair. In one hand he carried a small suitcase. The other held a cane.

As soon as the impression of a *young* man registered, it was overwhelmed by another: that of age. Streaks of gray shot through the black hair, and the eyes were dispassionate, surrounded with wrinkles formed by a sorrow that twisted fleetingly into ironic amusement.

"You blushed," he said, hobbling forward with his cane.

"Who in *hell* are you!" Anna cried indignantly, recovering her composure.

"Ah, you've placed me exactly," the stranger said.

Anna's initial conviction—that this was just some half-crippled man who had wandered in off the road, dressed in old corduroys and carrying an unprepossessing suitcase—shifted abruptly.

"I'm Jeremy Penn," he announced.

And Anna blushed again.

The stranger laughed. His laugh had a ragged,

unused sound to it. Anna wanted to be offended, but
he seemed to need the laughter so much that she
simply . . . blushed a third time.

The stranger took a deck chair, placed his case on a
white, wrought-iron table, and opened it, taking a
bottle of wine and one fluted glass from a tangle of
gray clothes. A corkscrew from his pocket opened the
bottle.

He handed the full glass to Anna and, for himself,
drank from the neck.

"Forgive me," he said, turning away. "Go ahead
and put your top back on. I didn't see a thing, you
know. The glare from the water blinded me."

Jeremy Penn's arrival was a matter of great moment
to Anna's parents. Mary's briefings had included no
mention of a son, and she was inclined to be suspicious. But Nancy said: "No, there's a Jeremy all
right," and then declined to explain how she knew.

That evening Anna was called upon to describe
Jeremy in detail, and her mother was much moved by
the cane, the wrinkles, the aura of tragedy. Curious,
she went to the main house, where Jeremy was staying,
and offered to prepare a meal. Jeremy, sitting quietly
drunk on the patio, said, "No thank you—Mrs. Ravine, is it?"

"Mary," she said, with her ingratiating smile.

"Mary," said Jeremy, and poured wine down his
throat. "But there is something I'd like to ask of you. I
need—peace, quiet. Please, let's keep my return between us?"

Mary thought it a strange request, but it was made
so sincerely that she agreed, and told husband and
daughters that she had promised for them too.

Lights were on in the big house as Anna and the
tired Nancy took their stations on the servants' porch.
As they talked and speculated, their groundless inquiries were broken by the sounds of Chopin. The playing
was amateurish, almost maudlin, Anna guessed. But

the music of the piano cast a spell that broke the pall of nothingness, and Anna nodded to herself, sure that her blushes, as with every other thing she did in true spontaneity, had been all right. Perfectly all right.

Anna and Jeremy crossed paths often. He begged her to feel free with the pool, and often when she sunned herself he dropped by to swim.

It was awkward at first. He came hobbling on his cane, a case of tremendous energy chained by partial affliction. He surged unevenly through space in a silken robe that was perhaps his father's and was certainly not apropos at poolside.

When Jeremy first shed the robe, Anna averted her eyes, to be, as she thought, polite. But she did watch Jeremy swim. It was his left side that was weak, and as he plowed with terrible force through the water, he tended to drift. He was fast nevertheless, and when he hoisted himself out, Anna looked.

His body was, to all appearances, almost perfect, marred only by a slight asymmetry that worked from his left calf all the way to the left side of his face. The left half was faintly atrophied, slacker than the other, and in the face there loomed an odd, nearly tortured expression which, though tempered by bemusement, seemed hammered into his very flesh.

"Do you want to see something really sad?" Nancy asked.

They sat in the living room. Usually Nancy watched television after the parents had retired, but since Anna's return she had taken to reading by music. Anna looked up from a magazine.

"Depends on what kind of sad. If it's depressing sad, no."

"No, not really depressing. Come on."

Nancy led her up the stairs. They stepped quietly past the bedrooms and to another flight that led to the attic.

Creaking open the warped door at the top of the stairs, Nancy switched on the light, at the same time taking a flashlight from its place on an exposed beam. The stifling odor of dry wood and condensed heat struck Anna.

"There's centuries of trash up here," Nancy said, unconsciously lowering her voice as they wound past three-legged chairs and old boxes. Finally, from behind a pillar, she dragged out a small blue carton.

"Here," she said. "Hold the flashlight." Anna sat on a crate, playing the beam while Nancy knelt before the carton and pulled back the flaps.

On top lay a pair of patchwork slippers.

They were oddly beautiful, sewn from diamonds of satin—orange, yellow, red, and violet—like a clown's motley. Fascinated, drawn to them, Anna leaned forward and took one of the slippers in her hand.

Nancy smiled.

"Neat, huh? And look," she said. "There's a card." She held it up. *Found these offstage,* it read. It was signed *Jeremy.*

Beneath the slippers was a bundle of letters, tied in naive red ribbon.

"I feel guilty every time I do this," Nancy said as she undid the package.

Anna slid a letter from its envelope.

Dear Catherine . . .

Her gaze slipped to the bottom of the page—

Jeremy.

—and then back up to the date: the letter was more than ten years old.

"The letters are nothing much, really," Nancy said. "Just about how great Yale is and how much Jeremy is—I don't know, *growing* or some such thing. And here are some pictures."

The snapshots showed Jeremy. It was recognizably he, in every shot. But the resemblance was distant, as though of a brother or a cousin—a relative vastly younger, more dynamic, happier. Even when caught in a somber mood, this Jeremy seemed somber in the manner reserved for straightforward, adolescent introspection.

There was no cane.

Nancy said, "See what I mean? I always thought it was sad, this stuff. Anna, I think they were in love. And yet somehow this stuff all got left behind, pushed into an attic—"

"But what's this box doing *here?*"

"Don't you see, Anna? She was like us, this Catherine. Just like us. This is how I knew there was a Jeremy Penn. Anna, can you imagine what she must have dreamed for herself? I can. And now—I mean, I've seen Jeremy getting around with his cane. And Catherine, she left these things behind. These pictures and these letters and these mysterious slippers. She left them all behind."

Nancy lapsed into a state.

The flashlight beam cast a stagy spot on the cardboard box. The satin slippers gave off a gay sheen.

"Very romantic," Anna said cynically.

Nancy glared at her, hurt and angry.

"Romantic," Anna continued. "But where is she now?"

❧ eight ❦

Anna had been through the routine a dozen times: the man sitting there pouring courage down his throat as the night stretched on and on, while she complied, drank, and watched him, wondering when the hell he was going to put down the bottle and suggest that they go to bed together.

With Jeremy it was different. Anna continued to use the pool—not just during the day, but at night as well, swimming under the clear starry skies of that sensuously warm spring. One evening when she climbed out, she found Jeremy seated in her lounge chair, a fifth of cognac by him on the table, two glasses.

Anna laughed.

"I think it's your turn to blush," she said.

Jeremy handed her a towel. He held out her robe and gave back her seat.

They drank half the bottle, taking a break to jump into the pool. Anna grabbed his ankle as he swam by and they kissed for the first time. His embrace was rough, inelegant, powerful. It shook the fun out of Anna, and as she rubbed herself with the towel she could not look at Jeremy. She gulped her next brandy like a refugee from a storm, damp and shivering.

He told her he'd been away from home for ten years. A decade had passed since he had seen or even spoken with his parents. Drink made Anna bold enough to ask if there had been some titanic fight.

"No," Jeremy said. "I just began to wander."

"So why did you decide to come back?"

"I think I may be tired of wandering," he said.

Anna listened to Jeremy's stories. He listened to hers. They got drunk before they knew what was hitting them, and it was she who finally suggested, as if to overcome a reluctance that was growing within her, that they go to bed together.

Anna and Jeremy became lovers of a sort, but exactly what sort Anna did not know and, as she often convinced herself, did not care. Jeremy was an energetic and vital man—twenty-nine, though he looked older—but he was remote beyond her abilities to gauge, and sometimes it seemed to her that he was only present physically. He slept little, and often when she awoke in midafternoon, having dozed in the wake of fierce sex, she caught Jeremy gazing at her in a way she could only interpret as disappointed. She decided they were occupying that large zone between indifference and attachment, and found to her astonishment that she had given up wanting or expecting anything more. At times she even thought of Catherine Dancer's bundles of letters, tied up in their little ribbons: at least she was not a fool of that kind. She could always go back to Jean, and another life.

One afternoon, Jeremy hobbled to the pool excitedly, and announced they were going into the city. "Friends of mine," he said. "Borders and Brook, they're in town. And bring Nancy, if she wants to come."

Nancy was thrilled. Her own life, she felt, was hopelessly bland. She lived at home. She dated lawyers. She husbanded her pay for forays into vast discount outlets where she joined herds of women clacking through racks of rejected designer clothes. She got drunk with other office drones in cute bars and tried to think up real careers for herself. She sorted documents and condensed testimonies, rattling into a dictaphone—"Defendant paren Johnson paren described automobile as late-model com yellow com with dented right front fender period"—until she was hoarse and bored to the edge of despair. She wanted to work hard and accomplish things, but she came to desire lunch breaks above all else and began to feel hateful and wretched.

Jeremy was exotic. Jeremy was romantic. "He has suffered," Nancy often observed, speculating on the nature and degree of that suffering and painting scenarios of high melodrama and noble loss.

To her, even from the start, Jeremy was something remote and unattainable, like all the other exotic and romantic prizes in the world. When she learned that Anna had taken that prize, and heard the hints of his sexual inexhaustibility and gothic sleepwalking, her heart sank. For Anna, everything was easy.

"Party! Party!" Nancy sang.

"It'll probably be some pitiful little gathering," Anna said. "Don't get so worked up!"

The three of them drove into Manhattan. Nancy read aloud from *Scientific American* because Jeremy wanted it, to keep his mind on course. Otherwise, he said, his attention strayed from the road. Anna had started the reading, but ran into trouble with the vocabulary, and as she sat beside Jeremy, listening to Nancy recite some tedious gobbledygook about particles, she wondered if everybody thought she was a moron.

Borders' apartment building was located on a chic block on the Upper East Side. Doorman and antique lobby downstairs—chaos upstairs.

It seemed to Anna that they started drinking even before they got past the door. Though only late afternoon, there was a mob of people who looked like they had been partying since January. Borders himself was a vague, lost, dark-eyed man of about thirty, with a southern drawl. Brook, the other, was a rangy blond with a wholesome glow and a cynical, fixed smile.

Anna gathered that Jeremy, Borders, and Brook had shared an apartment in Paris.

The doorbell rang and food arrived in gross quantities. Borders wanted to barter for it, but the confused Greek who had delivered the provisions refused the offer of: first, a wristwatch; second, a tape deck; and third, a first edition of *This Side of Paradise*.

Anna began to worry that Borders actually lacked cash to settle for the food, but in the end a wad of bills appeared and the delivery boy went away staring cross-eyed at his fifty-dollar tip.

The guests fell upon the food with beastly shouts of glee. Already Nancy was drunk.

"Are *these* fabulous people?" she whispered deafeningly into Anna's ear.

"Rich, maybe. Fabulous, no."

"That woman over there just ate a souvlaki in two bites!"

"She probably learned that at Brearley," Anna said. "That and how to lick cunny in closets."

Nancy nearly choked on her champagne.

Tall, blond Brook merged with Anna and Nancy.

Nancy asked: "How can you carry a bottle of—what is that?"

"Grain alcohol."

"Oh God! I was going to ask—I mean that *is* daylight coming in through the window, isn't it?"

"There's nothing we can do about that," Brook said. "They just turn it on and off with complete disregard for us."

"What," Nancy said, "the sun?"

"It's a torture technique," Brook said. "They do it to break down our resistance. To make us talk. We're determined not to pay any attention. Who are you again?"

"Nancy Ravine. I came with Jeremy," she added with a note of pride.

"You could have that printed up as a bumper sticker," said Brook.

Anna searched the room for Jeremy and saw him in a corner with Borders. Borders was laughing and clapping his hands, bent over. It occurred to Anna that Jeremy was pouring life into his melancholy friend. She hoped Borders was less insufferable than this sly cynic Brook. *There is nothing,* she thought, *worse than a lover with insufferable friends.*

There was nothing to do but get drunk.

Anna took more champagne. *Surprise, surprise,* she thought, *it works.* She found two nearly human beings, women who knew something about couture and were raving about a collection Anna had not seen and could not now afford to sample. Her own clothes won their appreciation even though she well knew that her breasts were too big and her height not enough to show off the best styles to advantage. It didn't matter to her: she knew equally well that models were creatures designed to exhibit women's clothes without exciting the hostility of women—which was to say, without exciting the admiration of men. The two women told her that Brook was a lawyer, but that he had been disbarred in some kind of cut-rate scandal four years earlier. Now, they told her in weary tones, he was devoting his time to "writing."

When she walked across the huge living room again, in search of Jeremy, Anna saw Nancy leaning out the window. Brook stood by her. He laid a hand on the small of her back.

"They just turn it on and off," Nancy was saying. "With complete disregard for us."

Anna wondered if she should do something to protect her little sister. Brook rubbed her the wrong way from the first moment, and Nancy, she could see, was as good as laid already. His being disbarred was not a favorable sign.

She found Jeremy and Borders in a room lined with books. Jeremy was on his knees stoking the fireplace, and the room was insanely hot.

"It's spring, you fools!"

Jeremy said nothing. He watched the flames rise. Borders began to sing quietly, and when Anna realized he was giving out with "North to Alaska," she fell into a chair in hysterics.

"If you're going to be absurd," she said, "be completely absurd and turn on the air conditioner."

It was done. Soon the library became a social center. Borders gave everyone cigars and the room began to cloud over, whirlwinds of smoke flowing up the flue. Anna absently held her cigar for almost ten minutes before throwing it down. People milled around her chair. She parted them with her hands.

"Borders," she said, "there are just too many buttocks in this town."

Borders howled and slapped his knee.

"Too many—too many buttocks!" he cried. Then he subsided into his peculiar, doe-eyed quiescence.

Nancy lurched in, followed—rather too closely, Anna thought—by Brook.

"This is totally demented!" Nancy laughed.

Night fell. More people came. In the big room the show featured music and dancing; in the kitchen, deep conversation; in the library, more "North to Alaska."

Anna wandered through the apartment, guessing and reguessing the rent, collecting second looks from men who seemed more interesting with every dose of Veuve Cliquot, and decided that she felt—happy.

Suddenly there was a mass movement, the gist of which was that everyone was going to embark on an epic journey to Borders's upstate cottage. Anna hated this kind of thing, but Jeremy was very sweet about it.

"I refuse to *jam* into any car," Anna said.

"You don't have to," said Jeremy.

"That's what they're talking about, isn't it? *Jamming* into cars and driving upstate?"

Jeremy said: "You and I will go alone."

Anna read from *Scientific American*. The highway

whizzed by the windows of the Mercedes. Anna read the "Letters to the Editor" aloud. She read "Science and the Citizen" aloud.

Fortunately, they pulled off the highway halfway through "Mathematical Games," and a few minutes later turned down a long, bumpy private drive that swerved through heavily wooded acreage and broke into an opening where Borders's "cottage" appeared. Anna guessed twelve rooms, minimum.

The main room was cathedrallike and bare of furniture, except for sofas along the walls. Music pounded brutally, hurled from a pair of monumental speakers. Brook and Nancy were dancing, Anna noticed disapprovingly, like two worms in warm mud.

Borders and Jeremy and Anna and a host of special guests left the din somewhat behind and rambled down the back slope to a creek that ran at the edge of the property. Two of the guests had been designated as native bearers. They carried a styrofoam cooler packed with champagne.

Then a blank spot.

Lances of yellow pierced the dark, wavering on black tree trunks. The epic journey had turned into a nature outing—with Borders, who had everything, providing flashlights.

"You'll love this!" he shouted, forging ahead in the lead.

"We're lost! We're lost!" voices cried.

Anna heard Jeremy laugh. She turned dizzily, and he pointed the flashlight up at his own face.

"What a ghastly effect," she slurred.

Borders called a halt to the procession. Anna found herself looking down the length of a small, shadowed valley. As the partyers deployed over the terrain, flashlights wavered everywhere, like huge fireflies, illuminating broken benches and walkways that terraced the slopes. At the end of the valley, like the head of a pale god buried up to its neck, stood an ancient marble fountain that bubbled water, causing a stream. The whole place, Anna realized, was a garden that had fallen desolate, strangled with grasping vines.

"The *grotto!*" Borders boomed.

"This isn't a grotto," Nancy called from behind the Cyclops eye of her flashlight.

"No?" Borders said. "What is it then? It's a grotto, damn you!"

"A grotto is, you know, a *cave.* This is more like a *glen,* a hollow."

"The *hollow* then!" Borders boomed. "But grotto sounds better."

Anna and Jeremy sat on the leaves. The flashlight winked out and her skirts went up. They fucked madly, and Anna had never felt anyone so drunk be so hard.

The hollow was deserted by the time they finished, and Anna and Jeremy made their way back alone. The leaves crunched underfoot in a rhythm that began to seem endless. Then ahead, the flashlights.

"Are we all here now?" Borders called when they had assembled on the lawn. His voice was terribly responsible sounding, and for a moment Anna took his tone to mean that Tragedy Had Struck.

Then Nancy said, in a voice garbled but firm: "Fourteen people went into the woods. There are fourteen people here."

They all drifted back to the house, cranked up the volume on the stereo, and had more drinks. Anna was fed up with the outdoors and ran into the bathroom to make sure her dress was intact.

Anna crumpled next to Jeremy on a sofa. Everyone was talking, knowing nothing would be remembered. Anna felt herself lapsing into dark sleep.

Anxiety about Nancy stirred her.

She kissed Jeremy and went looking. Nothing piggy was going on in the house, she discovered. She tried the outside world: the lawn was littered with bodies, some asleep, some embracing.

Anna found Nancy naked in the creek.

She fell behind a tree, her heart thumping almost painfully. The scene before her eyes reeled this way and that.

Nancy and Brook splashed out of the water. The only pale and visible things in the darkness, they stood on the bank and Nancy fondled his stiff cock. Anna heard her giggles. The giggles stopped when Nancy knelt and took the cock into her mouth. Her lips dragged along the length of Brook's shaft.

She can't do that, Anna thought dully. *She's my sister!*

But Nancy did that and more. She lay on the grass and parted her thighs. She threw her legs over Brook's back. She kissed him wildly.

Anna crept away dizzily.

Back at the house, Jeremy was pacing, his cane clicking on the hardwood floor. Anna towed him into a side room and her hands fluttered on his buttons, tore at the zipper.

Another blank spot.

They were driving in the Mercedes.

Anna floated up from unconsciousness.

"Good," Jeremy said. "Read to me."

The *Scientific American* again. The easy parts were used up. Anna plunged into an article about cosmology. The Mercedes weaved. When she came upon a word she did not know, she substituted a vegetable. "In this way virtual particles emerge at the avocado of the event horizon." It was a good gag, she told herself, and would remain so if they lived until sunrise.

Anna kept one eye out for highway signs. Come hell or being high, she prided herself on a fundamental sense of direction.

"That was our exit!" she shrieked at last, turning to watch it fade into the distance.

"We aren't taking our exit," Jeremy said. "We're going on."

Anna wheeled down the window and pitched out the

magazine. It flapped madly onto the highway, like a shot bird.

At length they turned off the highway and a smell of ocean poured through the windows. Anna nodded sagely to herself: the Hamptons. Rows of big beach houses appeared, separated by dunes and grass.

Anna dragged herself from the strange, musty bed. Unbarring and unshuttering the window, she let blazing sunlight in.

"I feel shitty—oh so shitty," she sang.

The beach was a white stripe of pain, and the waves were banging, banging. If Jeremy had stranded her here, she'd kill him. She wanted to be taken home immediately. She needed a glass of hot tea to nourish her guilt, the guilt she always felt after some wretched, pseudo-wanton binge. Soon memory would hatch a little parade of stupidities and humiliations, and Anna felt she couldn't face them in some shut-in, attic-smelling beach house. Sheets hung over the furniture. *Ku Klux Chair,* Anna thought abstractedly.

Smoothing her rumpled clothes as best she could— she'd awakened fully dressed—Anna started out of the bedroom. The memory struck her like a punch: searching for Nancy, finding her with Brook by the creek. Oh Christ, what if they'd spotted her spying? Brook's face loomed up, sneering in cold amusement. Anna chased it out of her mind.

The beach house was dark, like a black-and-white movie, slashes of sunlight humming through cracks in the shutters. Particles of sand grated under Anna's shoes. The place felt woefully abandoned: not just closed for the off-season, but positively untouched by human hands for God knew how long. Now *that,* Anna thought, was rich: having a house in the Hamptons and just letting it sit. A calendar on the kitchen wall was flipped down to May . . . ten years ago. Maybe all the Penns were eccentric.

Eccentric, Anna thought. She had never thought of

Jeremy as eccentric, but that's what he was, wasn't he? Somehow the idea comforted her. She headed up the stairs to the next floor.

A blank hall confronted her. Bird etchings lined the wall like feathered gargoyles. The doors were shut. In front of one lay a crowbar. A padlock over the knob had been pried open, cracking the jamb.

Anna edged the door open.

The room was dark. A triangle of gray expanded as the door creaked inward. Anna waited at the threshold while her eyes felt their way through the gloom. Finally, she stepped in.

The floor was spongy underfoot, and Anna realized that the walls were also padded with deep quilting. The only furniture was a large bed. Jeremy knelt beside it, his upper body thrown across the bare mattress. He was out cold.

Anna hurried to the window. She felt for the shutter bars, but found none. The window was boarded over with rough planks. A splinter jammed under her thumbnail. She told herself to let Jeremy sleep it off, but the room ate at her, burrowing through the gluey pain of her hangover. She got a crowbar from the hall and pried at a board. It moaned dismally—and then, as if yielding to the pressure of the sun's rays behind it, flapped open like a tall, narrow gate. A column of daylight toppled across the room.

Jeremy stirred. Soundlessly, he lifted his head. He shielded his eyes.

"What's this light?" he cried. "Not again. Don't let me wake up again."

Nancy did not come home until six days later, and then only for her things. Mary Ravine tore her gray hair as her youngest packed. Anna stood by with her arms crossed and tried reason.

"I love him," Nancy said for the sixth time.

"You can't," Anna told her.

"There's no can or can't about it. I do."

"Anna," Mary cried. "Who is he? Who *is* he?"

"He's rich, Mother. Don't worry about that," Anna said.

"But what *kind* of boy? Is he—is he decent? Is he—"

"He isn't rich, really," Nancy said. She closed one suitcase and opened another.

"Hold on," Anna said. She ran to her room and pulled her own suitcase out of a closet.

"Here," she said when she returned to Nancy's room. "If you're going to do this, you might as well have presentable luggage."

Nancy halted. She stared at the expensive leather, the brass trim. She had come home determined—grimly determined, it seemed to Anna—but now she almost burst into tears.

"It's just a suitcase," Anna said. "Anyone who can get emotional over a suitcase should really reconsider before she moves in with a man."

"You've never been in love," Nancy said, returning to her packing with a vengeance.

Anna ignored the comment and sat her mother down, and told her to be calm. It was not, she pointed out, the end of the world.

"It's the beginning of the world," Nancy said. "This *dress*. How could I *ever* have bought this *dress*?"

"I'm sure you loved it at the time," Anna said.

"No. No," Nancy said, casting it aside. "I never loved it. I needed a dress and this was on sale. I *settled* for this dress."

Fair enough, Anna thought. She sat on the bed.

"Nancy," she said. "I want to tell you right now that this Brook is a creep. You know he was disbarred?"

"He was framed," Nancy said.

"No. George Raft was framed. Jimmy Cagney was framed. Brook was disbarred."

"Do you know why?" Nancy asked righteously.

"No."

"I know. That's enough for me."

"He's really not rich, Nancy? A man like him, if he isn't rich, then he owes money. Is he that kind?"

"His parents are rich." Nancy threw open the first suitcase and began winnowing out the best from her wardrobe. She wanted it all to go in the good luggage.

"He's been cut off, then," Anna said, arms folded again. To be cut off was bad. She had made a go of it once, in the dark ages, with a boy who had been cut off.

Nancy Ravine then threw down the blouse she was folding, seized Anna by the shoulders, and pulled her to her feet.

"He's mine," she breathed fiercely. "He is mine."

She began crying.

"That's all," she sobbed. "That's the whole story. I'm in love with him. He's in love with me."

She said it a second time: "He's in love with me," and sternly continued with her packing.

"Well," Anna said, "well then. That will have to do, I guess."

Three weeks passed without a word from Nancy. Anna understood she was living in the city with Brook, but she knew a visit was out of the question. Nancy's sense of entrapment seemed to have bubbled over all at once into resentment against everyone in her family.

It was too bad, Anna thought. She wanted to know more. She told herself she was just being protective, but increasingly Anna felt a consuming desire for details. In her bed when she and Jeremy were apart, she imagined Nancy and Brook. In their apartment, with friends. And above all, under the sheets. She knew it was a trifle sick and demented, but there were images that struck at her in the quiet, coming with terrific vividness. Always they began with Nancy kneeling as she had been by the creek, Brook's sex in her mouth, stretching lips taut. And then positions, until Anna could not keep her own fingers from her mound, and she arched in bed, biting back the whimpers in her throat.

At the end of three weeks, a girl from Nancy's office rang, and it was Anna who answered the phone.

Jeremy and Anna had planned a trip into the city that evening. Not of the usual kind—Anna was subject to fits of boredom that could only be assuaged by lights, action, money. When the phone rang that morning, Anna was pulling her hair into various speculative shapes and wondering if there was anyone in America she could trust to perm and cut. Her last was growing out beautifully: she had long ago realized that that was one of the sure signs of genius in a hairdresser. Still, it was all beginning to look a bit ragged.

The caller introduced herself as Nancy's coworker and friend. She was relieved to find herself talking to a sister rather than a parent. Could they meet for lunch—that very day, if possible?

The appointment was sudden, but Anna sensed that the friend had made a spur-of-the-moment decision. The worry was plain in her tone, and it was contagious. Anna said of course.

They met at an Indian restaurant in midtown. A giant with a turban opened the door for Anna, and she found Nancy's friend at the bar. Her name was Gwen. She was tiny, with bobbed red hair and a freckled complexion.

"Have you ever met somebody and just *known* they were lying?" Gwen asked after another turbaned man had seated them. "Nancy invited me to this awful party somewhere on the Lower East Side—artist's loft of some kind. She really wanted me to meet Brook and of course I wanted to get a look at this living doll she'd been raving about. Oh, he was handsome all right. He shakes my hand and he's got this wonderful smile. But he's nervous. Deep down he's nervous. I may not be a genius, but I've got a sense of smell. I think that's why

I liked Nancy right away. She *smells* right, you know? She's real."

Anna smiled. She knew exactly.

"Brook smelled all wrong," Gwen continued. "I don't think I'd been talking to him for three minutes before he told me he was a writer and that he'd just sold a story to *Mademoiselle*. I said great—and then he says, 'And *Esquire* too.' Right away, my nose tells me this guy is lying. In a way, it's amazing—you know? I mean I've had people lie to me, but this was really the first time I'd ever met anybody who just *started in* by lying. Now, I don't know—maybe he *isn't* lying. That's the worst part. I don't have any proof. But Nancy was standing there and holding on to his arm and nodding. *She* believed him. Unquestioningly. If he said it, it was true—finished, done."

Anna ordered a drink and told the waiter they'd put off ordering food for a while.

"Nancy and I share an office over at Pierce and Winters," Gwen went on. "I'm like the first person to see her every day, and what I'm seeing I don't like. She comes in tired, her eyes all bloodshot, like she's been drinking all night, and she tells me about all the fabulous places Brook takes her to—restaurants and nightclubs. I say, 'Gee, this guy must be rich,' and Nancy says, 'Well no, but he's got money about to come in from his stories.' Then she tells me how much—and it's a ridiculous figure! *Nobody* gets that much for just a story. I don't care if it *is* in *Esquire*.

"Then later she comes in one morning and she wants to borrow money from me. From *me!* I'm a total spendthrift. I don't save a nickel. But Nancy . . . Nancy was the kind who was always saving up. You know—living at home, planning to quit and go to Europe to live. Always planning escapes and vacations. She talks about you a lot. About how you got away.

"But now she's trying to borrow from *me*. Something is *wrong*. I think this guy is ripping her off. She talks about him—you know, he's got problems, but he's brilliant. She tells me all the things he's done, and they don't add up. There are contradictions. I try to point them out . . . but have you ever been in the position of wanting to tell a friend her lover is taking her for a ride? I rehearsed it a dozen ways, and there's no way to do it. So I tried to lead her to draw her own conclusions. But when I point out the contradictions, she just gets kind of dizzy—like she must have gotten some of it mixed up.

"Well, yesterday, she told me she'd taken out a Mastercharge card in his name. *Her* account, *his* name. I blew up. I said: 'Nancy, you're crazy! You hardly know this guy. I wouldn't do this for Roger— Roger's my boyfriend—for Roger and we've been living together for two *years!*'

"All Nancy says is that she trusts Brook. 'Trust! Trust!' I said. 'What do you mean trust? What I want to know is why doesn't he have his *own* charge cards?' She says, 'Oh, they took them away.' We better order some food, Anna, or I'm going to get ulcers. Do you see what I'm talking about, though? I mean this is grotesque, isn't it?"

They ordered and food came and Anna grilled Gwen for more details. She wanted to know everything—to know if there was a chance that Gwen was wrong. But by three o'clock, Anna was shuddering a long, continuous pent-up shudder of outrage. What came across again and again was Gwen's description of Nancy's worried face. "We used to go out to lunch together," Gwen said. "But now she says she can't afford it. She brings a cheese sandwich. The same cheese sandwiches every day. I don't think she has a dime she isn't spending on him."

"But she's happy," Anna said. "Isn't she?"

"She's happy all right. But it's got to hit the fan soon. They're planning a *vacation* together. They're going off to the Caribbean for two weeks. At this point all I can do is put on a fake smile and go, 'Isn't that wonderful!' You know how they're going to pay for it? *Her* credit line, on *her* card. 'The money should come in from his stories by the time we're back,' she says.

"Where was I? All right—so yesterday I finally told her that she should consider, just *consider* that maybe Brook is . . . you know, only *hoping* to sell those stories. Maybe she could call the magazines and find out if he really did sell them. She went white. She almost blew up. But then I blew up first and closed the door and told her what I thought.

"It was scary, Anna. I mean it had no *effect* on her." Gwen sat back and sighed. "I don't think there's anything I can do."

Anna walked from the restaurant to the hotel where Jeremy had booked a room for them. The day was warm, with sunlight of almost unnatural clarity. Every person, every building, every detail of fenestration stood out, as if it had grown more real.

Nancy's was the problem of a girl making a fool of herself, the problem of the Bad Man, the User. Anna had met them in her time, and learned to back away fast, not because such men were unattractive, but because they were attractive to the worst part of her nature . . . of every woman's nature, she was convinced: that part where maternalism and masochism had a deadly pact. She had seen friends abused publicly by such dominating men, and then heard those same young women, in private, speak condescendingly of how their lovers needed help, were weak—were just children. If you needed that fix, Anna thought, have a baby . . . and find a man who'll tie you to the bed and whip you. It was better to have the masochism out in the open where you could see it and name it and realize what the sickness was. When she saw a man slighting a woman in public, or striking her, she wanted to claw the bastard's eyes out.

When the image of Brook's bloody eye sockets grew too vivid, Anna made a detour into Saks and went shopping. She could afford very little in her present state, but the saleswoman, noticing her clothes with expert eyes, treated her royally. She settled on a silk blouse that showed off her torso in a demure but alluring manner, and took it along to the hotel.

Jeremy was waiting. Having drawn the curtains, he was sitting in the gloom with—of all things, Anna thought—a Sony Walkman on the arm of his chair, listening through the ultra-light headphones. He seemed strangely at home among the impersonal but elegant eighteenth-century furnishings.

He gave a start when Anna appeared before him. Tearing off the headphones, he seemed on the verge of trying to hide the cassette player. Anna sat on the arm of his chair and ejected the cassette.

"Folk music," Anna mused, taking up the cassette. "Somehow I would never have guessed."

Jeremy held out his hand, and Anna deposited the cartridge in it.

"Don't go all taciturn on me," she said. "I've just heard some amazingly bad news about your tall-blond-and-handsome friend. I spent lunch with one of Nancy's office mates, and she says Brook's ripping Nancy off."

"Brook doesn't steal," Jeremy said.

"He doesn't *have* to steal. Nancy's giving him boxes of money, *all* her money. She's given him a charge card—the whole thing. Jeremy, she isn't rich."

"If she *were* rich, then it would be all right?"

"No. Well, *yes*. You're accusing me, aren't you? That's nasty, Jeremy. I just want to help my sister. We don't have to go into my past, for Christ's sake." Anna was about to add: *Unless we want to go into yours, too*. Then she glanced at the tape cassette. Jeremy was still holding it, like a talisman. All at once she recalled a detail of that awful room in the beach house—a wicker basket beside the bed, full of dusty cartridges.

". . . off?"

"What?" Anna said. "Sorry."

"I said do you think I can just go in there and call him off? It won't work, Anna."

"Tell me, Jeremy. Is Brook a—I don't know—a cad? Reassure me or something."

"I can't, Anna. Brook is no cad, as far as I know. A little blind, willful—but I don't think he'd purposely take your sister for a ride. Jesus, he could pick more lucrative targets if he wanted that. He knows all the right people. He's been in a tough position, hanging out with people who have lots of money, more money than they could ever spend, many of them. He hasn't got a dime of his own since his parents dissociated themselves."

"So he's using my sister's savings to lift his standard of living. Getting a charge card from her. That's cunning."

Jeremy laughed shortly. "Brook may be many things, but he isn't cunning. If he were cunning, I suspect he'd still be practicing law in Boston."

"He's weak then, weak and grasping."

"Yes. Yes, I think that's about right. And I don't think he even knows what he's grasping for."

"I feel like killing him!"

"It's just the money, then? Nothing worse?"

"Isn't that bad enough?"

"It's hers. Let her spend it."

"But *later,* Jeremy."

"Brook doesn't believe in later."

"You three are just a bunch of no-accounts!"

"I wish I could say you're beautiful when you're furious, Anna. Sit down again, would you? On the arm—here. Good, I see you bought something."

"Don't treat me like a pet! You don't even like me much, do you?"

Jeremy pulled her onto his lap. They kissed for long, struggling moments.

"That's no answer," Anna said softly.

Jeremy nodded at the Saks bag. "What is it, a dress?"

"A blouse. Do you want to see it?"

"I want to see it on," Jeremy said.

"I wonder what would happen to us if the sex went away, Jeremy. Sometimes I think we're immoral or something."

"Immoral," Jeremy said. "There's a word I haven't heard in a while." He clasped his hand around Anna's warm white throat. His eyes were dark as caves in chalk cliffside. A glint of fear sparked inside Anna.

"Try it on," Jeremy said. It was almost a command.

Anna swirled to a full-length mirror and removed her blouse. She felt Jeremy's eyes. After a second's hesitation, she unhooked her bra and released her heavy, upright breasts. They swung as she bent to open the Saks bag. She buttoned the blouse, and although she knew she could never dare to wear it this way on the street, braless, she was pleased with the effect.

In the mirror she saw Jeremy's expression cross a range. When she entered, he had been morose, sunk in his chair like an adolescent with the headphones clamped to his ears. Now he was watching her—his rugged face stony, his dark eyes glittering. It was when he looked like this, Anna thought, that he was at his most bewitching. She had learned the gentle art of teasing with her body early in life—unconsciously, on the laps of the old men at the Bird and Gun Club. But she had never met a man who responded as Jeremy did, with a complete and intensely vital seriousness. The transformation came over him, and he became—it was a ridiculous word—*noble* in his lust.

He took up his cane and hobbled forward. As he filled the mirror behind her, the cane toppled to the floor and he unbuttoned the new silk blouse. He held her breasts in hands that were cool.

Reaching down, he took the hem of her skirt and

lifted it, revealing Anna's long, tanned legs. She shifted slightly, her high heels clicking on the hardwood floor like the hooves of a colt, and his hand slid under the waistband of her panties. He held her mound almost violently. His fingertip slid into the slit and began working in the lubricated flesh.

Anna reached behind and unzipped him, her eyes half opened to the spectacle of herself in the mirror. Jeremy's cock jutted out, large and rigid. She fondled it with fluttering palm and fingers.

Breaking away, she began undressing him. He tried to reciprocate, but she said, "No, I want you naked first." She stripped him rapidly.

She ran her hands over the articulations of his shoulders, biceps, chest, stomach. He was beautifully muscled, not like the men she had known, with their tennis-player physiques, but like a boxer, with the boxer's tension and unyielding hardness. His sex was like a muscle too, and she grasped it in her fist, almost wanting to hurt him there, wanting to anger him, make him do things to her that were out of control.

She hiked up her skirt and stood on tiptoe to take his sex between her thighs. She swayed back and forth, kissing him on the lips.

Then she pulled back and stepped out of her skirt. Pulling off her panties, her breasts playing hide-and-seek behind the veils of her open blouse, she knelt on the floor. The wood was hard beneath her knees, and she could see herself in the ornate glass. She kissed Jeremy's cock and balls and, her hands planted on the hardwood, took the head in her mouth. Her lips dragged over the thick shaft, and for a fleeting instant, she saw Nancy and Brook by the creek.

Anna made Jeremy kneel too, and she turned sideways to the mirror, on all fours as he entered her from behind.

With Jeremy it was like unleashing a force of nature. Anna could have her way at the outset, humming an erotic tune to which they both could dance. But soon, and in the end, she always found herself pinned beneath Jeremy's merciless passion. Anna sprawled on the sofa, knees spread as Jeremy plunged into her. She lay on the bed, legs locked around his back as they came a third time. She sucked him in a frenzy as he worked his tongue into her sex. She could not believe the quantity as he shot between her lips. And more after that, until the boundary between day and night faded, and there was nothing but bodies.

At last he rose up, tousled, pale, and damp, the ceiling above him alive with moving shadows. His black eyes, so long distant and dull, focused suddenly on her. He gave his head a shake as if to clear it; a spray of sweat fell on Anna's face like warm rain. Then he smiled, his even white teeth like a crescent moon coming out of eternal eclipse.

"I love you," he said.

❧ nine ❧

The gathering was at a club in Nowhere, Manhattan. Nowhere, to Anna's mind, was a gerrymandered district that comprised all the areas between the places that were Somewhere. The Upper East Side was Somewhere. The West Village was Somewhere. Chinatown and Soho and Little Italy were Somewhere, and so was Chelsea, although only marginally. But Seventeenth Street and Third Avenue was part of Nowhere, despite the presence of this supposedly fabulous club.

There was no trouble getting in, though a crowd waited outside under the discriminating eye of the doorman. His eye, in its way, was no different from that of the saleswoman at Saks. The doorman could tell hip from unhip, and admitted only the former on busy nights—but Wealth he also knew, and also admitted, busy or not.

Inside it was loud, with video screens everywhere. The music was New Wave tapes; the bands would not appear until after midnight. Anna and Jeremy went downstairs to a room lined with television monitors showing a mosaic of scenes from aboriginal life in New Guinea and Australia. The contrast with the hard, futuristic music was strong.

Borders was there with his date, a sullen-looking blonde. Two other couples were there also—friends more of the blonde, Anna guessed, than of Borders or Jeremy or Brook, who sat at the tabletop, and when Nancy kissed her, Anna smelled heavy liquor on her breath. She was flushed and smiling.

Anna prepared herself to hate Brook thoroughly. She watched him closely, almost eagerly. Those beautiful, cool blue eyes, that sandy hair, perfectly tousled, the bright ivory grin—they added up to a mask of duplicity, Anna thought.

"I think your sister has a crush on me," Brook whispered loudly to Nancy.

"She'd better not have! This one is mine, Anna. I'm developing him."

"She thinks I have potential," Brook said.

"The question," Anna said, "is what kind."

Brook shrugged. "The unexamined life," he said, "is the only possible one."

He paid for the next round of drinks, producing a wad of cash. Anna watched Nancy's eyes as he peeled off bills for the waitress. Brook was all carefree largesse; the counting, the worry, was all Nancy's.

The horror of it, for Anna, was that Nancy might already be running out of funds. Brook did not seem vile enough to simply drain the girl and then dump her, but what would happen when Nancy finally let him know she was broke—when it hit the fan, in Gwen's words? Would Brook submit to a life of poverty-for-love's-sake? Get a job? Go to his parents on his knees? He seemed made for spending, for nonchalance. He had probably never tasted the grind of life. Did he sit at a desk and pretend to write as Nancy hurried to work each morning?

"Anna and I have a love-hate relationship, I think," Brook said.

"Looks more like a hate-hate relationship to me," Borders drawled. "Just keep 'em on opposite sides of the table and make sure they don't throw anything."

Borders forced drinks on Anna, and she drank them

like medicine. She knew she was being a complete drag, and ruining her chances at influencing Nancy, but she could not seem to stop herself from feeling steely. Besides, she knew it was nearly impossible, in general, to interfere with people's lives. It was like pitching a stone at a careening boulder: you deflected the boulder, but so slightly, and you could never tell in what direction.

No one wanted to stay for the live bands—"It'll get so fucking *loud* then," said Borders's blonde—so the group decamped to a nearby bar just before midnight, occupying a "garden under the nonstars," as Borders called it. There they dissolved into more alcohol and a good deal of hilarity. Finally everyone agreed they were hungry and fled to an eatery in Soho, making a three-cab caravan.

The eatery was neon-lined and at the peak of chic. The menu featured many species of outlandish nouvelle dishes; and Anna declared that if she even had to *smell* lobster in vanilla sauce she could not be responsible for the consequences. There was general agreement that kiwi fruit had made altogether too many inroads. Death to the kiwi fruit.

In every city of the Christian world, Anna knew, women sat alone in restaurants, making the best of their loneliness; brave or pathetic, according to the observer's point of view. But in the darkest corner of the neon-lit eatery, Anna grew aware—as one grows aware of chronic pain, suddenly realizing it has been there all the time—of a girl.

The girl's dress was white, catching the neon and softening it into an aura. Her face rose into shadow. She seemed weirdly headless, her pale hands wrapped around a glass of Coke, a plain sandwich lying untouched on her small table. They were girl's hands; the body was a girl's body.

Anna did not like to stare, but the girl was so still, like the super-real acrylic casts of people she had seen in a museum once, so alive-seeming that you said "excuse me" if you happened to bump into one. She gathered stillness around her, like an emblem of the quiet isolation Anna felt in the jaggedly hip crowd at her table.

"Don't go spacy on us, Anna!"

She turned back to her companions. Except for Jeremy, they seemed unutterably ugly and coarse—flung from the panels of a comic strip. She met Jeremy's eyes and for a terrible moment thought: *This is how he always sees.*

Borders, of course, knew of an after-hours club; and the caravan formed again, zooming through deserted streets. Jeremy kissed Anna, kissed her hard, in the backseat of their Checker. His hand squeezed her breast and held it until she could feel her heart beating in his palm.

The after-hours club was colorful high sleaze, with craps tables and even a roulette wheel. Anna was drunk. Small charges were detonating in her head, lending meaning to the word *blasted.* Jeremy was exuberant. He drank like everyone else, even more perhaps. But he never seemed to stagger or wilt.

"He never gets drunk," Anna whispered to herself. Then louder: "He *never* gets drunk!"

"It's true! It's true!" cried Borders, who had had one year of medical school and was the resident authority. "It's an objective fact!" He drained his glass and inverted it over Jeremy's chest.

"Pulse is steady," he announced solemnly. "Too steady."

Everyone laughed and ordered more drinks and soon it was hold-back-the-dawn time. Anna sensed deeply, with a suddenness that was almost shock, that without Jeremy this reeling constellation would fall apart: Borders would sink into the despair that walked beside him, step by step; Brook would turn, inside and out, into a creature of cynicism. The party would break up, and not dawn, but total night would descend on the friends—friends who could raise their glasses to toast each other amid the rattle of dice and the rise and fall of love's passion, which was nothing more than another rattle of the dice. . . .

"Anna's going maudlin," Brook said.

In the Neanderthal bathroom Nancy caught up with Anna and asked if she could borrow fifty dollars. In the back of Anna's mind, like a little mouse scuttling back and forth, was the knowledge that this graffiti-streaked pissoir was not the place to set up a trade in Truth About Boyfriends, but Anna unpacked her wares nevertheless.

In the end, Anna thought, Nancy acted like a junkie. Yes yes and no no, but I need the fifty dollars. She had always been the money-careful one, Nancy, and with the end of caution had come a great yawning anxiety. She told the one about Brook's stories, and Anna heard herself laugh. It was a laugh she had heard before, from old, face-lifted women on balconies where servants moved invisibly—the laughter of too much experience, throaty and knowing and derisive. Nancy told the one about the stories, and Anna shattered it—not gently, but with a hammer blow. In the morning she would wish she had been drunker, drunk enough not to remember. She gave Nancy the fifty dollars, leaving herself nothing. In that room of stained cream tile and blue trim, she pulled the gold watch from her wrist and offered that too. As she held it out, they both began to cry.

"Give it to him," Anna sobbed. "Give him everything. If he loves you, really loves you, give him everything. Because it will never happen again. Does he though, Nancy? If he does—if he does—"

Nancy gave back the watch, convinced her sister was insane. Anna simply would not stop sobbing, and Nancy found that she was chagrined at having to comfort her in these dreary surroundings. Hell, she was crying herself. Anna upstaged everybody and everything.

Nancy laughed. "If he doesn't," she said, "I'm out some money."

They staggered back to their table, arm in arm.

"Oh shit," Borders said. "High drama in the powder room." The blonde was asleep in her chair. The other two couples had winged into the night. Brook stood and took Nancy by the arm like an invalid, casting a harsh glance at Anna, as if to say, *What have you been doing to her?* "It's time," he said, "to break up this scene."

As spring matured into summer, it seemed to Anna that Jeremy was beginning to open up. A black cloud had been hanging over both of them, she realized. Hers was Jean, the past, the bleak prospect for the future. Jeremy's cloud remained an enigma, although she began to glimpse aspects of it. But with the coming of long, sun-filled days, both clouds began to thin. Anna and Jeremy rose earlier in the morning to hit the beaches or drive upstate. They played in the surf of the South Shore, and laughter seemed to come more easily between them. Where the nights had been powered by alcohol and desperate, insatiable lovemaking, they now featured moments of warmth. The silences seemed less like bottomless pits, and when Anna broke them, Jeremy welcomed her conversation. It was like being in love.

They saw less of Borders, and nothing of Brook, shunning the city, spending evenings on the patio or the pier. One evening they even went to a drive-in double feature and ate three boxes of popcorn. Anna had remembered the drive-in as a place for locking limbs, a scene of carnal struggles. But she and Jeremy parodied it all, fumbling at each other idiotically until she giggled herself sick.

Later that night they stationed themselves on the

patio with lemonades. The sky was mottled with underlit clouds that marched slowly over the bay, lights glittering on the far shore. Anna said: "Jeremy, how did you get your limp?"

Jeremy flashed her a hot glare of betrayal. Anna recoiled inside.

"At birth," he said shortly.

"That's not true, Jeremy. I've seen pictures of you from before. You weren't in Vietnam or anything, were you?"

"Hardly."

"Oh. Oh well, there goes that theory."

"It was an accident, all right?"

Silence fell.

"What kind of accident?" Anna asked carefully.

"A drug overdose," Jeremy said. "Pills."

"Oh Christ. Were you heavy into drugs?"

"I was that day."

"But I don't understand how it—your left side—"

"That was the side I was lying on when I went out. That's all I know."

"You were sleepwalking again last night."

Jeremy nodded.

"Do you ever remember?" Anna asked.

"No, not really. But I can . . . *feel* that I've done it."

"It's eerie, you know. You always go to the window"—she pointed to the picture window behind them—"or to the sliding doors. It's like you're keeping watch. Then I lead you back. Did the sleepwalking start after the overdose?"

"No," Jeremy said, "it started when I came here."

After that he asked her if she'd learned enough for the night. Anna said yes, thanks. They talked about the views they had seen, the places where they had sat, like this one, with drinks in their hands. Anna found herself telling too much about school and lovers, and about Jean.

"Is that really why you left him?" Jeremy asked.

There was a note of incredulity, even cynicism, in the question. It was Anna's turn to glare.

"You don't know, Jeremy. There are so many—there's an army of rich, lonely women out there."

"Rich, lonely men too," Jeremy said, thinking of his stepfather and the marriage to a secretary.

"Yes, but if you're a man, you can buy yourself a nice young companion. Do you know what it's like when a woman does that? Do you know how people look at her? Somehow it's contemptible for a woman. I think it's contemptible all around."

"So it's loneliness you're afraid of? That's no privilege of the wealthy."

"No, it isn't loneliness. I'll never be lonely," Anna said. In the big quiet night, it sounded like bravado to her.

Jeremy looked at her seriously.

"Not if I can help it," he said.

He looked away, out to the bay, took a drink from his glass, and set it down with a click.

"And you will never wander," Anna heard herself say.

Anna rolled over to reach for Jeremy and touched nothing. She sank back into sleep . . . then jerked awake. She sat up in bed, swaying in the grainy dimness. *Oh Christ*, she thought, *it's happening again.*

Sighing, she threw on a robe and slipped out of the bedroom. Secretly, she had come to like finding Jeremy at the window. Once or twice she had taken a seat on one of the sofas and watched him, moonlight bathing him as he stood at the glass in nothing but his pajama bottoms. He was very beautiful then. She liked leading him back to bed and putting his head on the pillow, shutting his eyes with gentle fingers. At first it was a little frightening. Anna wasn't superstitious, but she was still dreadfully afraid of awakening him. The stories she remembered said he would drop dead—or was it go insane? She clucked this nonsense away, but if his "nocturnal strolls," as he called them, were somehow a side effect, mightn't something awful happen anyway? So she led him carefully, like a child pulling a wagon stacked high with boxes. It was nice to feel needed, and as she wrapped an arm around him under the sheets, Anna felt she had recovered something.

She padded downstairs. At night especially, the house seemed like a big summer place waiting emptily for guests. Anna peered across the huge living room.

The place at the window was bare. Moonlight poured across the floor.

"Jeremy?"

Anna poked around the ground floor and found nothing. Had he strayed outside?

It was a sultry night, but Anna pulled the robe tight as she stepped onto the terrace. The lawn sloped gray in the moonlight, and below, the pier jutted like an arrow into the bay. The houses on the far shore were distinct as toys. But as she scanned the grounds she saw no sign of Jeremy.

Then a flash of motion caught Anna's eye from the enclosure of the boxwood garden, and she gave a sigh of relief. There he was, walking sound asleep among the marble planters and rigid statuary. With a little smile she set off across the grass toward the boxwoods, grateful that the fears she had been beating down— Jeremy drowned, Jeremy struck on the road—had come to nothing.

But at the hedges Anna stopped short; flashing between them she glimpsed not only Jeremy but someone else, a girl in white.

She hesitated, reconsidering. Well, Jeremy wasn't sleepwalking then. Well then, he was out walking, in the absolute dead of night, with a girl—a young girl by the look of her. And she, Anna, had on nothing but a bathrobe. It was not exactly a standard-issue social situation, but Anna was damned if she'd go back up to the house. She had her line and she decided to play it.

She strolled into the garden.

"Jeremy!" she said with a small cry. "I thought you were sleepwalking."

Jeremy said nothing. The girl said nothing.

Anna vibrated by the hedges. Her mouth opened again, and then closed without a sound.

Moonlight cast a spell over the garden. The black walls of boxwood, like walls of night, cut off the world. Flower beds lay lush and heavy, the blossoms gray in the darkness like otherworldly blooms. The rich perfume of summer hung in the motionless air. Waves lapped distantly.

Jeremy and the girl walked slowly around the flower beds, he a head taller, dressed only in black pajama bottoms. His eyes were open but bland, as if gazing at the farthest horizon.

The girl walked in white. Her skin was completely pale, framed by long raven hair and set with large, sorrowing eyes that seemed to see nothing and everything. They were a grim and luminous couple.

Anna glanced to the girl's feet, as if to reassure herself that she had weight, could leave an impression on the grass.

On her feet the girl wore patchwork slippers.

Anna backed away, her chest rising and falling jaggedly. She stumbled back, back, out of the garden, the black hedge-wall receding like the inner room of a forgotten dream.

A cold hand clutched at her wrist. Anna gave a strangled cry.

"Shh!" came a hissing voice.

An old woman twisted before her. She was disheveled, her white hair a bedraggled halo. Her eyes stared angrily from sunken sockets. Her grip was powerful and obsessive.

"Let go of me!" Anna shrieked.

"I will!" the old woman said. "There! Now—now

go, get on! Go back to your own bed." She lowered her voice to a menacing whisper. "Can't you see they shouldn't be disturbed? Can't you see?" She finished with a shout of triumph:

"Can't you see they're in love?"

Anna shook out the three tranquilizers and gulped them down. She slapped the medicine cabinet shut and propped herself on the sink, eyes closed, praying for the pills to take effect. She had heard the phrase "shaking like a leaf" but she had never felt it. Now she felt it: there was nothing to her but a shudder. Dots swam in a field of pulsing black.

She went to a credenza in the living room and pulled out a bottle of vodka. She splashed vodka over the credenza, missing the glass, but when she hit the glass she filled it and drank it clean to chase the pills.

Immediately she felt better. She sat on a sofa. She got up and sat on a chair. She got up and went back to the bedroom with the bottle. She was trying not to think, not even to be, because when she thought she thought a skull, and no force of thought could rid her of a cloying sense of death.

She sat in the bed, being ordinary, clutching the idea of ordinary the way a woman will hold a dead child. She drank from the vodka and then the tranquilizers broke through the wall, climbing over her like friendly animals. She flicked out.

When she woke up, it was the gray edge of morning. Dim light filtered through the curtains. The furniture threatened to dissolve.

Anna spun in bed and found Jeremy beside her, sleeping expressionlessly.

Then she looked up in time to see a wisp of white fabric flashing out the bedroom doorway.

She fountained out of bed, her heart hammering painfully. She looked at Jeremy. She looked at the door.

She surged into the hall, down, and into the living room, where she caught a glimpse of white vanishing at the far end, where the library lay.

The library door slammed shut.

Anna seized the knob and pulled. The door bulged out and bounced closed. Anna could feel the girl's weight on the other side.

"Anna! What's going on?"

It was Jeremy, limping fast. Anna leaned back hard on the doorknob and said: "It's Catherine, isn't it?"

Anna watched Jeremy's face turn ugly. Ugly with shock. Then uglier with hope. He pried her fingers from the door and pushed her away. She slammed back against the far side of the hall.

The door flew open and Jeremy rushed in. Anna hesitated. Then she followed.

In the morning softness she saw pale oak paneling, shelves of books, cream leather club chairs, and desk.

She whirled to left and right, saw nothing more—

—saw curtains billowing at one window, even as Jeremy saw too.

He ran to the window and climbed out. Anna heard him thud to the grass.

Incredibly, dawn became day and the sun rose into a sky of painfully clear blue. Anna sat on the terrace, clothed and rigid, watching daylight transform the estate. Where was Jeremy? Insects whirred and Anna felt that if they were to suddenly stop she would flicker out of existence.

What she had felt with Jean in the end, what she had felt in the sepulchral offices of the Swiss bankers—all the leaden burden of lifelessness she had felt then she now felt a hundred times more. She had no ideas, she was too broken for ideas, but she needed no ideas to smell what she could smell, what she had smelled, at the last, in Jean and his world—the stench of morbidity.

"Yo-ho!" a cheerful voice called.

Anna turned her head slowly. Her bleary eyes followed.

It was Brook, striding tall, clean, blond across the expanse of bright green grass between servants' quarters and terrace. He gave a jaunty wave.

Anna broke from the table and ran toward him. He slowed with a puzzled look.

"Get me away from here, please," she said. "Can you? Your car?"

"Parked there." Brook nodded worriedly toward the parking area.

"Please," Anna said. She took his arm and they walked to the old Plymouth. He patted her hand and asked no questions.

Anna threw herself in. The door chunked shut. Another door shut and Brook was beside her gunning the engine.

The car lurched into reverse. Brook straightened it out and soon they were passing through the gate.

"Brook," she said. "Where—where are we going?"

Nancy read the letter again and again, stalking the apartment she had shared with Brook. She read it until it burned her to the quick. Then she found a bottle of cognac and got drunk and read it again. On the coffee table lay Caribbean travel brochures. She swept them to the floor. When the first bottle was drained, she found another, Armagnac, and dispensed with the glass. She plunged into the bedroom and spat on the bed. She threw open the closet door and clawed down Brook's beautiful suits, tearing and shredding them.

She smashed his photograph. She rushed back into the living room and hurled books from their shelves and records from their sleeves. Each shatter lashed her nerves. She located the letter in the rubble and read it again. She poured Armagnac over it and set it on fire. It burned with a low, mysterious flame until she stamped it into ashes. Then she lurched into the bathroom and threw up and crumpled to the tiles and began to cry.

It was unfair, unfair, unfair!

"Anna!" she raged aloud as she fell back against the bathtub. "Anna, you thief!"

❧ ten ❧

Rivulets of rain streaked the glass. Anna and Brook had fled to Martha's Vineyard, and Jeremy had decided to follow them. Ahead two islands floated black in the North Atlantic waters, silhouetted against the night sky. Jeremy checked his watch. The ferry would soon make the channel between them. The larger island of Martha's Vineyard lay an hour beyond.

The big cabin of the ferry was all but empty of passengers. Smells of salt sea, engine oil, and the lingering odor of hot dogs filled the air. Despite the roaring of the engines, the cabin seemed silent in its scrubbed whiteness, its unused booth waiting for more animated seasons.

On the phone Brook had said, "Christ, what's the proper formulation? I've ripped you off, old friend." Pacing to the rear of the cabin, Jeremy watched New Bedford dropping away, a cluster of lights on the black mainland.

Jeremy had said, "Let me talk to her," but Anna refused to take the receiver.

Jeremy told himself he only wanted answers, but he wanted something more. He wanted Anna. The roar of engines filled his ears, punctuated by the slapping of the prow as it tilted over the choppy waters.

What pulled him toward Anna was physical. Not a refined thing, but a desire that had solidified into a need, a need that had burned white-hot until it glowed to a steady ember of something close to love, closer than Jeremy Penn had felt in the decade since.

Yes he had run, but no he had not found the Catherine Anna had seen. What he found were empty lawns and empty road. He had searched for hours and only when he was done did he stop to consider how long he had searched, how earnestly, how believingly.

He had wandered for years, and why had he come home? Because in the world there walked no Catherine. Because the opium of Marseilles, the hashish of Morocco, the whores of Hamburg could not bring him to his senses. Because he wanted to return his senses to the last place those senses had seen, heard, and felt a girl long dead.

He had called for her in the night a thousand times, and now—he had realized it only as he searched in the dawn for a thing that Anna had seen—and now he had stopped calling, because of a woman, a woman as strong and desperate and, in her way, as wandering as himself. It was an irony, and of all the things life had prepared Jeremy for, irony was foremost: he had crossed the globe, yet only in returning home did he find the stranger who freed his memory.

A thin, driving rain spattered the glass. Past the barren deck, the sea churned darkly. Farther out, sea and sky merged in a vague horizon.

Anna, Jeremy thought, *what did you see? Nothing more than a moment when sea and sky, life and death, merged without a break?*

Or did you see her?

He understood, he understood why Anna fled, and he would try to make her feel that this had welded them together. He sensed that this thing showed the oneness of their hearts. He had thrown into her the deepest need of his soul, even as she had made, at last, that need wane.

Finding an abandoned newspaper, Jeremy left the

window and returned to his booth. For a moment, he thought he caught a glimpse of white on the deck outside. *A seagull,* he thought.

The tabloid teemed with incidents of crime and death and extraterrestrial wonder. Ads guaranteed weight loss. BIGFOOT ADOPTS HUMAN BABY, a headline read. Starlets leered from the pages, giving their reasons for divorce.

Jeremy gave a start. He was sure, now, that he had seen a flash of white through the glass by his elbow. A voice inside told him not to turn, not to look.

He turned. He looked.

He saw a girl behind the rain-streaked glass.

Her eyes were the eyes of a homeless child looking in at a feast. Her black hair was pasted to her forehead and neck. Her white dress clung wetly to her slim figure.

She seemed not to see him, staring over his head searchingly.

Stepping back, she dissolved into the veil of rain.

Jeremy threw open the hatch and lurched out onto the windswept deck. The sharp rain stung his face. The hatch boomed shut behind him. Gusts blew loudly in his ears, and the open sea had a sound of infinite restlessness.

The downpour hung like a mist over the deserted deck. Light from the cabin cast yellow rectangles on the plating. Further forward, the pilothouse gave off a diffuse glow. On the dark waters the ship was like a solitary prairie house.

Jeremy strode ahead, peering into the gloom cast by the superstructure of the ferry. The silver tip of his cane clacked on the deck.

"Come out!" he shouted.

Suddenly Jeremy drew back, possessed by a fierce urge to return to the cabin. An awful foreboding welled up in him.

It was then that the girl drifted shyly from behind a cowling.

The wind whipped at her clothes. She glowed luminously in the scant light. But she was *there*. Jeremy saw how her hair hung in drooping strands, how her white dress lay plastered against her small breasts. He strained to see through her to the railing beyond, but she was solid.

Jeremy began to speak. His voice faltered.

"Tell me who you really are!" he managed to shout. "Tell me your real name!"

The girl stared back wide-eyed.

"Tell me!" he shouted over the howling wind. "What is it? Is it Jane? Is it Carol? Who are you really?"

The girl stepped closer, like a wan melody growing louder.

"Don't you remember me?" she asked. "Doesn't anyone know me here?"

Jeremy felt his heart stop beating.

"Catherine!" he whispered.

The girl beamed happily and ran up to Jeremy. Leaning on his cane, he put out a trembling hand, almost as if to ward her off. The girl took it. He felt a terrible warmth.

"You're alive," he rasped, looking her up and down. "This hand—this—you're alive."

"Only," Catherine said, "as much as you."

Jeremy pulled away. A gust of wind jostled him like an invisible mob. Suddenly he felt the need to lean against the hatch.

"What do you mean by that?" he asked with a surge of anger. Dizziness almost overwhelmed him. He felt his own chest. "Here, here I am! Touch me, I'm—"

Catherine gazed at him pityingly.

"No," Jeremy said.

Dazed, he began pulling at the hatch.

"No," he muttered. "No."

"We went together," he heard Catherine's voice—and it *was* her voice—say behind him. Her tone was quiet, as if she were reluctant to hurt him. "Can you remember it, even a little? A long, long slope, everything gray, a whole river of us moving down and down."

"No!" Jeremy shouted.

But he did remember, from a dozen dreams, the kind so dreary and sluggish that they seemed to bring their unreality with them into the waking day.

"You turned back, Jeremy, remember? I think I know why. Maybe you had too much life still in you."

Jeremy's hand relaxed on the handle of the hatch. He felt an easeful silence opening up inside him.

"I wanted to stay," he said distantly, as if he were trying out the words.

"Yes you did. You wanted to stay with me. I believe that, I held on to that. But more than that you wanted to go back into the sunshine. We all did, you know. But you were different. You somehow—" She paused. "But you never really did, did you Jeremy? You never really did find the sunshine."

Jeremy turned to face her. He felt lost in a dream, certain he must be dozing over his newspaper, *there,* in that very booth he could see obliquely through the nearby glass.

"You told me I could try, didn't you?" he asked.

"Jeremy, you were never meant to come along. It was my road to walk alone. I always said that. Can you remember? We stood still while the gray river of people streamed around us. You kissed me and said goodbye. I turned to watch you pushing your way against the current. I waved, but you never looked back."

Against the current. It was strange, Jeremy thought, but that was how he had felt all these years: as if he were swimming against a current . . .

From the pilothouse came a deafening toot. Jeremy looked around, half hoping to awaken. The ship was making the channel. On either side the two islands loomed darkly, glittering here and there with points of light.

When he glanced back toward Catherine, he almost expected her to have vanished.

But she was still there, silent and waiting.

For a long time they stood wordlessly on the deck. Rain battered them. Around their little dimlit stage the sea churned like angry obsidian.

"You want me to come back with you," Jeremy finally said.

Catherine turned her face away to look out over the black waters. She moved to the railing.

"This water," she said, "is cold and dark. But not for long."

She glanced at Jeremy with a guilty look. He came to the railing with her. The rain pricked his face. He could hear the heavy, rhythmic pounding of the ferry's prow as it slapped the waves.

"And that place," he asked. "Is there nothing more to it? Is it gray"—he shuddered—"is it cold and dark and nothing else, nothing else for all eternity?"

"I don't know, Jeremy. Everyone else moved on. Only I stayed in the grayness. Some people talked about a Light at the end, others said no, that we were just slowly fading. But all of us, I think, hoped for the Light. I guess that hope, in the end, was all we had. I still hope."

"But you. You didn't fade."

She smiled. "Because you kept calling, Jeremy. Now . . . now can we hope together?"

When the ferry docked at Edgartown, Martha's Vineyard, two passengers—one with a ticket, the other without—stayed on deck. In the dark and the rain no one noticed. At last a weary crewman threw off the lines and the ferry pulled away, homeward bound.

More than once—as the ferry made its way, between the black islands and to the old, embracing harbor of

New Bedford—more than once Jeremy walked to the rail with Catherine and peered into the black sea.

But when the ship tied up at home port he was still aboard. He watched as Catherine ran desperately to the gangway and clattered down to the pier.

There, in the harsh glow of a sodium lamp, a gray-haired woman stood waiting.

❧ eleven ❧

Before long, Nancy Ravine broke down and told her office mate that the romance with Brook was over, finished. Gwen said, "You're better off without him," and meant it. But when the whole story came out, she pursed her lips, whistled, and plumped into her swivel chair. "You poor little bastard," she said. Nancy shut the cubicle door and cried. "Your own goddamned sister!" Gwen raged. "Jesus, and she seemed like such an okay person."

The office was the worst place. In the cool, air-conditioned hum, Nancy ground through the tedium of searching for documents, indexing, and digesting. Not long ago, she remembered, the boredom had been eased by thoughts of Brook, a melody that played in the background and made her long for five o'clock.

Now she longed for nothing. The apartment greeted her with hollow emptiness. The nights stretched on and on, sleepless. Even the memories were worthless; there were too few of them. She had only begun to close her hands around love when it had crumbled into dust, into the smudge of ash on the carpet. The apartment wasn't even *hers:* it smelled of Brook. It was as if she were still living inside him.

Bills kept coming in. The rent, as usual. But also notices from the credit companies. She had spent an appalling amount of money. *Brook* had spent an appalling amount of money. In the mornings, when depression hit her the hardest and she wanted just to lie there in the twisted sheets, she remembered how much she owed. Anxiety forced her out of bed and into the shower, suffocating her, steeling her for the eight-hour ordeal at the brown formica desk.

"Nancy," Gwen said, "maybe you should think about moving back home."

She resisted. Home. It was like admitting failure. But then a wave of fresh bills came in the mail, like a series of punches. Restaurants Nancy had forgotten she'd dined in. Clothes she'd forgotten having bought. She had spent the money with abandon, but now she writhed with worry over the deadly interest charges. There was nothing left to fall back on. She spent whole evenings figuring how much she owed, her bank book open. It would take more than a year to pay back. And the rent. The rent was the biggest bite.

Nancy edged herself homeward by stages. First, a weekend. Her mother kissed her and asked no questions. Big Bill grinned madly, and at dinner he glowed.

The second weekend ended with Nancy buying a commutation ticket. Now *this*, she thought, was really too much—adding commuting costs to her already impossible budget. She called the landlord and said she was vacating immediately. Gwen's boyfriend popped by with his car, and the three of them drove Nancy's belongings back to the big estate on Long Island. Home.

The evenings brought long hours on the porch, surrounded by fragrant cordwood and stacks of newspapers. The new summer's air was warm and healing. But from the main house came, from time to time, the strains of piano music.

Nancy's mother reported that Jeremy seemed depressed. He wanted to be left alone, and would cook his own meals, thank you.

Sometimes at night, when insomnia kept Nancy from her sleep, she could see him wandering the estate, looking haggard, his limp more pronounced than she remembered, leaden.

The sounds from his piano had changed too, she thought. Melancholy, hesitant, discordant—they were all stronger than they had been before, strong enough to catch Nancy unawares and chill her. Sitting on the porch, she listened, wondering what precisely Anna possessed that she could take and take and take—that she could travel and never hold a job and make people miserable, even her *own sister*, even handsome men, and still have everything she wanted.

Friday nights, Gwen rode the train out with Nancy and stayed over. Together they would sit on the porch and consume dead man's whiskey while Nancy became absurdly maudlin and bitter by turns. On Saturdays Gwen returned to the city, and Roger.

On one of these Friday nights—the last of them—Gwen and Nancy drank too much and excavated their respective pasts. All the old boyfriends were paraded for inspection. All the old mistakes and all the old good times were reviewed. Even the parents were dragged in.

"I let myself get too sheltered," Nancy said. "That was my big mistake."

"All that means is you were a virgin until you were nineteen. What's that make you, a *nun?*"

"I don't mean sex only. I did everything close to home. I went to college where I could be close to my parents. I stayed here when I started working. And I'm back. Back again."

"Ah, so what? You could *live* with your parents, at least," Gwen said. "I ran off screaming. Your folks are nice. You think if you get a one-room cave in the city, you'll turn glamorous?"

"My folks aren't nice. They're like old beat-up

furniture. Someday I'll be old beat-up furniture too. Already I feel like old beat-up furniture."

"That's because you've been beat up, that's why. Look, you got screwed."

"Royally," Nancy said.

"Royally screwed. Boy, you're going to have some great family reunions, you and Anna. Don't you just want to strangle her?"

"I did at first. I wanted to strangle them both. But now I just feel . . . tired."

"Oh, bullshit! Last Friday you still wanted to strangle them. Get mad, for Christ's sake! They're up there in Martha's Vineyard having fun! They screwed you! Get mad!"

"It *would* be nice to kill them. I hope they're miserable. He really *was* a rotten pig, wasn't he, Gwen?"

"You know me. I defended him from the first."

"But I'll tell you what I realized, though. They're— they're alike. You know? Anna and Brook."

"That's why they'll be miserable," Gwen said. "They're *both* leeches."

"Gwen, she's my *sister!*"

"Too bad she didn't remember that."

"Gwen!"

"They're both leeches. Okay, *nice* leeches. Cuddly leeches. But they don't know how to work—I mean, has either of them ever earned a day's pay?"

"Brook, before he was disbarred. Besides, earning a day's pay isn't a virtue. It's just what you have to do."

"If you aren't a leech," Gwen said.

"Or rich."

"Or rich."

They gazed through the wire screen, down the curving driveway to the big house.

"Oh Gwen," Nancy said, "I was so tired of my life. Tired unto death. Somehow I'd managed to do everything I thought was right and still have nothing in the end. Nothing but a job I hated and a bed with nobody in it and stretches of boredom that felt like they'd go on forever. So I went out and made a total fool of myself. And now I don't even—I can't even go on *vacation!*"

Nancy began to bawl.

"Jesus, this is fun," Gwen said. Then, in a whisper, "Nancy, how much does Brook owe you anyway—between that credit card you gave him and everything?"

"Four thousand *dollars!*"

A spectacle of tousled brown hair and pale, wet skin, Nancy gazed apprehensively at Gwen, expecting a torrent of abuse for her stupidity.

Instead, Gwen began to cry too.

Big Bill came out from the house and stood behind the screen door.

"What happened? What happened?" he roared.

"Nothing, Daddy. Go back to sleep."

"What's everybody crying for?"

Big Bill lumbered back into the house, muttering.

Later Nancy said again, "But they *are* alike, Anna and Brook," but by then it was after one, and Gwen had subsided into a doze. Nancy shook her awake and led her up to her room—Anna's room.

"Aha, the traitor's quarters," Gwen said.

Nancy was in her stocking feet to keep the noise to a minimum, and as she made her way back down, she slipped on the polished stairs and slid to the landing.

Gwen appeared at the head of the stairway.

"Nancy, are you okay?"

"I'm drunk, drunk."

"Nothing broken? If you say 'only my heart,' I'll come down and kick you."

"Go to bed," Nancy called up as she staggered to her feet. "I'm going to go back to the porch and get even drunker. Life stinks, Gwen."

Gwen's face grew serious at the top of the stairs.

"Oh Nancy," she said. "It does not. It really doesn't. Why don't you read me a story or something?"

"Go to bed, Gwen. Ow, my back."

"Did you hurt your back?"

"I'm crippled. Go to bed. I'll just drag myself along the floor. Boy, does life ever smell."

"Okay . . ."

"I'll just slip into my iron lung and get drunk through a tube."

"Good night, Nancy. And it really doesn't you know. Not really and completely."

"I know, I know. Just the part with me in it."

Back to the porch. Bottle, glass. The bottle said "Clark" on it in Magic Marker. It was some kind of Scotch that didn't even exist anymore. The crickets chirped and every once in a while a car zoomed by on the road at the edge of the estate.

Nancy remembered the day when Anna had been packed off to the school in Connecticut. Anna sat in the front seat of the car during the interminable drive while Nancy had the back to herself. Her memory was bad; all she could recall was the horrible sense that the whole family was being punished for being poor. And the school itself, dignified and isolated, and the strange mix of emotions on Anna's face. That day had marked the beginning of Anna's escape . . . while, for herself, the ride home to the club had been the first of many such returns. Home, always home, wherever Mary and Big Bill were. Where little sister lived.

No, life didn't stink. Not completely and really. Only if you were a sheltered little coward . . . and a little fool who imagined men were in love with you.

Eventually, Nancy began to feel genuinely ill. Sitting in one place made her dizzy, and she had to work actively to keep her head from spinning off and her dinner from coming up. She took a walk.

Her stockinged feet thudded heavily on the grass. She felt heavy and gross. Yet if she could have seen herself then, weaving and disheveled, long brown hair awry, and dark eyes milking tears—more beautiful at her worst than at her best . . .

"Life is p-u-u-t-rid," she sang.

She ambled down the slope, past the pool and the boxwood garden, past the cabañas at the foot of the pier, and out on the long, spindly-legged black dock itself.

It was a night of appalling beauty, the bay dark and still, lights on the far shore, the distinct sound of boats chunking against their moorings. At the end of the pier, Nancy looked down at the low-tide wavelets and thought about—

Girl overboard. Tragedy. What a tragedy. How could I have done this to my own sister! I never loved you, Anna! I loved her! And now I have lost her forever!

Suddenly, amid these overwrought and idle musings about self-slaughter, Nancy grew afraid that she would fall off the pier and actually drown. Very carefully, she lowered herself to the old boards and sat. The whirlies returned with a vengeance, but Nancy, like a cat up a tree, felt immobilized. The stars were clear and many and dimly seen . . .

When she awoke, the boards were rough against her cheek, and she felt sore all over. It was still dark, and the salty fresh air struck her nostrils, bringing a recollection of how she had come to the pier and passed out. It was disgusting.

Then she heard the footsteps on the boards, clear and hard, felt the vibration through her cheekbones.

A voice said: "Green, then wet for a long time. Then green again."

Oh God, it was Jeremy! Looming above her, Jeremy! Nancy gathered herself together, hot with shame. She had been *groveling* on the pier, completely smashed. She knew she must stink of whiskey. A sour little songbird began to chirp that this was the end: she had degenerated totally.

Brushing herself off with what she hoped were self-possessed motions, Nancy got to her feet and piped, "Hello, Mr. Jeremy."

She nearly swooned with the stupidity of this. What was she, a pickaninny? *Mr.* Jeremy!

Jeremy said, "See that house there? You can just make out the windows through the trees. It looks like a Frank Lloyd Wright."

Nancy spun, but she saw only lights that all looked alike, peeking through the trees that covered the hills rising from the edges of the bay.

"This place?" Jeremy said with a small laugh. "I don't think this place was designed by anybody! It just grew."

He's in his bathrobe, Nancy thought. She did not want to turn around, but the first look she had had of him came back: bathrobe, cane.

"It's lovely," she said.

"At night the whole facade is lighted," Jeremy said. Nancy strained, but saw nothing.

"So you must go to school here," Jeremy said.

"Yes—well, no. I mean—"

Jeremy laughed. Nancy edged away and turned to face him.

"I've heard it's that kind of place," he said.

Nancy fell silent. Jeremy hobbled to the edge of the pier.

"Oh Christ no." He smiled. "They wouldn't dream of sending me anywhere else. The pier, though—I swear it's dangerous. I guess your father will be going at it pretty soon?"

"I don't understand," Nancy said. The fog of alcohol had been momentarily cleared out of her head, as if by a cold gust. Jeremy's eyes were focused on the distance, but an animation and happiness suffused his features—and Nancy found it terrifying. He was like a madman.

"Jeremy?" she asked.

"Summer is like that," Jeremy said.

142

Abruptly, Nancy reached out and took this strange man by the shoulder and began shaking him.

Just as abruptly, he dropped his cane and wrapped his arms around her. For a suffocating instant Nancy thought he was going to kill her.

Then she kissed him.

She would wonder later why. She would tell herself that she had been confused or drunk. She would tell herself that life had seemed so poor and hopeless that she had been driven by instinct to take one chance— one real chance. She would remember, also, how lost and infatuated Jeremy had seemed.

The kiss was brief. Jeremy pulled away.

He reeled back, unsteady without his cane. He glanced from left to right, disoriented, a wild look of terror shooting from his eyes.

"Who are you?" he breathed.

"I'm Nancy Ravine."

"Nancy Ravine. Nancy Ravine. Yes. Yes, Nancy."

Jeremy clutched his face. Nancy recovered his cane and held it out to him.

He stared at it dumbly.

When he began to cry, Nancy was aghast. She watched him stagger back down the pier, leaning on the railing, off balance and out of control.

Finally, he crumpled to the boards. Sobs tore from his chest.

Nancy ran to him, knelt by his side.

"Here," she said, pushing the cane into his hands. "Take this. Get up. It's all right, really it is. It's—it's Catherine, isn't it?"

Jeremy unfolded himself. He looked at the cane. He looked at Nancy. She felt herself falling into his intense black eyes.

"Help me up?" he said.

She gave him her hand. His grip was powerful, and was she dreaming or did he hold on to it an instant longer than was necessary?

"I'm sorry," he said. "I grabbed you, didn't I?"

"Not really," Nancy said.

"Oh, I did. And you—"

Nancy colored.

"No," he said, "none of it happened. Let's forget it, all right?"

Nancy nodded quickly.

"Did I say anything supremely ridiculous?" he asked.

"Just rambling on. About spring, I guess, and a house across the bay. And school. You seemed—very happy."

Part of a laugh escaped Jeremy.

"You're out pretty late," he said.

"I got drunk and fell asleep on the pier. I must look like a total mess."

"Don't suppose I cut too elegant a figure in this bathrobe, either. So, Nancy, we both got dumped, eh?"

"I don't even want to talk about it."

"Hate her? Your sister?"

"Yes. No. Hate's too big a word."

"You shouldn't, you know."

"And how about you?" Nancy asked. "Do you just roll with the punches?" Then suddenly: "Don't tell me who I should hate! If I want to hate her, I *will!* Maybe you don't hate her. *Great,* you're philosophical. But what she did was the rottenest thing I ever heard of!"

I'm acting like a raving idiot, she thought distantly. *He's just been crying and now I'm screaming.*

"Hold on, I didn't mean to—"

"Aren't you pissed off or *any*thing? Maybe you didn't love her. But *he.* He was *mine!"*

"I think . . . I think she suddenly needed someone, and he was there."

"Tell that to the goddamn judge! Your Honor, I suddenly needed a car, so I stole one! What's the difference! She's a *thief!"*

Nancy ran to the railing, bent over, and threw up. When she was done, she hung over the rail like a

144

bundle of clothes. She felt Jeremy's hand on her shoulder.

"Leave me alone," she wailed.

"Come on to the house," he said. "I'll give you a couple of Alka-Seltzers and a cup of coffee."

"How about a length of rope and a chair?"

"Don't ever talk like that," Jeremy said.

"Will you please stop telling me what to *do?*"

Nancy collected herself. The taste in her mouth was awful. It occurred to her that the man she'd been shouting at was—well, her parents' employer.

"I need a grape soda," she said, starting off for her own house.

"No you—I mean, most hung-over individuals don't really require a grape soda. They may *think* they require one. Come on with me. Please."

Nancy considered through a fog. "Will you play the piano for me?"

"You don't want to hear me play," Jeremy said.

Nancy drummed her fingers on the railing.

"That is," Jeremy said, "I don't believe you really do. I'm being humble, see? Not telling you what you want. Oh hell, let's go."

They walked.

"I want a grape soda," Nancy said, not realizing that she was weaving. "And another drink. We'll get maudlin and bitter."

"Great plans for a Friday night. I don't particularly enjoy getting maudlin, *or* bitter."

"Not over Anna, anyway," Nancy said.

Jeremy halted. "Let's forget it," he said with controlled anger. "Why don't you just go back to your pink little bed."

"I know all about Catherine," Nancy said. "I've got a box full of all her old letters and things. I know what she looked like. I know how she thinks. What happened between you and her, anyhow?"

"She died," Jeremy said, and walked on abruptly.

Nancy blinked. She ran after him.

"Oh Christ," she said. "Forgive me, will you? I'm a fool. I'm just retarded, Jeremy, *please* forgive me!"

"Do you really have a box full of her things?" he asked.

"Yes, yes! In the attic!" Nancy pointed to the windows of the servants' house.

"May I see them? Sometime?"

"Now! Let's go and get them! There's lots of stairs, though . . ."

"I'll *crawl* up them," Jeremy said dryly.

They made their way to the house. "We'll have to be very quiet," Nancy said. "Everybody's asleep."

They crept up two flights of stairs to the big attic door. Nancy found the flashlight. Its beam swung over the crates and furniture and exposed rafters. But the box was gone.

"It was *here*," Nancy whispered. "Right here behind this post. A blue box, about yea by yea big. Look, you can see in the dust where it was. It was full of pictures and letters—and slippers, little satin ones made of patches. What could have happened to it? Maybe it got moved."

Nancy began to search, nosing into dusty corners.

"Nancy," Jeremy said, "give it up. It's gone."

Nancy insisted on searching. "You don't believe me," she said, lost behind a stack of wooden gin boxes.

"I believe you," he said.

Nancy peeped out from the stack. "But I *liked* that box," she said. "It's got to be around here *some-where*!"

They went back down.

"It was so—I don't know," Nancy whispered. "Beautiful. Poor Catherine."

She saw Jeremy to the porch.

"Good night," she said. "Sorry about barfing and the box and everything."

Jeremy shook his head. "Come on," he said with a wave of his hand. "Grape soda. I'm sure there's some in the larder. There's everything."

Nancy shrank back shyly.

"No, I don't really want any grape soda, I don't think. You were right."

"The piano, then. Alka-Seltzer." He reached through the doorway and took her arm.

"Okay, but I've got to brush my teeth first. Hold on. You know, the taste. Bleh."

Nancy ran up to her room and sat panting on her bed. *It's not pink,* she thought. *It's blue.* Should she change her clothes? What was she wearing, anyhow? Run to the mirror. *I look terrible.* She was keeping Jeremy waiting. You were supposed to do that. *What am I thinking? What did I come up here for? Teeth.*

She ran to the bathroom and worked her mouth into a lather. She gargled with mouthwash. She splashed her face, brushed her hair. *Do I have time for makeup? Why am I such a jerk?*

She ran back down.

"Ready." She smiled.

They decided on coffee. Nancy darted from counter to counter in the kitchen while Jeremy did the brewing. He was trying to make her feel like a real guest and not like the housekeeper's daughter, she thought. But still, she wished he'd give her something to *do.* Quick, something to talk about . . .

"How about some Irish whiskey for the coffee?" she asked.

"Always struck me as a contradiction in terms," he said.

"How?"

"It's what you have when you can't decide if you want to be drunk or sober."

"Oh, then let's have all whiskey," Nancy laughed.

They carried their coffee to the piano.

"Still want maudlin and bitter?" Jeremy asked. He hammed up a few bars of Beethoven.

"I can play 'Raindrops,'" Nancy offered.

"Ah, well, the epitome of the classical repertoire." He moved over on the piano bench.

"I had lessons when I was a little girl. Let's see. This is the really cunning part." She began a little vamp of tinkling rain sounds.

On the other end of the keyboard, Jeremy added ominous rumblings.

"Thunder," he said.

"It's not that kind of rain."

Jeremy kissed her.

Nancy kept playing "Raindrops." She missed notes.

"I don't even know if I like this," she said.

"It's never been one of my favorites."

"You know what I mean," Nancy said. "And don't tell me I started it." She gave up on the song and laid her hands on her lap. Her blue jeans felt tight. *I'm fat,* she thought. *I've been miserable and I've been eating, and now I'm fat and I won't take my clothes off. I refuse.*

"All this trading off," she said. "It's not right."

"All I did was kiss you, for Christ's sake. And besides, you started it."

"Nobody ever just kisses anybody anymore—and I asked you not to say that! I'm going home." She stood up.

"Shall I call you a cab?"

"Trying to drive me crazy, is that the plan?"

"There is no plan," Jeremy said.

Nancy stood motionless, eyes half closed. In that instant she wished Jeremy would strike. The instant passed, and she made for the door. The whole evening had been tremendously exciting, she thought, and now it was time to sit in her bedroom and sort it all out.

"Nancy," she heard him say, "I wish you would stay."

He sat on the piano bench, leaning forward on his cane, long black bangs tousled over his forehead. Nancy had never noticed before how lopsided his face was, one side nearly frozen with the paralysis, the other mobile. A rough face, a jagged face. The piano spread darkly behind him.

"You just like mashing the serving girls," Nancy said. "That's all."

"You aren't a 'serving girl' and you know it."

"I'm not like Anna." Immediately Nancy was embarrassed by the words.

"We can just talk," Jeremy said. "People do still just talk, don't they?"

Nancy remembered the human wreckage that Jeremy had been not long before, crumpled and sobbing on the pier. She felt sorry for him. The intensity of his need was visible, and maybe it *was* nothing more than a need for human company. But there was more. Something else that made Nancy want to escape. No, just talking was out of the question, Nancy thought. If only she didn't feel so *fat*. The thought of going to bed with him, of being compared line by line to Anna: she could never measure up.

She sat on the sofa and crossed her arms.

"Okay," she said. "Tell me about Catherine."

Jeremy recoiled.

"Or about the weather," Nancy said. "Or about anything. Anything in between."

Forty-five minutes later, Nancy was unbuttoning her blouse. She sighed with the inevitability of it, and Jeremy laughed. She glared at him. They were side by side on the sofa.

With a hushing sound, he placed his finger over her lips.

"Why don't you just rip my clothes off?" she said, lips moving against the fingers.

Instead, Jeremy removed his robe. He was wearing only pajama trousers, and Nancy sent a glance toward his crotch. He was already getting hard. Quickly, he unbuttoned her blouse. *He's done this a few times,* Nancy thought. She tensed as he unhooked her bra. How many times had she watched Anna undress, and these incredible tits spill out? Her own, she was convinced, were strictly mediocre.

But Jeremy did not pause to take stock. He crushed Nancy in his arms, and suddenly her heart was racing. She turned up her face, and his kiss was powerful. Her breasts flattened against his chest, which was like warm wood. She groped toward his crotch, but he brushed her hand away.

He held her for a long time, saying nothing, his lips on her forehead. Nancy closed her eyes. Finally she tried again for his sex.

Jeremy said, "You don't have to. We can just stay like this."

"Maybe *you* can."

Pulling away, Nancy wriggled out of her blue jeans. Her panties had a rip in them, so she whisked them off quickly. She lay back on the sofa. She had read in *Cosmo* that lying down was the most attractive position if you were overweight. Jeremy smiled and began kissing her stomach.

"This is all pretty funny to you," Nancy whispered. "Isn't it?"

Jeremy's head shot up. His face darkened with anger. Climbing upward, he pressed his lips against hers. When he was done, Nancy looked up at him, wide-eyed.

With brisk motions, he stripped off his pajama trousers. Nancy felt his sex pressing against her. Her thoughts began to spin. *Free, white, and twenty-one,* she thought. *The break of day,* she thought.

"Jeremy, fuck me," she said.

It began with the finding of the angle, awkward, nosing. Then in.

"Oh, yes," said Nancy.

Then the laying on of bodies. He was strong. She said, "Jeremy, Jeremy." His breath was warm on her face, scented with coffee. He pulled away, he came back. Pressure and release. Her knees climbed up his sides and held on.

"You, you, you," she panted.

Pushing against the mound. The motion, back and forth, going there, travel.

Nancy came up for air. She felt the fabric of the sofa against her back, saw the living room, vast and carefully furnished, lost in shadow. She gazed up at the face. Driving. He had her in his hands.

She shuddered upward.

"Jeremy, Jeremy!"

He smiled, and it became a grimace.

"Come in me," she said.

"I love you!" she cried, crashing her hips against his.

"Sorry," she said. "I'm just one of those idiots who yells things like that."

Next Sunday afternoon, Alice Dancer came to pay a call.

There was no sound of door chimes, no knock. She opened the servants' entrance and breezed in, surprising Nancy in the kitchen with a wave and a greeting: "Is Jeremy in?"

Nancy pointed with a carrot. "Out on the patio," she said.

"Thank you," the woman sang.

Jeremy sat hunched over a white wrought-iron table, a book spread open and a lemonade at hand. He heard the faint echo of a voice from the house and looked up suddenly. The voice was familiar, but how?

Sun glared on the glass panes of the french doors. Behind them, a woman in silk blouse, trim skirt, with silver hair and pearl-drop earrings was waving to him as she worked the handles.

"Oh my God," Jeremy whispered.

An image flashed before his mind as he watched Alice Dancer cross the flagstones, bathed in sunlight: it was the image of an old woman on a darkened dock in New Bedford, shaking with rage and demanding, "Where *is* he?" and striking Catherine when the girl

151

gave no answer. The two of them, mother and daughter, moving off together along the glistening, wet pier . . .

It seemed impossible to Jeremy that this could be the same woman. "Jeremy!" she cried, extending her hand. "How wonderful to see you again after all these years!" A wash of matronly perfume spilled from her. Jeremy did not shake her hand.

In the kitchen window of the house, he saw Nancy making quizzical grimaces. He shook his head quickly, and she ducked out of sight.

Alice Dancer took the other chair and pushed Nancy's lemonade out of the way. "Oh, you look so wary," she said, wagging her finger. "Don't worry, I won't bite you. I only thought it was time for you and me to have a talk."

Hesitantly, Nancy moved to the french doors for another look. She felt like a fool for spying, but the visitor had piqued her curiosity—or not the visitor, so much as Jeremy's reaction to her: shock, dismay, then complete stoniness. Who was she?

Their postures were rigid. Suddenly Jeremy raised his voice.

"Jesus Christ!" he fumed. *"What are you doing to her?"*

He lashed out and seized the woman's wrist. Nancy edged closer to the doors, trying to catch more. But Jeremy calmed himself, released the visitor.

Creeping to another window, Nancy peeped out. The conversation appeared normal, but she could make out the strain on their faces.

The woman got suddenly to her feet. She was smiling at Jeremy, but there was no happiness in the smile. Jeremy also stood. He bowed mockingly to the woman. She shuddered with suppressed rage.

Then abruptly she glanced toward Nancy.

Trying to seem nonchalant, Nancy slid away. She paced deep into the house, heart pounding and face flushed. She wrung her hands. Oh, she was tacky, tacky beyond belief! A cut-rate little spy!

Maybe from the upper window . . .

Stop that!

She had to get out of the house; there was no way around it. She picked up her purse and headed out the front door. The gravel of the circular driveway crunched underfoot. At the gate she turned toward town.

She walked quickly beside old brick walls topped by iron spikes. The stroll was a familiar one; she had taken it many times to the grocery and the town's only bar. But now Nancy's mind was churning.

Anna had made her paranoid, she decided. She'd gotten ridiculously careful and watchful after Brook. She wasn't clinging, though, was she? She'd just kill herself if she turned clinging. But damn it, there was just no way of escaping Anna! Anna was the biggest bigmouth in two counties, and she had told Nancy everything about Jeremy, every detail. How he talked, how he ordered from a menu, how he tipped, how he reacted to liquor, how he stirred in the night to sleepwalk. How he made love. At every turn during the last week, Nancy had found herself comparing all that with the Jeremy *she* was getting.

And it was different. Not only different, but less— he wouldn't even let her spend the *night* with him, for God's sake! What was she, a leper? And the other part, the sex. Anna had told of endless fucking. "I don't know how he stays so hard," she'd said. She made it sound like a complaint, with the soreness and all.

Nancy kicked a pebble into the road. The road sloped down to the Public Library and then the little shops of the town. "Violent." That was the word Anna had used, worldly-wise.

On the first night with Jeremy, Nancy had braced herself for some of that violence. After the first time, she asked, "Did you come?" "Yes." "Then why are you still hard?" "It happens to me," Jeremy said. "Come on, really?"

Nancy was full of offers, but Jeremy had hushed her down and stroked her hair. "Just lie next to me," he had said.

And then he told her to go home, the bastard.

She had gone back to her bed and cried bitterly, certain that there would be no more. But the next afternoon he had called. They spent the day together on the beach.

Maybe Jeremy was violent with Anna, but with her he was nice.

"Nice," Nancy muttered, loping past the vacuous storefronts. Anna stoked the passions, but to her he was *nice*. *That's me*, Nancy thought. *White cotton panties*.

She halted outside the Methodist church. It wasn't just Anna she had to compare herself to, she thought. There was Catherine too. Even after ten years, the dead girl had a hold on Jeremy's imagination and his heart. It would take somebody very special to shake him free, Nancy decided.

She was getting squeezed in the middle; that was the problem. The dead Catherine was still the big romance. And on the other side, that fabulous body of Anna's. Sultry, sexy Anna.

Which meant Jeremy carried the flame for one, brought out the passion for the other—and handed out niceness to the one in the middle.

Me.

When Nancy returned to the house, Jeremy was gone.

❧ twelve ❧

By the gate sat a teenager. He asked if Jeremy was one of the auditors. Jeremy leaned out of the window and said no, he had come to visit the Dancers. The boy gave directions to the servants' building.

Jeremy drove a full quarter mile down the tree-lined drive before catching sight of buildings. The main house was a baronial mansion of the early Long Island type, immense and substantial. The driveway split to the right, and Jeremy followed it to a stone cottage.

"Why—why it's Jeremy!"

A slim, aging man cut the engine of a tractor and left it standing outside a nearby tool garage.

Jeremy recognized Mark Dancer. He slammed the car door. Anxiously, he scanned the windows of the cottage. Sunset cast long shadows and tinted the facade pink.

Mark Dancer smiled. "I'm glad you came." He drew nearer, blinking mildly. "The missus is over at the museum, so you picked a good time. The museum, that's what I call the main house. Come on in."

The interior was saturated with the rosy tones of the dusk, like a chapel with its stained-glass windows. The television was on in the little living room, a weeping face also in pink. Behind the cleanliness, the homey order, Jeremy picked up an animal-cage smell.

Mark Dancer stripped off his work gloves and tossed

them on the TV. Jeremy watched him in wonder. The man seemed jaunty. Happy. He remembered how much Dancer had adored his only child.

"I'll go up and tell her you're here," he said, backtracking to the stairway. "You want something? A drink?"

Jeremy gazed around the room. He counted four vases filled with flowers. The Catherine touch.

"No, no thanks," Jeremy said. Suddenly he heard soft footsteps above.

"Daddy?" a voice called from the top of the stairs.

A shuffling of slippers on steps. Jeremy shot to his feet.

Catherine's face peered down over a railing.

"Catherine," Dancer said, "get back into bed. You know you shouldn't be up."

"Jeremy," Catherine whispered. Tears brimmed in her eyes. She raced down the stairs in her robe and flung herself into Jeremy's arms. "I knew you'd come," she sobbed, trembling lightly against him. "I knew you would."

She turned up her face. Her eyes shone.

Jeremy tried to hold back, but he couldn't. He kissed her. His arms folded around her body and pressed her. He felt her small strength. He felt the inner stillness of her, a quiet circle drawn around the two of them, a peace.

Catherine pulled away. Her eyes drifted shut.

"Listen," she said. She took Jeremy's hand and held it against her chest. He felt nothing.

"It's gone now," Catherine whispered. "But it was there for a second." She smiled up at Jeremy, and then across the room, where Mark Dancer was beaming like a beacon.

"Daddy," she said. "It was beating."

"That's the girl," Dancer said.

Catherine swayed, and her father ran forward to support her. "Let's get her back to bed," he said.

Jeremy followed up the stairs and down the corridor to a darkened room. He pulled back the covers and pushed aside the menagerie of stuffed animals. As Dancer helped her in, Jeremy stood back, farther and farther, until he bumped against a chair and sat suddenly.

In the bedroom, three more vases of flowers. The stuffed animals. Beyond that, nothing. The walls were bare. No knickknacks decorated the dresser.

"She seems awfully tired," Jeremy said.

"Oh no, don't even think about leaving." Mark Dancer finished arranging the covers. "You don't want Jeremy to leave, do you, Cathy?"

"No," Catherine whispered.

"I'll be downstairs if you need me." Dancer closed the door behind him.

"Sit closer?" Catherine said.

Jeremy took a chair by the bed. Catherine sat up against the pillows.

"Dingy in here, isn't it?" she asked. "The light hurts my eyes, though. When the sun's all the way down, we can pull up the shades. If I left it up to Dad, all I'd do is lie here in this old bed. How are you, Jeremy?"

"Catherine," he began, "the reason I never came—"

She held up a hand, as if to say "I know."

This was not what he had expected. On the ferry, in the driving rain and the intensity of the moment, everything had seemed so different. But to sit by Catherine's bed and see her face glowing, giving off its strange fervor, to hear her talking about shades and her dad—it shook him. It was familiar beyond words. Jeremy realized that though he had known Catherine in the sunlight and in the full flower of her exuberance, it was only when she began to fade, only when illness began to claim her, that he had truly loved. He pulled his chair closer.

"These animals." He smiled.

"Pretty dumb, huh? I can't believe they saved them. It was Dad, apparently. He thought I'd be mad if they threw them out."

"Would you've been?"

Catherine shook her head. "A lot of things stop being important," she said. "But it was nice to find them here," she added quickly, toying with the ear of blue beagle.

She's still so young, Jeremy thought. The ten years had brought no change in her features. The dark eyes were sad, but then they had always been tinged with sadness. The hair was long and black. The complexion was pale, but then . . . then it had always been pale, just like his own. The outline beneath the blanket was slim, but Jeremy had grown accustomed, in the last days, to a scarecrow Catherine.

He said it: "You're still beautiful, Catherine."

"You're still Jeremy, Jeremy . . . It's so *quiet.*"

"You don't have your music."

"Oh, it isn't like that anymore, Jeremy. I'm not dying, you know. I can't. Poor Jeremy, my poor wanderer."

He took her hand. For a long time they were silent.

Then he said, "Do you remember what it's like out there?" with a nod to the shaded window.

"We remember—we remember the feelings, that's all," Catherine said. "But we remember . . . all of them. Do you know what I mean? I think people learn to remember only some feelings, some good and some bad. But we remember all."

"Do you miss it? All of it?"

"Yes," Catherine said.

"Even the pain?"

She hesitated. "Yes," she said. "Jeremy—"

"I can't go, Catherine. Nothing has changed. What you told me, about where you've been. I don't belong there—"

"And do you belong here?"

"Yes! Yes, this *is* where I belong! You can't see it

anymore, Catherine. I—for a while I wasn't sure. But now I *am*. There's so much here. And where you've come from—on the ferry you told me something. You said that you all lived in hope. I can't live on that."

"Is there more here?"

Jeremy looked into her eyes.

"Vastly more," he said. "Even for me."

"Nothing but that hope," Catherine said. "You make it sound like nothing at all."

"Isn't it? 'I have hope.' That's what we say when we've got nothing else."

"Have you ever had so much that you *weren't* hoping?"

Jeremy stood up. He looked at the wall, struggling with what he had come to say. He glanced at Catherine, lying in bed with the covers up to her neck, her arms out.

He couldn't leave her just now, he decided. Not yet.

"You're all right here," he said awkwardly. "I mean—your mother came to see me today, and some of the things she told me . . . I began to wonder. I'm afraid I got pretty mad at her. But it seemed like she knew everything about us. Everything we'd talked about. Everything."

"She can be very persistent," Catherine said.

"I was afraid she'd been coercing you."

"Please, Jeremy. I can't talk about it. I don't want to."

"I check for signs in the morning. To see if you've been with me in the night. Doors open that I left closed, my cane in a different place. I've been sleepwalking, I know that. Have you been with me?"

Catherine nodded. "Once or twice."

Jeremy sat. He leaned forward intensely.

"We can stay here together, Catherine. Here. Together. Catherine, this is the place. You've got to see that this is the place!"

Violently, he hauled her from her bed. He spun to the bureau. She stood tottering.

"Here!" he said. "Put on some clothes. We'll go out. You've got to get out of this—this tomb!"

As Catherine dressed, some of the old excitement returned, a feverish desire.

They descended the stairs, Catherine refusing to lean on Jeremy. In the living room, Alice Dancer was waiting, a rictus of a smile on her face. She was delighted; they were going out. How nice, how wonderful. She nudged her husband. "Have her back by one," he said. "I will, sir," said Jeremy.

Jeremy buckled her into the Mercedes. "Drive fast," Catherine said. "Drive very very fast."

Wind blasted through the window. Jeremy wished it were day. He churned possibilities, and finally pulled into the parking lot of a seafood restaurant they once had favored.

"No hesitations now," he said. "We're going in."

It was a weeknight, and they were able to get an outside table overlooking the water. Jeremy ordered a bottle of champagne. The steward poured it and Catherine leaned forward.

"I don't drink," she said.

The food came.

"I don't eat," she said.

Music drifted across the bay. On the far shore, Jeremy could make out colored lights. He drank the bottle of champagne himself. A hurricane lamp cast a soft glow over the table. A pitiless anger grew in Jeremy.

Catherine tried to be gay, but it had never been her strength to seem other than what she was. All at once, she heard the music too. She reached across the table and took Jeremy's hand.

"Dancing," she whispered. "Across the bay. Listen."

Jeremy stood and threw down his napkin.

"Dancing, then," he said.

They drove around the bay to a newly resurrected town which had recently rebuilt its dockside. Along the water hung paper lanterns, and a small orchestra was playing waltzes. A smiling fireman sold Jeremy two tickets.

A crowd gathered around the dance floor, herded in a U with the bandstand at one end. The white masts of sailing yachts rose beyond, nodding like a dozen slow batons. A smell of beer and ice cream and marijuana wafted through the bodies as Jeremy and Catherine wended their way. Jeremy felt her slim waist beneath his hand. She slipped eagerly between the onlookers and craned to look at the swirling dancers.

No one was decked out for the occasion; it was come-as-you-are. They couldn't waltz either, most of them, Jeremy noted. But it made no difference under the summer night's sky.

"Would you honor me with this dance, Catherine?"

Hooking his cane over the back of a chair, he offered his arm.

She turned up a nervous face. It struck Jeremy how like a consumptive heroine of Italian opera she was. He dashed the thought.

"Should I?" she asked.

"Perhaps you should get your chaperon's approval," Jeremy suggested.

"You won't let me fall? You won't let me stumble?"

"I'll carry you out if you want."

Catherine laughed and spread her arms. Jeremy gathered her to him and they glided onto the dock, merging with the gleeful waltzers.

Their first waltz ended almost immediately, and they joined the others in dutifully applauding the musicians. Another melody began, by Strauss out of Mancini, designed for an easy *one*-two-three, *one*-two-three. Jeremy and Catherine fell into the lulling tempo.

"Spin me, Jeremy!" Catherine cried.

161

They whirled and turned, orbiting, filled with the intoxication of movement, the music singing through them.

One waltz succeeded another. Jeremy swam in the dark, merry eyes of Catherine, and it seemed to him that the body he held was warm with exertion, flushed with excitement, that the heart below his own was . . . beating.

The orchestra took a break and the dance floor emptied. The rhythmic tread of feet on yielding boards ceased. Catherine broke from Jeremy and swirled, skirts rising to reveal legs and thighs.

Jeremy thought: *She's still a virgin.* It struck him with amazement as she spun, head thrown back, long tresses flying.

"Jeremy," she said. "I feel reborn. I feel such strength."

She staggered and fell like a bundle of rags.

A scream sounded from the sidelines. Jeremy knelt over Catherine, shouting back the crowds with cruel orders.

"She's all right!" he roared. Then softer, "Just a little too much champagne."

Scooping her up, Jeremy carried Catherine away. She was light. The crowd fell aside, making a human aisle. At the gate the fireman said, "What's the matter here?"

Jeremy pushed through to his car without a word.

He buckled her into the car. The engine, trusty, mechanical, started easily, and bare nameless night rushed past them. The highway.

The pitiless anger rose again, like writhing weeds from a garden so recently fresh. Each of Jeremy's thoughts was a curse. He rode the gray eraser of the highway until he felt that he himself was gone. Beside him in the car, lights shifting across her, Catherine stirred and moaned.

At the Mills estate Jeremy got out and opened the

gates himself. By the time they reached the servants' cottage, Catherine was able to walk a little.

Inside, the television droned. The late movie cast a traveling light over Mark Dancer, asleep. Alice Dancer sat awake. She looked like an Egyptian icon, with the body of a woman and head of a cat. Alice Dancer sat with hands on knees, erect, eyes fixed on the screen.

She swiveled her face.

"Was it a lovely evening, children?"

"Beautiful, Mother," Catherine rasped.

"No," Jeremy said, waving her away. "Don't bother. I'll take her up, Mrs. Dancer. You understand."

And he winked at her.

"I can't make the stairs," Catherine gasped.

"You can," he urged.

She made the stairs, step by painful step. Jeremy pushed her on. A wild, immortal pain sparkled in his veins. Catherine fell into bed like a bag of sand. Jeremy turned away in revulsion. Anger raged over his eyes like a curtain of red. When it parted, he found himself staring into Catherine's closet. On the floor lay a blue cardboard box.

Above it hung a wedding dress.

Not an ordinary wedding dress, but a full-skirted white gown, its narrow bodice fantastically encrusted with hand embroidery. Jeremy stepped closer and fingered the material.

Up close, the gown gave off a must of years, and he saw that the lace was no longer truly white. Time had yellowed it.

Jeremy sat on the edge of the bed.

"Don't say it. Don't say it yet," Catherine implored. "Stay a minute. Keep me company. We're alone, Jeremy, you and me. Nobody can keep us company but each other."

She looked into his eyes and read everything there.

"Then I'll have to find my way back alone," she said.

❧ thirteen ❧

"I don't know why you have to sew out in the yard tonight," Big Bill said, playing out the extension cord.

"Because it's beautiful out," Nancy said. She carried a floor lamp in one hand, a radio in the other. They passed through the back door.

"That lamp'll get rusted," Big Bill grumbled. "Don't leave it out all night."

"I *won't.*" Nancy switched on the lamp. It threw a circle of yellow light on the patch of lawn. The old webbed chair cast a spidery shadow. Pulling up a bench from the picnic set, she put down the radio and hooked it up. Her mother trundled out, plump and smiling, and handed her a pair of overalls.

"I marked them," she said.

"Thanks, Mom."

The screen door snapped shut and Nancy was alone on the little expanse of lawn that belonged to the servants' house. High picket fencing all around cut off the view of the estate, and under the summer night's sky Nancy felt she could be anywhere in America. With needle and thread she sewed patches on the knees of her father's gigantic overalls. It was not something she had to do, but it made her happy. The music played softly on the radio, she hummed, the crickets chirped.

She was on the second knee when a face appeared

above the fence. A cane landed on the lawn. A moment later, Jeremy hopped over and picked it up.

"Oh gasp," Nancy said. "How athletic."

Jeremy sat on the bench and watched her sew.

"Run away with me," he said.

"All right. Where should we go?"

"To Borders' place upstate. Now. Tonight."

Nancy stopped sewing.

"You almost sound serious."

"I am. Will you go?"

"Jeremy, it's Sunday night. This little piggy has to go to work tomorrow."

"Forget work. Call in sick."

"I did that about twelve times in May. Are you drunk?"

Jeremy pulled her to her feet. They kissed.

"You're not drunk," she said.

"Let's walk," he said.

"There's actually a gate in this fence if you want to use it."

Jeremy hopped over the way he had come. Nancy went by the gate. They walked across the estate, meandering toward the fountain. The moon had set. It was dark. They sat on the lawn and slowly lay down.

Suddenly it was like high school. Not the fumbling or the uncertainty, but the pent-up, desperate bodies. Jeremy pushed his fingers into Nancy's hair and kissed her until she could hardly breathe. They struggled on the grass.

"Someone will see us," Nancy panted.

"No, they won't. I don't care."

He eased up her skirt and began stroking her. Her parents' house was a small nest of lights far across the grounds. The smell of salt water mingled with the fragrance of flowers, grass, the soft earth. Nancy kicked her panties off and lay exposed to Jeremy's touches. He slid his hand under her top.

She caressed his face, pale and serious.

"You need a haircut," she whispered.

"You can give me one later."

"Forget it. Too much responsibility. Here." She unzipped him. "I'm better at this."

Jeremy smiled at her, and for a second it seemed to her that he was about to cry. He lifted her top and kissed her nipples.

"I'll bet this never gets soft," she said. "You just tuck it under your belt when you want to walk around. Let's do it, Jeremy. Wait, let me take off your pants. Okay."

She lay on her back, her legs parted. He knelt between them. With both hands she fondled his cock and balls, pushing aside his shirttails. The stars twinkled behind his head.

"You do like me, don't you, Jeremy?"

He lay over her and entered.

"Yes," he said. "I think I love you."

"Oh no," Nancy breathed. "You don't mean that. You just—you're just—"

They rocked on the grass. Nancy opened his shirt and pressed her breasts against his smooth chest.

"—you're just one of those idiots who say things like that."

Nancy collected her panties and they went up to the main house. Jeremy ducked into a bathroom and ran water.

"Let's hit the showers," he said.

"Oh boy, fun," said Nancy.

They left their clothes in a heap outside the bathroom door. When they came out, a cloud of steam followed them, and they were wrapped in big towels.

Nancy tripped into the kitchen and found a bottle of red wine. "I can't work this *cork*screw," she sang. Jeremy opened the wine and Nancy carried the glasses into the vast living room.

"Take off that towel," Jeremy said.

Nancy shook her head.

"Why not? It's warm enough."

"Shy," she said.

Jeremy put down his glass of wine and wrestled it off her.

"Lie back," she laughed.

He lay back on the sofa and Nancy knelt on the rug. His own towel had torn loose, and he was hard. Nancy parted her lips and took his sex in her mouth. She ran her tongue around it. She slid her lips up and down the shaft. Then she got to her feet and straddled him, ass on his knees as she aimed the tip into herself and wriggled closer.

"All this skin," she said. She grabbed a handful of his long black hair and kissed him. She bounced softly in his lap, and then they rolled to the carpet.

They went to Jeremy's bed for the third act; when it was over, Nancy kissed him and got up to leave.

"I know the drill," she said.

Jeremy pulled her back onto the covers.

"You want to stay," he said.

"Don't tell me what I want!" she laughed.

"You want to stay."

She gazed into his dark eyes.

In the middle of the night Nancy tried to roll over and felt a tug at her wrist.

"In a minute!" she piped through a fog of dreams. She made to haul a pillow over her head. She felt the tug again.

"It isn't even light yet!"

She awakened. Rubbing the sleep away, she looked at Jeremy sleeping beside her.

He had tied a length of silken curtain sash from his wrist to hers.

In the morning Jeremy repeated his offer.

"Just for the day," Nancy said. She called the office and told the receptionist she'd be in Tuesday. She felt rotten about the lie. It was too much like the bad times with Brook.

Jeremy was eager to go, no delays for breakfast. They climbed in the Mercedes and soon the highway was under them. The clear night had given way to a sky the color of smeared grease, but Nancy was happy. Happier, she thought, than she had ever been.

He told me he loves me. Well, actually he said that he *thought* he loved her, but that was the kind of thing men said, except for the doggy type who instantly wanted everything on a romantic basis but really felt the minimum. From Jeremy an "I think" was worth a lot.

Nancy was sure he'd never said anything like that to Anna.

Driving, Jeremy seemed preoccupied. No, more, Nancy thought. He seemed disturbed. He was driving fast: at least—she leaned over to glance at the speedometer—twenty miles over the speed limit. Maybe he could afford the ticket, but she hated sirens and the feeling of being run to ground by a patrol car.

"Playing hooky is habit forming," she said. "I used to do it all the time in school. How about you?"

"Yes. All the time. Hated classes."

He was barely listening, Nancy thought.

"I still get nightmares about being gone so long I can't find my locker," she said.

"I don't," said Jeremy.

"Well, I guess it doesn't make for too much of a nightmare. But usually it's the day of a test and I haven't studied and I need my books. You know, lost, roaming around the halls, worried I won't remember the combination even if I do find the locker." Nancy paused. "Eating frogs, standing on my head, breakfast with God."

"Yes," said Jeremy.

No, he wasn't listening at all.

On I-95 Jeremy began pounding the steering wheel.

He pulled the car onto the shoulder. Nancy became alarmed.

"What's the matter! What is it, Jeremy?"

"Nothing," he said. "Just a little numbness."

She took his hands and rubbed them. He smiled at her.

"It seems to be getting worse the further we go," he said.

"We can go back if you want."

They drove on.

Nancy began talking about food. She was hungry. As they pulled off the highway and into the succession of narrower roads that would bring them to the cottage, she suggested they stop for groceries. They passed a supermarket, and she made Jeremy turn back.

Jeremy stumbled as he got out of the car.

"Just a little stiffness," he said. But Nancy worried about his limp as he hobbled across the parking lot toward the enormous supermarket. He was leaning heavily on his cane.

Nancy pushed the cart toward the meat aisle.

"What'll we have?" she wondered aloud. "These pork chops look good. You like pork chops? Pork chops, then. We're not even *looking* at those cakes. How about lunch? They've got a deli."

They wheeled over to the deli counter.

"I think I'll have the number-two special."

"What am I doing here?" Jeremy asked.

"Getting lunch and dinner, dummy."

But Jeremy was gazing around vacantly, holding his cane as if about to change it into a serpent, waving it at the long, brightly lit aisles. Housewives piloted shopping carts bearing babies and mountains of food. Goods stretched in endless, colorful array.

Nancy ordered two number-two specials and towed Jeremy to the vegetables.

"Potatoes and broccoli okay?" she asked. "And a salad with lunch."

As they waited in the checkout line, Jeremy studied a *Newsweek*. His expression was puzzled.

Nancy was relieved when they got back to the car. "I think I'd better drive," she said.

They arrived at the cottage around noon. It was unbearably musty inside, and Nancy went about opening windows and lifting shades, crying: "The dust!" Sunlight poured into the big room. Jeremy sat on one of the sofas along the wall.

She had given up trying to talk to him. Even Anna had reported these moods of his, silent and morose. Nancy only hoped he could snap out of it, or the day would be a bust. She decided the best tack was relentless cheerfulness.

"Lunch'll be ready in a jiffy!"

She tore up lettuce in the woody old kitchen. "You know," she called back, "if we cleaned this place up a little it could be nice for weekends. We could come up here and hide out."

No answer. Nancy sighed and peeled carrots into the salad bowl, carved tomatoes, and dumped bottled dressing on top. Unwrapping the sandwiches, she put them on plates. She found two six-packs in the refrigerator. She managed to balance plates, bowls, and beers in her arms and headed back for the cavernous main room, where she set the meal on a card table.

"Lunch," she announced.

Jeremy sat motionless on the sofa. His eyes were wide and unblinking.

"Jeremy?"

Nancy hurried to the couch. She shook Jeremy by the arm.

Suddenly she arched back, her heart triphammering in her chest. She grabbed Jeremy and shook him violently.

He slumped over like a doll.

"Jeremy! Wake up! Wake up!"

His eyes stayed fixed and glassy. Nancy took his wrist.

Oh God there's no—
She felt his throat.
There's no—
She tore open his shirt and pressed her ear to his bare chest. Lurching to her feet, she ran left and right.

"There's no pulse, there's no pulse, there's no pulse," she stammered.

The telephone.

She ran into the kitchen and clawed the receiver off the wall phone. She dialed 911. There was no ring. She depressed the hook and waited for a dial tone.

No dial tone.

Jesus God it's disconnected.

Racing back into the big room, she bent over Jeremy and shook him and shook him. The staring eyes.

Put him in the car! No, don't move him!

Nancy's hands clutched and unclutched at her blouse. She hurtled toward the front door and out.

Where were the nearest neighbors? *Think, think!*

Nancy flung open the door of the Mercedes and climbed in behind the wheel.

The keys!

Plunging back into the house, she found the car keys in her purse. Jeremy lay on the couch, feet still on the floor, cane in his lap.

Nancy rocketed outside and into the car. Dirt and gravel flew as the tires spun and caught traction. The Mercedes heaved backward, and Nancy pointed it out the long, unpaved drive.

Trees shot past as Nancy aimed down the narrow channel in the forest. She could feel Jeremy growing cold—as if it were her own body. She could feel his brain dying. Hopelessness swarmed over her, choking her.

The car careened onto a gravel road. Up ahead, Nancy glimpsed a mailbox. She jerked the car into a driveway and leapt out of it as it rocked to a halt.

She flung herself at the front door of a white frame house.

"Help! Please help! Emergency!"

Oh god there has to be somebody home.

Inside, a quick shuffling of feet. A voice sounded behind the door. "What do you want?" a woman asked suspisciously.

"I have to call an ambulance and my phone's out! Please!"

The door opened a crack. Nancy slammed into it and it flew inward. She pounded into a quaint entry hall.

"Where is it! The phone!"

The woman, old and shambling in a bathrobe, pointed her to a parlor that reeked of violets. Nancy ran to the telephone and seized it, dialing with a shaky hand.

She made contact with the police. She garbled out directions. Then smashing down the receiver, Nancy sprang to her feet and rushed back to the car. Backing out of the driveway she sideswiped the mailbox.

At the cottage she exploded out of the Mercedes and through the still-open front door.

Jeremy lay on the couch, unmoving.

She listened to his chest. Nothing. She realized his flesh was cool to the touch, and recoiled.

She sat trembling on the sofa.

Oh God he's dead.

A few minutes before she had been thinking how much she hated the sound of sirens. Now she longed for them fiercely. Gasping, she trembled away from the couch, unable to sit with the body. How much time had passed? Five minutes? Ten? Was there anything anybody could do?

She reeled out of the house and stood craning every sense toward the possible approach of help, checking her wristwatch obsessively.

Minutes passed.

Slowly, panic gave way to blunt despair. Jeremy had complained of numbness. In the supermarket he was disoriented. Now he was—

He was.

From the distance came a thin, warbling wail. Of sirens. It grew louder, until it became a shriek in Nancy's ears. The shriek of *too late too late*.

"Send them away!" a voice cried.

Nancy spun.

"Nancy! Send them away!"

She bolted into the cottage.

Jeremy was sitting upright on the sofa. Nancy shook her head uncomprehendingly. Her fist went to her mouth.

The next morning, Nancy drove home to get her things. There was no question now of going back to work. Jeremy needed her, at least for a few days. He still seemed dazed.

The ambulance attendants had very nearly tried to take Jeremy against his will. But he drew himself up and sent them off imperiously, anger churning beneath a facade of cool.

Nancy's head spun when she recalled her own total panic. She had been ready to volunteer for the ambulance herself. The police were very kind and soothing and somehow everybody's attention turned to her.

Poor hysterical Nancy, she thought. But there was truth in it. Jeremy explained that he occasionally suffered from these passing, trancelike states—a side effect of his long-ago accident. His pulse had only been subdued, and she had gotten overexcited in the extreme.

As she drove, Nancy tried to store the whole event under the category of Things I Will Laugh About Someday. But it wouldn't store. The terror and, in its wake, the feeling of total stupidity, was still with her, a metallic taste on her tongue.

Jeremy refused to let the ambulance men examine him, and even after they had left and he was actively calming her down, Nancy was afraid he would suddenly keel over again. Only when evening fell and they made love, she drunk on a bottle of wine mined from the cellar, did she feel certain he was all right. Afterwards, she barely had the energy to call her mother and let her know she wouldn't be home that night. She slept twelve hours.

The sign ahead said TOWN OF OYSTER BAY.

Maybe I should find another boyfriend.

Nancy's reception at home was strained. She had only returned home two weeks earlier, her mother said, and here she was packing again.

"It's only for a few days, Mom!"

Still Nancy could sense that her mother was disturbed. She didn't like it that *both* her daughters were making time with their employer's son, and though so far Nancy's involvement with him had been kept under wraps, it was all pretty plain now. Mary Ravine was ashamed.

Jeremy's name was never explicitly mentioned, until Mary said, "There's a man who's been waiting all morning to see Jeremy. I told him I didn't know where he was or when he'd be back, but he wouldn't leave."

"Do you think I should see what it's about?"

"I leave it up to you."

Nancy decided to see the man. Her mother said, "I don't much like the look of him. He used to work here, and I think he wants money."

"But he asked for Jeremy? Not Mr. or Mrs. Penn?"

"I don't know how he found out he was here. I didn't tell him. But wait. Before you go. There's a letter for you. It's from Anna. I put it on your dresser."

Nancy closed her overnight bag.

"Don't you want to read it?" her mother asked.

"No."

Mary trundled to the dresser and held out the envelope with a pained expression.

"Nancy," she said, "it's from your sister."

Nancy took the letter and tore it into four pieces.

"There," she said, whipping the quarters into a waste-basket.

The visitor was waiting in the foyer of the main house. He was a bald, mild-looking man in a cheap sports jacket. He jumped up when Nancy entered, and she could see he was distraught. He fumbled nervously, introducing himself as Mark Dancer.

Dancer. The name sent a jolt through Nancy. She was possessed by curiosity.

"I've got to talk to Jeremy," Dancer said.

"He's not in now, but I can take a message for him."

"No, I've got to tell him directly. It's—personal. Urgent."

"I'm afraid he's out of town now."

"Damn," Dancer said. "Is there any way I can reach him?"

"There's no phone where he is."

"Is it far?"

"You couldn't see him now, Mr. Dancer. He's not well."

"Not well?" Dancer became alert. "Is he—" He stopped in midsentence. "This is urgent," he said. "I can't tell you how urgent. I know Jeremy will want to see me."

"You can tell me," Nancy said.

"No, I can't."

"I'll be seeing him in a few hours. You can write it out and I'll take it to him. Come with me."

She led Dancer into the library and gave him materials. He wrote furiously, sealed the envelope, and pressed it into Nancy's hands.

"Please hurry," he said.

As soon as Dancer had left, Nancy carried the envelope back into the library and held it over the brightest lamp she could find.

Jeremy,
    Catherine has tried to shoot herself. Her mother

has locked her up. She won't let her go back. Catherine is [here a word was scratched out] falling apart. I can't do anything. You've got to help. She is desperate.

Mark Dancer

Nancy slipped the letter into her overnight bag.

So she isn't dead, Nancy thought as she headed the Mercedes toward Connecticut. *That whole tragedy was just a story. Everything Jeremy told me, made up. But why?*

There was only one answer, and it sank Nancy's heart.

He's still in love with her.

In love the way people are only once, Nancy guessed. In love so deeply they wander around at night imagining they're back together like in the old days.

"After ten years!" she cried aloud.

Catherine must have given him the dump. Again, why? Nancy remembered the photos she had seen. She was beautiful.

More beautiful than me.

No, that wasn't the way to put it. Catherine was beautiful. Nancy was . . .

Pretty. You're very pretty, Nancy.

Catherine had a dramatic face. Pale and soulful. Nancy was sure *she* wasn't soulful. No chance of that. She resolved to be more soulful in the future.

She tried to shoot herself. . . .

How can you *try* to shoot yourself? Bullshit, Nancy thought. You get a gun and aim at your heart and *blam*! Curtains. If you really try, you can succeed.

She hadn't tried to shoot herself, Nancy decided. She's been grandstanding, trying to grab center stage. Catherine knew how to bring Jeremy running. She even had her father running hither and yon, carrying so-called desperate messages. Everybody had a technique, Nancy thought. She also thought she should learn some of her own.

When she arrived at the cottage, she found Jeremy working at a window sash with a steak knife.

"These damn things were mostly painted shut," he said.

With a shove, the window opened.

"Only two more to go," he said.

"Let's have a picnic by the creek tonight," Nancy said.

"Why not?" said Jeremy.

She decided she wouldn't show him the letter today. Maybe tomorrow.

❧ fourteen ❧

Anna had two appointments that day. The first was—
God help me—a job interview. Brook had already left
for his own job and Anna busied herself making the
bed. The apartment was so small that even the slight-
est untidiness racked her nerves. Compulsively, she
aligned the clock radio on the night table.

As usual, Brook had left a mess in the kitchen.
Anna threw his plate into the sink. *I'm turning into a
goddamned wife,* she thought disgustedly. She got
coffee going.

The prospect of the interview filled Anna with
despair, but it was a must. They needed the money.
Anna had not worried so much about money in years.
There was simply no way to earn a serious dollar in the
Vineyard, it seemed. All the jobs were seasonal and
touristy—retail clerking, cooking, waitressing. Brook
had wrangled office work at a local law firm, but he
was, Anna knew, no better than a secretary.

Anna decided *to hell with the dishes.* She drank her
coffee and felt the horrible anxiety attacks come on.

She had passed a rough six weeks since fleeing Long
Island. Her periods had stopped. She felt always on
the verge of an outburst, unsettled, dismayed by the
tiniest failures. Perhaps it was just the piercing awareness that she was, after everything, without a dime in
the world.

Running off with Brook had been the maddest act of her life—part and parcel of the maddest day of her life. She had imagined Brook as rescuer, there on the spot with strong arms, a clean, knowing face, and a chariot. At the time it had seemed so right. Even the element of betrayal—*poor Nancy*—had only added to the Desperate Moment.

But time dulled all. The routine of daily life dulled all. Her hysterics over Jeremy were just that, she realized now. The world was all too concrete.

All too concrete, Anna told herself, and tried to think no more about it.

For the second time in her calculating life, Anna had been possessed by impulse. It was liberating. Brook approved; he never calculated. But the lack of money stifled impulse, narrowed its scope to the pitiful. It was one thing to fly off to Rio for Carnival on impulse, and another to spring out for an ice-cream cone. Even worse to quit a job on whim, as Brook had already done once. Anna was quite sure they were both miserable. She could not stop dreaming about Jeremy.

She glanced at the clock. *Oh God,* she thought. *The interview.*

The apartment sat right on Main Street, Edgartown. It was a hot, clear day, and tourists were streaming in and out of the pseudo-seaport-style boutiques and cafés. Anna was thankful for one thing: she still had clothes. Her mother had packed the wardrobe and shipped it to her. But every stain, every sign of wear, stabbed Anna. She could never replace these things. A future of rummaging through discount bins spread before her, and she winced. She forced herself to remember that the future was far off. There were always detours, and for now she was wearing a simple, shell-white silk dress and heels that had thrilled her when she found them in the eighteenth arrondissement. For now, the men were still staring.

She turned into a Colonial-style seafood restaurant. It was quiet inside, only the soft clatter of preparations for the lunch crowd. Anna asked for the manager and was led into a dingy, windowless office.

The manager was a paunchy, bleary-eyed character of premature middle age, the kind Anna had always imagined as secret purchasers of bondage literature. He looked Anna over with dead precision. He asked where she had worked before. Anna reeled off the lies she and Brook had formulated: an American café in Lyons, a nightclub in Rome—all uncheckable references.

"Okay," the manager said. "Do you want to start today?"

Anna nearly panicked.

"I—I can't," she stammered. "I have a doctor's appointment."

"Tomorrow. See you at ten."

She felt sick as she left the restaurant. She had a job. Hooray. The tips would be good. Hooray. She would wear a uniform and smile and show off her tits and legs. She, who had dined regularly in establishments where the head chef of this dive would not be permitted to chop vegetables, would now have to lug eats to the *turistas*.

Look upon my restaurants, ye mighty, and despair.

She walked to the docks and found a bench. The boats pounded against the pier, the thudding of her pulse in her head. Maybe she really was ill. The thought cheered her up. A quick, dramatic disease. *Good-bye, shitty world.*

She passed a wretched half hour and then decided to get a late breakfast before seeing the doctors.

The doctor said: "Of course, you could be pregnant."

Anna laughed.

180

"Doctor," she said, "I have but one religion. The Pill. I take it devotedly."

The doctor shrugged and smiled. "Possibly your estrogen level has just increased, and the contraceptive is interfering with your menstrual cycle. There's a gynecologist in this building. I think you should see her. As for the rest, it sounds like stress to me. Would you like a prescription for some Valium?"

Oh God, Anna thought. *I am* turning into a wife.

"Brook, I'm simply terrified. I don't know how to wait tables!"

Brook grinned.

"Oh, don't give me those flashing all-American choppers. Help me!"

"Just be thankful you don't have to cook," he said. "You'd be out the door in five minutes."

"How supportive you are."

"You could have salted this chicken, at least."

"Salt's bad for you." Anna picked up the shaker and slammed it in front of him. "There! Salt. Tomorrow night's your turn. You can show me how it's done."

"I really don't know what you're so worried about, Anna. You'll knock them dead."

"Knock them *over*, more likely."

"Bah."

"Brook, you talk like this is going to be a bathing-suit competition."

"Isn't it?"

"You've got to take orders, make out tabs, handle all those dishes—"

"You'll do it all with style, Anna. The salad's good, by the way."

"Thanks. That's right. I'll have good comportment. I'll have that on my side."

I'll drop a tray and cuss everyone out, she thought.

"But maybe they call out orders in a special way," Anna said in a fresh burst of anxiety. You know, 'two over, one pig'—that kind of thing. A code. Oh God, Brook. I'll be expected to know a *code*."

"Tell them they had a different one in Lyons. Hey, listen, call your mother. Maybe she'll know something."

"She never worked in a *restaurant!*"

"Oh."

Later, Brook proposed they go out and have a few drinks.

"No, go on without me," Anna said. "I couldn't take that crowd. Besides, if I start to drink tonight, I won't be able to stop."

"I don't want to leave you alone, Anna."

"Go ahead."

"You won't suffer?"

"I'll read."

As soon as Brook left, Anna ate a Valium. She read a mystery. The tranquilizer took effect. She switched to a magazine. Two hours later, she took another tablet.

Through a happy haze, she wondered where Brook was. She crawled into bed alone and fell asleep.

In the middle of the night, Anna felt Brook get in beside her. She was dimly aware of whiskey breath. He said something and she said "sh-h-h . . ."

When she woke up, the bed was empty. She clawed at the clock radio.

"Oh Christ," she wailed, "it's quarter to ten!"

Anna hurled herself into the shower, jammed on clothes, and headed out the door. As an afterthought, she backtracked and got her bottle of pills.

There was no code. The headwaiter filled Anna in on basic procedure: where to call orders, where to pick them up, the tab and penalties for error on it. Another waitress helped her rummage through uniforms until a reasonable fit could be found.

Used clothes, Anna thought bitterly.

"There's a mirror in the bathroom," her helper offered.

"No thanks," Anna said. She didn't want to see herself in sackcloth. When the waitress left, she shook out a Valium. "Give me strength," she said to the little pill.

Anna was assigned the most remote grouping of tables. The headwaiter gave a few last instructions in a cynical tone which Anna took to mean, "I know you were hired for your cantilevering, and you probably won't survive the day."

Loathsome faggot, Anna thought.

Her first customers were a party of two, and they wanted blissfully simple things. They were both men; and from the way they ogled her, Anna knew they would forgive her anything.

She passed through a swinging door to the pickup station, calling the orders politely and clearly into the kitchen through a cutout in a separating wall. The appetizers came immediately, and she carried the oysters to the table with a feeling of triumph.

With a second set of customers things became a level more complex. Then four tables were occupied. Anna slid into the bathroom and shook out another Valium.

"Oh, the poached salmon isn't yours? Excuse me."

Anna knew she was fucking up on a massive scale, but she felt lighthearted and at peace. She beamed radiantly at the customers, and they beamed back—all except a trio of disgruntled old women.

"We've been waiting half an hour for our trout!" one crowed.

"It must be prepared freshly," Anna said, marveling at her own professionalism.

"What are they doing, waiting for it to come into season?"

The other two women chortled.

You are three putrid old sluts, Anna thought.

"I'll see what's holding it up," she said.

The kitchen noises had escalated into a maddening din. Waitresses crowded into the station, dancing around each other with plates in hand. Anna found the three orders of trout. They were cold.

"Could you heat these up again?" she asked in a small voice.

The headwaiter was seating a fifth table when Anna emerged with the trout. The thought of juggling another set of orders sent her mind reeling. Thank God they were only two, and men at that.

"There you are," she said to the old women.

Picking up a couple of glasses from the water station, Anna set them in front of the two men.

"Can I offer you gentlemen a—"

Anna choked in midsentence. She stared at the two customers.

It was Jean and his driver, Armand.

Jean glanced up in shock. To Anna's tranquilized imagination, an ironic smile played over his lips.

He stood immediately, as if to wait until she was seated.

"Look again, Jean," Anna said, plucking at the bodice of her uniform. "I work here."

"I have bribed him," Jean announced. "He has left."

Anna held open the door to the apartment. She wished she could summon the vehemence to order him out, but she felt too drained and humiliated.

"You're dreaming!" she said.

"No, it is very real. I have given Brook cash and he has left. It was simple."

"He may have taken your money—"

"He has given me his word. I think he was re-lieved."

Relieved, Anna thought. That was just possible.

"How much?" she asked.

184

"That is my business," said Jean. "We did not bargain."

"How long has all this been in the works, may I ask?"

"I approached Brook last evening. Armand drove him to the ferry this morning."

The little—Anna searched her memory. Brook had come home very late, and drunk. He had tried to talk to her. To tell her what? Forgive me, Anna, but I just sold you?

And now he was gone.

"I can't believe you did this! I can't believe you— you think this will gain you anything! Do you think I'll fall into your arms now that Brook's out of the way? You must be crazy! Get out of here!"

Jean sat down and glanced around the barren little apartment.

"Is this the best that you could do?" he asked.

"We wanted our own place," Anna said. "We were tired of favors. Some of us have to *earn* our incomes, you know."

"Brook was not tired of favors," Jean observed.

Anna strode over and slapped him.

"I asked you to leave," she fumed. "Now get out or I'll call the police."

"Police," Jean said, "are usually cooperative. Anna, you realize that I could have remained silent about Brook? He would have disappeared from your life and you would have never known why."

"He would have told me."

"No, that was part of the agreement."

"You wanted to save it for yourself then? As a little treat?"

"No. You do not understand. I met with Brook and made him an offer. It was not kind of me to make the offer, but he accepted it. I did not expect that. I could then have let him leave. I could have let you remain ignorant. Perhaps then I could have slipped back into your life. But this morning, when Armand called to tell me that all was well, I decided that you should know what had been done on your behalf."

"On my *behalf!*"

"Anna," Jean said, "he has taken the money. Don't you see that this makes him a—scoundrel?"

After the slap, Anna had retreated to the furthest corner of the apartment. She gazed contemptuously at Jean, but it was a practiced expression. In reality she did not know what to think. If there was a morality underlying Jean's actions, it escaped her. It seemed to her that he was only justifying his bribing Brook.

Brook, Brook, you shit!

Jean sat impassively, one cheek still red. It seemed to Anna that Jean had aged—had begun, at last, to look his fifty-two years. The body was trim, the eyes glittering, the hair a bold shock of gray. But weary lines had appeared on Jean's face, and he carried an air of desolation.

"You despise me," he said.

"You guessed it. You're despicable and you make other people despicable. That's your talent, Jean. That's your *métier.*"

"Will you believe me if I say that I have never before done anything of this kind?"

"This kind in particular, or this rotten?"

Jean was silent.

Anna stared out the window. She wanted another Valium. Somehow she had made it through the lunch shift, after Jean had left without ordering. The head-waiter had quizzed her suspiciously, but Anna managed him. She would still have the job tomorrow.

But now the dim, contented flux of the tranquilizer was gone, and all she could think of was Brook. Brook sitting in his favorite bar, the one just down the street. She could see it from the window, its facade blue-gray in the evening light.

She could see him clearly saying yes to Jean's offer. An envelope full of cash. Impulsive Brook meets

Mephistopheles. It came to her again, her moment of madness with Jeremy. There was in Jeremy something of Jean's implacability and control, something even of his aquiline face. Now that Jean had returned, Anna realized she had been acting out some half-baked psychodrama that day, projecting onto Jeremy all the dread she felt of the bankers, of the contracts, of Jean's virile, active, but somehow suffocatingly lifeless existence.

Yes, she could see it clearly, Brook and Jean sitting together over a drink. But Jean was no Mephistopheles. He was a beautiful, elegant machine.

"You're dead, Jean," she said, not turning to face him. "And I want you to get out of here before you kill me too."

The gynecologist said: "I don't believe you'll like this. You're pregnant."

Anna gave her the line about the Pill being her religion, this time without laughing.

The gynecologist, a maternal type, was not amused.

"Then I'm afraid your faith has failed you," she said.

Anna grew enraged. "You mean I'll have to have an *abortion?*"

"No . . ."

"I've never had an abortion in my *life!*"

"Have you ever had a baby?"

Oh God, Anna thought. *This woman's a pro-lifer or something.* Dismay washed over her. *An abortion, how grim.*

"I'll sue the company!" she said. She rummaged in her purse. She was ready to dash off to an attorney, pills in hand. Then she remembered she kept them at home in the medicine cabinet.

"When you get home," the gynecologist said, "read the enclosure. There is no such thing as a perfect contraceptive, short of sterilization."

From the purse, Anna pulled her datebook. She

kept track of her periods, and now she went back over the months. She remembered having cramps in the Lyons airport.

It isn't Jean then.

And afterwards . . .

Anna did not need to page through the little book. She had missed every period since then. It could not have been Brook. It could not have been Jean. It could not have been the American boy that last night in the chateau. . . . It could only have been—

Anna laughed aloud.

"Would you like a tranquilizer?" the gynecologist asked.

❧ fifteen ❧

The phone buzzed.

"There's a Mr. Halpern to see you," the receptionist said.

Nancy clutched her palm over the receiver.

"Oh, my God," she said, "it's Brook!"

Gwen left her desk. "Don't see him," she said.

"But it's Brook."

"Don't. Don't do it."

"But what if he wants to—"

"Think, Nancy! He ripped you off! He took advantage of you and then he ran off with your sister, for Christ's sake!"

"Maybe he wants to apologize and take me to lunch."

"Yes, and maybe he wants a loan," Gwen said witheringly.

"A loan? But I'm broke."

"You've still got your credit cards, though, don't you?"

"Just barely. You think that's it? A loan?"

"Why else would he try to corner you in the office?"

"Who does he think he is?" Nancy said. "Tell him I'm tied up," she said into the telephone.

Silence.

"He says he'll wait," the receptionist reported.

"He'll wait, Gwen."

"Okay, let him wait then. Let him wait forever."

Nancy smiled maliciously. She told the receptionist.

Nancy and Gwen jumped up and down in their cubicle, clapping their hands.

"This feels great," Nancy said. "Wouldn't it be wonderful to call the police on him?"

"Oh yes! Have him dragged out of the building by security!"

Five minutes later, Gwen dialed the reception desk. Brook was still waiting.

An hour later, he was waiting still.

Nancy felt depressed. "This is awful," she said. "It's like he's *lurking* out there."

"He's trying to psych you out," Gwen said.

The door to the cubicle opened.

"Hello, Nancy," Brook said. His expression was somber, but he was flushed with excitement.

The receptionist brought up the rear. "Mr. Halpern!" she cried. "Mr. Halpern!"

"She doesn't look tied up to me," Brook said, not taking his eyes off Nancy.

"Get out of here!" Gwen screamed.

Nancy's throat dried out. "That's right," she said. "Get out."

"I just got back into town, Nancy. I wanted—"

In the outer office, necks craned. Nancy's color rose. *Oh no,* she thought, *a public spectacle.*

Gwen leaped out of her chair. She gave Brook a shove, the top of her head level with his armpit.

"Get security," Gwen told the receptionist.

"Nancy, this is between us," Brook said. "Would you call off this little beast?"

"Please," Nancy said. "Just *leave.*"

Two men came behind Brook. Nancy recognized one as a partner. The other was a summer associate.

"Young man," said the partner.

Good-bye job, Nancy thought miserably.

"Get your hands off me!" Brook threatened. "Nancy . . ."

Nancy hid her face.

"Creep!" Gwen cried. "Thief!"

Brook grew stony. He reached into his jacket pocket.

"He's got a gun!" Gwen shouted.

The lawyers vanished.

Brook drew out a thick envelope. Nancy watched as he removed a wad of cash. He crumpled the envelope and pitched it aside.

"Here," he said. He began counting out bills. "Here, I want to—"

Nancy stared at him in stunned embarrassment. Tears were flowing down his red cheeks.

"Here!" Brook exploded. He threw the entire stack into the air. "Take the whole fucking lot, you mercenary bitch!"

He turned and stalked off.

The associate put his head in the door. "Everybody okay in here?"

Money fluttered onto chairs, desks, and floor in the little cubicle.

"Did you *hear* what that bastard called you?" Gwen said.

Nancy was on her hands and knees.

"Gwen!" she said. "Be quiet and help me pick this up! They're all hundreds!"

Jeremy burst into a smile.

"Brook! I thought you were living the simple life up in the Vineyard. Come on in."

Brook stood hesitantly at the doorway. "I'm sorry, Jeremy. I acted like a total prick. It seems I can't do anything else these days."

"This is not the carefree Brook I know," Jeremy said. "Are you growing a conscience or something?"

"I stole your woman. Aren't you going to kill me?"

"No, but if you step inside, I'll consider punching you out."

Brook turned to wave. A bright yellow taxi backed off in the early evening light.

"What's this?" Jeremy said. "No car?"

"I left it to Anna."

"Is it over then?"

Brook nodded.

"And you left her your *car?*" They went into the kitchen. "Then you really are growing a conscience." Jeremy pulled two cold beers. "Here," he said, holding one to Brook's temple. "Apply this until it shrinks."

They sat at the kitchen table.

"I've blown everything," Brook said morosely. "My life is a shambles."

"Brook, no offense, but your life has been a shambles for years."

"It's a worse shambles now. I—hell, I sold Anna."

"What do you mean, *sold?*"

Brook rubbed thumb and forefinger together. "Like for money," he said. "Did she ever tell you about this character Jean—the one who asked her to marry him?"

"Yes."

"He came to the Vineyard and paid me off never to see her again."

"Nobody does that," Jeremy said.

"He did."

"How much?"

"Twenty-five thousand. Cash."

"And you—"

"I took it."

"Jesus, Brook, you really are a total prick."

Brook grew agonized. Jeremy had seen him this way before, full of self-pity and guilt.

"We weren't happy," Brook said. "We were . . . wretched. This bastard held out the money and I thought, oh fuck, it's just a matter of time before Anna and I break up, anyway."

"Sometimes," Jeremy said, "it isn't a matter of time."

"It was for us. There was no real feeling. I think she just ran off with me because she was pissed off at you."

"And who were you pissed off at?"

"Nobody. Myself." He paused. "I just came back from seeing Nancy."

Jeremy said nothing.

"I went to her office. Big mistake. She wouldn't see me. Kept me waiting. I must have waited two hours. Finally I got mad and charged in. I—I threw the money at her. I can't believe I did that."

"Maybe it's what you meant to do."

"Sure, *some* of it. But she had this little demon in there sharing her office. They were really in a state, the two of them, real wildcats."

"Things got out of hand."

"They wanted to call security on me! The other one started screaming that I had a gun, for Christ's sake!"

"So you threw the money at Nancy."

"I was not sane. I mean that's still my money, damn it. How can I get it back?"

"Ask her?"

"Get serious."

"Why not? You came here to see her. See her. Talk to her."

"You don't know her, Jeremy."

Jeremy said nothing.

"You don't know about her and money. That's the bizarre thing about it. I mean—I've never done that to a girl before, taken her for a ride like that. And it had to be *her.* I can't explain it, but it was like she *wanted* me to rip her off."

"Uh-huh," said Jeremy.

"No, no. Really. Giving me money—for her, that was big-time commitment. It made her desperate, but I swear she liked being desperate. She wanted to live at the edge—and fuck it, you know and I know, we've lived at the edge. There is no edge, really. There's just being hard up or too high or all alone—or going to too

193

many parties and meeting too many assholes. But for Nancy, spending too much money, that was the edge. And that's where she wanted to be. Blowing her life savings was the roller-coaster ride for her. It showed—hell, it showed she wasn't some ordinary office drudge."

"It showed she was in love," Jeremy said.

"Exactly. So I had to be domineering Brook. What a lousy part."

"Shitty explanation, Brook."

"Well, I had to get out of it, that's all I know. We were running out of cash. Then what? End of reel, that's what."

Jeremy got two new beers.

"Now I haven't even got fifty bucks to live on," Brook said, with a significant glance.

"You need?" Jeremy asked.

"If you've got," Brook said. "Until I can get that—Jesus! I still can't believe it! All that cash! In the air!"

"Hold on."

Jeremy went to the bedroom he shared with Nancy. He opened the dresser, took out his wallet. He had only fifty-two dollars. He thought a moment. Nancy always kept cash around. Brook was right about her attitude: she had a fixation.

Jeremy searched through the dresser. *She's probably buried it in the backyard,* he thought. In the bottom drawer, beneath Nancy's blouses, he found an envelope with four fifty-dollar bills.

Beside it lay a second envelope, marked "Mr. Jeremy Penn."

"Hey Jeremy, are you still in there, or did you go to sleep?"

An eternity later, Jeremy folded the sheet of paper and set it beside him on the bed. He got two fifties for Brook and returned to the kitchen.

"Let me call you a cab," he said dully.

"A cab? What's up? Hey Jeremy, are you okay?"

"Here's a hundred. I'll come see you in the city."

"Borders told me the phone was disconnected," Brook said as Jeremy dialed.

"We put it back in."

"Wait a second. The train station's only about three miles from here."

Jeremy felt the numbness rising from his feet. By sheer force of concentration, he kept himself in one piece.

"That's right," he said.

"Listen." Brook took the phone from Jeremy's hand and hung it up. "I'll walk then, save the fare. It's a nice day, what the hell."

"You could catch the seven thirty-five," Jeremy said.

Nancy drove back to the cottage from the train station. Her head was still whirling. After the debacle, she had been called into the partner's office for a grilling and emerged with her job hanging by a slim thread.

She took a short lunch and deposited the cash in her savings account. She knew she would remember the look on the teller's face for a long time. She wanted to go home early, but stayed until five-thirty to make an impression of conscientiousness.

All that money! Nancy still couldn't believe it wasn't a dream. She hugged the steering wheel in her excitement.

On the last stretch of road she saw a tall blond man hitchhiking in the opposite direction. At first she was sure it had to be Brook. Then she told herself she was crazy; then she realized: *Maybe it* was *Brook.*

Hitchhiking. Oh, that was nice, Nancy thought. *I've got all your money, you stupid bastard!* And better, he had been to the cottage. Maybe he had realized . . .

Even in the office, Nancy had wanted to cry out: *Get out of here! I'm in love with Jeremy, and he's a better lay than you'll ever be!* Thank God she had stifled the impulse.

195

But maybe now he knew. *Good. Good.*

Nancy bubbled with excitement as she turned into the driveway. She sprang from the car, feeling breezy and full of possibilities.

Immediately, she sensed an emptiness in the house. She traced a path through bare rooms, to the doorway that framed her bed.

"Jeremy," she said. "I'm . . ."

Jeremy was sitting on the bed, a letter open in his lap. He raised baleful eyes from the page.

The smile melted from Nancy's lips. She shrank back. *She's afraid of me,* Jeremy thought contemptuously.

"Sit down," he said. He held up the letter. "How long have you had this?"

"Just three days," Nancy said. "I was going to show it to you, Jeremy."

"Do you know what it says?"

"No," Nancy said.

When she lied, he could always tell. Even if the lie was an insignificant one, and until now they had always been so, he saw through it instantly. Now it was as if he were peering directly into her soul. He saw her trembling under his gaze, small and worried and guilty. He felt a darkness spreading through himself like spilled ink.

Jeremy, he read again. *Catherine has tried to shoot herself. Her mother has locked her up. She won't let her go back. Catherine is falling apart. I can't do anything. You've got to help. She is desperate. Mark Dancer.*

After *Catherine is,* a word had been scratched out. The word was *decaying.*

Alice won't let her go back, Jeremy thought. *She's locked her up.*

Nancy sat beside him on the bed.

"Jeremy, I'm *so* sorry," she said.

"Very good," he said flatly. Then: "Were you afraid I'd go back to her? Was that it?"

196

Nancy nodded, confessing the earlier lie.

"You have so little faith in yourself?" he asked.

"But Jeremy," she pleaded. "She was—I mean I knew that once, she was your big romance. You lied to me about her. You told me she was dead. I wanted to ask you and give you the letter, but then I let it go. I didn't want to—to mess things up."

Jeremy pulled Nancy's overnight bag from the closet and threw it on the bed.

"Pack up," he said. "You're leaving."

Nancy burst into tears.

"I'm sorry! I said I'm sorry!"

Jeremy pulled a drawer from the dresser. He dumped the contents on the bed. He threw the drawer across the room. It landed with a crack of splintering wood. Nancy shook.

"Pack," he said. "You messed things up. I want you out."

He pulled the other drawers and upended them. Nancy began packing hysterically.

I'm being kicked out, Nancy thought. Her hands flew over the jumble of clothing, stuffing blouses and underwear into the bag. *Why didn't I show him that letter? Why?* Jeremy was on the verge of hitting her, she knew he was.

She tried to control herself. It was important to do this with dignity. If she moved deliberately, if she gave Jeremy a chance to cool down, maybe he would relent. She felt him looming behind her.

"Hurry up," he said coldly.

Nancy closed the overnight case. Without turning, she carried it out to the car. She could hear Jeremy following, but she maintained her poise, irritated with herself for crying before, and for snuffling now.

In the car, Jeremy started the engine so mechanically, so expressionlessly, that she burst into tears again. She stopped him from shifting into first.

"Are you going to see her?" she asked.

"That's my business."

"Why did you pretend to me that she was dead?"
Jeremy glared at her. "Because she is," he said.

Dead to him, was what Nancy thought. The phrases of the letter came back to her. Was Catherine now insane? Was that the tragedy that had broken Jeremy's love? *Won't let her go back,* the letter had said. Back to an institution?

"Then why are you so *mad* at me?" Nancy wailed.

"I'm not," Jeremy said. He engaged the clutch. Then: "I said she's dead. Doesn't that mean anything to you?"

"Jeremy . . ."

She reached out to touch his face. He brushed her hand away.

Jeremy felt nothing but contempt. It was like being made of steel, lifeless but powerful. He could feel Nancy's soft desperation beside him, but he was unmoved.

I don't give a shit, he thought. All he could think of was Catherine and her days of agony; Nancy's cowardice, and her days of deceit. The letter lying fallow in the dresser, accumulating pain.

He brushed Nancy's hand away. *Empty gestures,* he thought. Still she was there, weeping and prodding. He felt a great disgust. She loved him, wanted to keep him. She would do anything to defend her piece of human territory.

And Brook, with his pitiful weakness, his uncertainty. It was all of a piece. The road unreeled. He pulled into the train-station parking lot. The train was there.

Jeremy reached over Nancy's lap and pushed open her door.

"Get out," he said.

Nancy thought: *What would Anna do?*
Would Anna cry and plead and cling, making herself

feel like she was worth ten cents? The train was already in the station, a grimy old diesel. A few homeward-bound commuters stepped down and ambled toward their parked cars.

Anna would be strong, Nancy thought. *Anna would be sophisticated.*

Anna, she thought, *would get mad.*

Nancy got out. She dragged her case from the backseat. Without a word to Jeremy. She shut the car door and trudged toward the train, feeling lost and weak.

"Nancy?" It was Jeremy calling.

She turned and saw him hobbling toward her, cane clicking on the asphalt. He halted a few yards away, pale and intense. A station wagon passed between them. His long dark hair stirred in its wake.

"Nancy," he said, in a broken voice that made her shiver. "You don't belong with me."

He watched her as she turned away and walked to the platform, drooping with the overnight bag in one hand. He returned to the Mercedes and glanced at the dashboard clock.

This train, he thought. *It's the seven thirty-five.*

He watched her board, and thought: *Godspeed, Nancy.*

The train was virtually empty. Nancy was grateful for that. She sat in the smoking car, too feeble to move, until a gross man plumped down across the aisle and lit up a cigar. The fumes were revolting, and when he began grinning toothily at her, she wearily walked forward to the other car, wondering miserably what would become of her.

Then she remembered her new money, and felt comforted. *All those hundreds,* she thought. The train jerked into motion. She swayed as she shoved through the doors into the no-smoking car. She visualized the neat bundle of bills sitting in a vault, with a tag on it that said "Nancy." It wasn't really that way, she knew, but it was nicer to think of.

She felt so tired. It would be good now, she thought, to have an apartment of her own to go to. One with pretty curtains, flowers, pillows. Not a big place, but hers, and a color TV at the foot of the bed, so she could drink lemonade and be safe. She could go shopping and come home with packages and lock the door. She could have friends over to listen to her new stereo, when she got one.

Jesus Christ, it's Brook!

At the same moment, Brook, who was making his way up the car to the lavatory, recognized Nancy.

"Where's my money!" he cried.

"Conductor!" Nancy shouted. She pressed back against the window, wrapping her arms around her purse, as if he would try to snatch the few dollars she had there.

Brook sat down.

"Go away!" Nancy said.

"I tried to see you, you bitch! All I wanted was to pay you back!"

"Well you did! Thanks!"

"Not *that* much! I lost my head!"

"So did I, otherwise I wouldn't have let you make a sucker out of me!" Nancy said.

"How much did it come to? How much?"

"More than you can *ever* repay."

"Fuck that! How much in *money?*"

"A bezillion dollars!" Nancy cried.

"You stupid child! Not more than three thousand!"

"All my savings!"

"So what?" Brook said. "What were you saving it for? You gave, I didn't ask!"

"You asked. You asked all right."

Brook fell silent.

"Nancy," he said. "I *need* that money."

"What for? I'm the one who needs it. Who cares

what you need? You gave me that money. Everybody saw it. What'd you do, rob a bank?"

"No."

"Rake it off some old slut?"

"Nancy, you have got some decidedly twisted notions about the world."

"So you got it legally?"

"Yes, of course."

"Good. Then it's *mine*."

"I need it, Nancy. Nancy, I just came to—I just wanted to—"

"That won't work, Brook. Being pathetic just won't work. I mean it's a great effect. You're six-feet-two, you look like some Nordic god, and then when you go pathetic you expect us to break down like the world has got to be coming apart. Grow up, Brook."

"You're such a peasant."

"Okay. Fine. I'm a peasant. Now leave me alone. I've got what I want. What do you need it for? The money."

"To get reinstated," Brook said.

"In what? The human race?"

"The bar. So I can practice again."

Nancy paused.

"You lie," she said. "This is a calculated lie."

"You—"

"I'll call the conductor!" Nancy warned.

"Do I lie? Have I ever?"

"Yes, and worse. You betrayed. You think I'll give you your—*my*—money back? Forget it, Brook! I don't know how you got it, but did you earn it? I doubt it."

"I earned it," Brook said.

Night began to fall, and the train rolled on.

❧ sixteen ❧

The road. Across the bay to Jeremy's right hung the necklace of lights. He could almost hear, through the open window and above the thrum of tires, the remembered sound of waltz music in the summer air. With every note he was leaving Catherine further behind.

I won't go to her, he thought.

He knew it was wrong.

"It's not the gentlemanly thing," he said aloud, and laughed over the steering wheel. The Mercedes's headlights stabbed into the lonely dark.

It was wrong but it wasn't wrong. He had helped her, he had come to her in her sickness. He had conducted her into the underworld—and then had turned back.

Could anyone want more? Could anyone ask more? Cathrine, vulnerable, beautiful.

Jeremy laid his head on the wheel and felt the nubbled coolness on his brow. An oncoming car honked.

He jerked upright.

If he went to her now and helped her now, no longer a teenage boy desperate for life, would he be able to turn back? Or would he follow?

Across the gray depths, down the twilit slope. With the gathered mass of the dead, he and she holding hands.

The headlights cut into the lonely dark. The yellow line disappeared beneath the wheels. To Jeremy's right the bay vanished. Trees took over.

He could feel Catherine, a figure in a small window, a window in a big blackness. The figure and the window grew smaller with every mile, the blackness larger.

He was the Loser. He had lost. Lost Catherine, lost Anna, lost Nancy. Lost one to Death, lost another to Death, lost yet another to Death. Death was against him, seizing Catherine like a raider. Death was beside him, a mask to frighten Anna. Death was in him, a demon to chase Nancy.

Jeremy wiped sweat from his brow. Understanding was worse than not understanding. Because death was in his heart now, and in the whole lost, unthinking world only he could come to Catherine's aid.

With every mile, she fell further behind.

He heard an old song on the radio, a Beach Boys number, all sun and pleasure.

On the night road, a hardy bicyclist heard a mad laugh zoom past. And so it went, until the dark, jeweled towers of Manhattan began to show themselves across a primeval river. Suddenly the driving changed, funneling into a dense traffic, hurtling down ramps, over an awesome bridge and into canyons.

Jeremy walked the street in long, hurried, aimless strides. Faces and bodies passed him, laughing or isolated, smug, in despair, full of ambition and tragedy in the night glow of Manhattan. Ahead he saw a crowd, and joined it in the hope of distraction, nudging forward, craning his neck.

At a nondescript door stood a big man in a formal jacket. The man gazed impatiently over the crowd, and wherever his eye traveled, the crowd seemed to rise on the balls of its feet.

He pointed at Jeremy and waved him closer.

Beside Jeremy a slim, pale girl with black hair styled

like the plume of a Roman warrior's helmet seized his arm and whispered, "Take me." The crowd parted; a corridor of people formed, peering back at him as if trying to decode him.

The girl laughed. The plume of her hair nodded. "Well move, silly," she said. "We got in, get it?"

A note of triumph sounded in her voice, a low victorious chuckle. Jeremy looked at her again; she was pretty, nervous, artificial, just a fragile girl done up radically saucy. She waved back at her friends, breathing quickly under her leather jacket as Jeremy soberly led her through the crowd.

Inside the door, already at the border of a pounding, nocturnal music, Jeremy paid for both of them. They passed through a long corridor lined with stuffed birds and small mammals. The girl on Jeremy's arm began chattering a mile a minute, picking up steam and rhythm. They broke free of the corridor and stepped into a pulsating room lined with animal cages and terrariums. In the center, bodies swayed on a tiny, packed dance floor. A weight of deafening music bore down on Jeremy. The girl shouted some insanity— "The Theme Is Animals!"—into his ear.

"My name is Carrie!" the girl yelped. Jeremy told his. She dragged him to a bar that somehow seemed underwater. A towering dog asked him what he wanted.

He turned to Carrie. "We can split up now," he said. "You got in. Is it so hard to get in?"

"Impossible!" Carrie said, showing a gap between her upper front teeth. She smiled at him, wounded. "Do you want to get rid of me?" she asked.

He understood then. The doorman had picked him out. He was magical. And she, she was from—he placed the accent—Staten Island.

"No," he said. "Not at all."

Suddenly he took Carrie's face in his hands. She never stopped grinning.

"Come on," she piped, "let's dance. I hate drinking."

She had dragged him to the bar, now she dragged him to the dance pit. They danced to an enormous song. Carrie looked all around with quick, penetrating glances, her eyes flashing in dark-painted sockets. Jeremy longed for Anna—saw her, all at once, laughing on the terrace, her dark hair tumbling on her shoulders, her breasts high and important beneath a flowered blouse.

The song ended. The girl said eagerly, "Okay, now let's have a drink."

She said, "I never want to leave!" He had stunned her with champagne at delirious prices. But leave they must. She ran ahead on the street with shouts of joy.

The street lay silent, storefronts and bars darkened, a lone cab zooming by from time to time. Buildings loomed up into a peaceful night that soon would be a harried day. The girl waited for Jeremy to catch up, rocking back and forth.

"Why do you wear that leather jacket?" he asked. "It's damned hot, isn't it?"

"To get in," she said.

For breakfast they went to an all-night restaurant with neon inside. She was famished, laughing when food half fell out of her mouth. He ate almost nothing.

"You are *so* cool," she said dizzily. "I want you to know that."

"Will you stay with me tonight?" he asked.

It was all right going in and all right checking in, but when he shut the door and she toppled on the bed with a giant sigh, Jeremy knew that he could not, that he never could.

Because death was inside him.

He pointed at her, said, "Take off that jacket."

She did. He lay beside her.

She said, "You can if you want to." Her eyes were like unwound springs, madly happy.

He kissed her, and in the snap of a finger she fell asleep. He pulled off her shoes, put the blanket over her, and left a note. It was a maudlin note in a way, but he wrote it and did not tear it up.

In the morning, Carrie woke up clutching her head and making faces. She found and read the note, and smiled.

In the morning, in the early morning, Jeremy drove and drove, edging his way deeper into America. In the morning he pulled his Mercedes over to the shoulder, got out, pounded the hood.

Over him towered a road cut where engineers had blasted through a Pennsylvania hill. He could see the layers of ancient time, before people had been, or history.

Did that place exist then? he asked, thinking of the gray place. Was it made and waiting? Waiting for the parade? Waiting for Catherine, waiting for me?

He raked the hair out of his eyes. Early as it was, the highway roared with cars. They were going westward, going his way.

Except only one person was really going his way, and only he was going hers.

"Don't find your way back alone," he decided aloud. "We'll find the way together."

❧ seventeen ❧

The abortion clinic was a bright, airy floor of offices one flight up on East Seventy-ninth Street. It had been mentioned long ago by a school chum as "positively the best," and Anna wanted the abortion done in New York, where the whole procedure would be professional and impersonal: the Vineyard was too provincial for a job like this, she decided. She drove Brook's car, and in the back of her mind was a plan to return the old Plymouth to him. Once she did that, and terminated the pregnancy, the circle would be closed. She could step away.

On the phone, the secretary had recommended that Anna come with a friend, or at least arrange for someone to pick her up after the procedure. *Nonsense,* Anna thought. *I'll be perfectly all right, and if I feel weak, I'll simply take a cab.* But the secretary's suggestion left a bad taste: Anna had begun to realize that she *had* no friend to accompany her to the clinic—not even to pick her up afterwards. Dragging her parents into the act would only complicate things. *Once upon a time,* Anna thought, *it might have been Nancy.* But not now.

Like many women whose lives revolve around men, Anna traded in social lives each time she traded in lovers; her friends were her lovers' friends, and by slow degrees she had lost touch with her own. To a wedding she might have invited many of the women she had known over the years, but an abortion was an occasion that called for intimate friendship, and it depressed Anna to know she lacked that. She rode the elevator to the clinic alone.

There was something dental about the place, no aura of sickness or surgery. A cheerful aide ushered Anna into a niche where a detailed medical history was taken, then blood pressure and a blood sample, which hurt only fleetingly. Anna was directed to a bathroom to provide a urine sample. Breast and pelvic exams followed, with a pap smear and that unpleasant sensation of having one's insides scraped. The doctor moved efficiently and delicately, with a smile on his face and firm-voiced requests.

Anna was shown to the waiting room, and for the first time found herself with a group of other women who were preparing for the same procedure. There were seven including herself, but only four were patients. The others were friends, and once again Anna fought off a sense of isolation at being the only one who had come alone.

One of the women, a rather overweight blonde, was visibly upset and uncertain. Her companion whispered into her ear, held her hand. Anna felt irritated: why make such a fuss?

Anna had not even bothered to sort out her own feelings except to note that abortions were undeniably tacky. She had heard of women going in with her attitude, having the abortion, and then bursting into tears at the first sight of a baby in the street. She doubted this would happen to her. It wasn't like having a tooth out, exactly—she knew she was cutting short a small life—but after all, she could get pregnant again. And a *baby, now* . . . There was no question about it; the whole farce was a disagreeable necessity. Anna supposed that some women felt they had to dramatize everything.

Still, she was nervous. She didn't much care for the

idea of a vacuum-cleaner hose in her insides and tried not to think about it. Where she sat, she could see long, white corridors lined with doors. One of them opened and a young woman emerged.

She had just had her abortion and everyone seemed relieved that she looked fine. She went into a recovery room. Anna realized the whole thing would be done with street clothes on. Really, she thought, it *was* more like having a tooth out.

One by one, the others were led down the corridor, their companions alongside, until Anna sat by herself in the waiting room. Only then did she begin to feel frightened and guilty. She began thinking about babies and knew tears were on the way if she didn't beat down the ridiculous emotions that were overwhelming her.

I told Jean he was dead. I told him he was a destroyer. But am I any better?

A frantic girl rustled into the waiting room, distracting Anna. Not a day over seventeen, she was alone and already crying. The girl plumped into a chair and buried her face in her hands.

Anna glanced around anxiously, hoping a nurse would come by and do something. She wondered if she should fetch one. Finally, she got up and sat by the girl.

"I'm so scared," the girl sobbed, her slim body shaking.

"I'm scared too," Anna said.

"Scared of dying," the girl said.

"Come on, now, pull yourself together. Nobody *dies* during these things."

"I'm going to," the girl said. "I can feel it!"

The girl's terrors were so extreme and groundless that Anna felt a rush of maternalism. She got out a handkerchief. Gently, she pried the girl's moist palms from her face. She gave her the handkerchief and held her hand. Miraculously, her own fear began to evaporate.

Soon, a nurse came for the girl and led her into the corridor, opening the first door. The girl turned and gave a little wave to Anna. Anna made a fist and winked.

Minutes passed, and Anna began to feel disgruntled at having been made to wait so long. *They took that teenager before me,* she thought.

Suddenly, Anna heard violent noises from the corridor. A thin voice cried, "I want to go home!" The first door burst open, and a disheveled figure flew out, blood-pressure gauge dangling from one arm. It was the frightened girl. A nurse sprang out after her, trailed by a doctor with speculum in hand.

Anna leaped to her feet to intercept the girl. The girl struggled briefly and then gazed desperately into Anna's face.

Seeming to realize what a scene she was making, the girl took a deep shuddering breath.

"I was wrong," she said. "It's not dying I'm scared of. It's living. This." She put a hand on her abdomen. "This is what I was afraid of."

The doctor, the nurse, and now an aide closed in. Anna found herself saying, "Let me talk to her. Do you want to go outside?"

"Yes," the girl said.

"The gauge," the nurse said. "The blood-pressure gauge."

The nurse unstrapped the gauge. Anna and the girl took the stairs to the street.

"I won't kill it," the girl sobbed.

"Listen," Anna said, ignoring the stares of passersby as she walked with arm around the girl. "I can't argue the whole philosophy of this—"

"Neither can I!"

"—but what's the point of wrecking your entire life? You'll still be able to have babies, you know."

"Yes, but I *have* one already! This one!"

They walked twice around the block.

"You aren't going back then, are you?" Anna asked.

"No," the girl said fiercely. "There is no going back. It's—destiny, you know?"

"You dope," Anna said. She hugged the girl on the street. "You idiot."

To herself she decided not to go back. At that instant the idea came to her, compelling and fully formed, that she must find and see Catherine Dancer.

Anna staggered back on the sidewalk. It seemed to her that she could almost see a figure in white in the heat shimmer of the street.

The girl said, "Are *you* all right?"

It was easy: directory assistance found only one Dancer in Suffolk County.

"Could I speak to Catherine, please?"

"Catherine?" said a man's voice. "Who is this?"

Anna said her name.

"Catherine's sick. You can't talk to her. Hold on a minute."

Anna heard whispered conversation. A woman came on the line.

"Miss Ravine?" the woman said in saccharine tones: "Of *course* you can speak to Catherine." The voice was almost familiar. Anna wondered if it was the voice that had crawed at her outside the boxwood garden, the night she first saw Catherine.

Next came a weak voice. The placid sound of it sent a shudder through Anna as she stood in the telephone booth.

"Hello, Anna Ravine."

Anna drove. There was no time involved, or space. Only a distance of emotions. The sun beat down on the old Plymouth's hood and on the highway. Air blasted through the open window.

She had Jeremy's baby inside her.

Only now did she realize it. It was a king-sized concept. Having chosen not to rid herself of it had somehow—

—she was confused.

Somehow, she felt strong feelings, romantic feelings. They wouldn't go away.

"The child must have a father!" she announced in gruff tones—

—oh definitely, definitely confused.

Anna thought of all the times she had made love to Brook, thinking of another face. Of all the men she had known, only Jeremy—

—only Jeremy what?

Only Jeremy.

Anna caught herself singing to the endless road.

As the teenager sitting by the gate let her in, Anna had doubts.

"You with the auditors?" the boy asked.

"Yes," Anna said. "No," Anna said. In a flurry of words the boy gave her to understand that the estate had been in probate for years, since the owner's death. The auditors were long past due. "They're lost," he said. "Good and lost."

He opened the great, wrought-iron gate and she drove into a cathedral of trees.

The Alice Dancer who answered the door was charming. She welcomed Anna in with an offer of tea. Flowers graced the small, neat living room, though the tiny cottage windows admitted only faint sunlight.

With tea came cookies and sharp, probing inquiries —designed, Anna saw at once, to uncover the depth of Anna's relationship to Jeremy. Anna diverted the conversation to Catherine. She could hear the clattering of feet above.

Soon Mark Dancer led his daughter down the steps. "You must understand," the mother whispered. "She hasn't been at all well."

Catherine had the pale, damp appearance of someone who had been confined to bed for a long time.

Dressed in robe and slippers, she leaned heavily on her father as they shuffled into the living room. Her eyes were large and luminous.

Anna thought: *She doesn't look seventeen anymore.* It struck her that Catherine looked to be no particular age at all.

"Come sit by me," Alice Dancer said, patting a sofa cushion. In slow motion, Catherine broke from her father and drifted to the couch. She gazed wide-eyed around the room, as if she had never seen it before. She smiled at Anna.

"Mother," Catherine said. "Do you think we could sit outside?"

Alice Dancer shot a quick, suspicious glance at her husband. "Now, Catherine," she said sweetly, "you know you're not well enough."

"But it's warm out," Catherine said. "The day is clear. There's no wind in the trees. Could I sit in the sun? Just out in the back?"

The wistfulness of Catherine's voice melted in Anna's chest. She spoke as if the outside were a rare and special treat. Without waiting for an answer, Catherine got to her feet and began to walk toward the kitchen.

"Catherine!" her mother said sharply.

"Mother, Anna and I want to talk alone, don't we?"

"If that's all right, Mrs. Dancer. I would like to—"

"Your father and I will be watching!" Alice Dancer said.

Catherine nodded. She stretched out her arms, holding out her hand to Anna. Anna rose and took it. Catherine's grip was weak and cold. Her touch sent an odd thrill through Anna.

They went out the back door to the yard. Catherine winced at the brightness. A soft breeze played at her robe. Hedges fenced in the square of lush green lawn.

Catherine said: "From my window—you can't see it from here—I can look out at the bay."

"It must be beautiful," Anna said dutifully.

"It is. On clear days, I can even see the far shore. Sometimes it's veiled in mist, but still I can see it."

"Catherine!" the mother's voice rang out from the house. "Don't tire yourself out."

Anna took Catherine's elbow and helped her to a webbed chaise longue. Beyond the hedges she caught a glimpse of the father.

"Do they always keep you under surveillance like this?" Anna asked, taking a lawn chair.

"They're very careful of my health," Catherine said slowly. "Especially my mother."

"May I ask what's wrong?"

"Don't worry," Catherine said. "It isn't contagious. I'm very weak, though." Then: "I'm so sorry if I upset you. I've been so foolish. No, please let me say it. I've been gone a long time. When I came back, I wanted to see Jeremy very much. Once we were . . . very much in love. But I was afraid to come to him directly."

"You shouldn't have been," Anna said.

Catherine smiled. "The sun is so nice," she said. She reached down and stroked the grass. "I'm grateful you came," she said. "If only for this. He came to see me too, you know."

"Who? Jeremy?"

Suddenly Catherine glanced at Anna's middle. Anna stirred uncomfortably and wondered if she was showing already. No, that was impossible. Yet she felt certain, as Catherine looked up again, that this person knew, had sensed her condition. She saw a flickering light come into Catherine's eyes.

Catherine leaned forward. "He loves you," she said.

Anna nodded. Then she wondered why she had nodded.

"And you?" Catherine asked.

Anna heard the unspoken question: "Do you love him?" All at once she felt that Catherine was not twenty-seven—as she must be—but eighty-seven, a wise old woman giving gentle advice.

"You won't find him easy to understand," Catherine said. "You'll need strength. All the strength in the world, to love him as he really is."

Anna sensed there was a question buried under Catherine's words, as if she were asking: *Do you know who he really is?*

"I don't know if I have that much strength," Anna said.

"Will you tell him something for me?"

"Of course."

"Tell him I'm—tell him I'm fine, will you? Don't let him know you've seen me like this, sick and everything. I made a mistake in coming back. I know that now. Tell him that for me?"

"I think he'll want to know if you're ill . . ."

"No. Tell him you saw me in the garden. Tell him you saw me in the sun. Tell him I said that I hope you will be very happy together. Please tell him those things for me."

Catherine spoke in a quick, soft, impassioned voice that penetrated Anna like electricity.

"I will," Anna said.

"Catherine!" the mother shouted down from a second-floor window.

"Oh no," Catherine said. "She's been listening."

"Come inside at once!"

"How can you let her talk to you that way?" Anna whispered.

"She had a dream once," Catherine said quietly, as if to herself, "and I was part of it. Now it's become a nightmare. And I'm a prisoner of it."

Alice Dancer surged out of the cottage. She glared at Catherine. She seized her daughter's arm. She glared at Anna.

"Come in," she said. "Now." And as an afterthought, to Anna, "You too."

Anna suddenly wanted out. She wanted out fast.

"I must be going," she began.

"Come in!" the mother ordered curtly.

For a moment, Anna fell under the spell of Alice Dancer's obsession. She followed as the woman dragged her daughter into the house, through the kitchen, and into the living room. Tea service and cookies still rested on the coffee table.

"Please, have a seat," Mrs. Dancer said.

They sat. Mark Dancer shambled in quickly, and at his wife's order, also sat. Anna felt trapped in a sham family life, a surface under which some nameless thing was writhing.

"I've got to go," she blurted.

"No! I want you to stay. Stay long enough to see something."

With these words, Alice Dancer jerked Catherine to her feet. Catherine struggled.

"Mark!" the mother cried. "Help me!"

Reluctantly but obediently, the father helped restrain his feverishly thrashing daughter.

"Go, Anna!" Catherine wailed. "Please!"

"Just long enough," the mother said, her eyes flashing, "to see, and to tell him!"

Anna rose quickly, but not quickly enough. With horror and shame, she looked on as Alice Dancer pulled open her daughter's robe and, with one brutal motion, ripped apart her flimsy nightgown.

"There!" the mother cried triumphantly.

Anna backed away in shock. She fell against the sofa.

Catherine stood naked in the living room, her head thrown back, dark hair flying as she pulled feebly at her pinioned arms.

The body Anna saw was the color of boiled pork, a sheath of gray flesh covering a skeletal frame. Covering Catherine's breasts, stomach, and thighs were ulcerous sores, like a dozen purplish mouths. Below her left nipple lay a dark red wound the size of a dime, and as Catherine struggled the wound began to trickle blood.

Catherine crumpled sobbing to the living-room floor.

Anna Ravine realized in terror that she was in love.

She realized as she ran from the little stone cottage, the image of Catherine imprinted in her brain. She started the old Plymouth. It screamed with rage and leaped heavily. Her hands slipped wetly on the steering wheel. She rocketed through a corridor of trees, the sun piercing through in unreal shafts of cathedral light.

She realized as she headed for the gate and another car nosed through and she slammed her brakes with visceral dismay.

She realized as she saw Jeremy climb out of the Mercedes and race toward her. Realized, as she buried her face in her hands and heard through the blackness Jeremy's voice through the window.

"I love you," she said, realizing. "I love you."

He said "Slide over" and took the wheel, pulling the Plymouth to the side of the drive. He helped Anna out. She shook violently, leaning against him as they walked to the Mercedes. Jeremy could feel her body through her summer dress. The flesh of her arms was cool to the touch. He smelled the perfume of her dark hair. A little bracelet of coral dangled around her wrist; it struck him as a vulnerable thing and it dawned on him, as if for the first time, how small Anna was.

He took her. He held her. He kissed her.

They went away. They drove, far away it seemed to Jeremy; not far at all, Anna thought. The end of the world would not have been far enough to be from where she had been. They walked on a beach holding hands. The waves crashed at their feet as they carried their shoes.

The sun set mammoth red on the horizon. It sent a

carpet of red to them. Anna laughed. She turned her face to Jeremy.

"I was just thinking," she said, "that I'll never need to eat, never need to drink, as long as I have you."

She turned her beautiful face to the eternal face of the sea. She shook the waves of her dark hair.

"How wrong," she said. "How wrong that is."

Night grew deep. It was Anna who said, "We have to leave the beach." Jeremy had grown silent, and as they drove again, headlights cutting the deep night and the road, he became all silence. No motel was right, no hotel good enough.

Finally Anna stopped him. They pulled into a blank parking lot. A tall sign reading VACANCY reigned, and a wall of numbered doors two high.

"Go to her," she said. "But come back to me."

❧ eighteen ❧

Catherine stalked the room. A wave of darkness crashed over her and she clung to the wall. Edging weakly to the window, she pressed her face to the small opening that had been left in the nailed-up boards. She peered out at the lawn and the bay, with its distant lights twinkling in the night. It was almost the hour when her father came with the bowl and the rags. Catherine wondered if he would come tonight.

A clicking sounded at the door. It creaked open and a hand reached in, setting a bowl of water and a soft bundle on the floor. Catherine lurched across the room and seized the arm.

Mark Dancer drew back in shock as the door flew wide. He pulled away slowly, unable to meet Catherine's eyes.

"We'll escape," he began suddenly, his voice quiet and fervent. "Just the two of us. We'll take the car and go—go where she can't follow." Just as suddenly, he sagged, and the light dimmed in his face.

He shut the door and locked it, leaving Catherine alone. Catherine took up the things and carried them to her night table. Opening her robe, she began washing her wounds. Every night fresh ones appeared, and the old grew deeper, as her flesh mottled into a darker gray. She wiped away the streak of dried blood that had trickled from the hole below her left breast.

Shifting the robe off her shoulders, she cleaned her back as best she could. The exit wound blasted by the bullet gaped raggedly beside her shoulder blade. *I should have aimed for the brain,* she thought.

She prayed for Jeremy to come, prayed for him not to come. If only she had another chance with her father's gun, she would be less cowardly. *It was vanity made me aim for the heart,* she thought. *I couldn't stand the thought of my face blown apart.*

With the brain destroyed, surely she could not go on as she was. But the gun was out of reach now; her mother would have seen to that. She wondered how much longer before her vanity would mock her and the face begin to decay as the body had. If Jeremy came, there would be no escape for either of them. They would be trapped in this room together, filled with loathing and remorse.

She would have to get the gun again. She would have to rouse her father into action if she could. He could lay hands on a weapon and bring it up to her. It was nearly hopeless, but she had to try—

The lock clicked, and Catherine wrapped herself in the robe. There was a time when her father would have done anything for her, given her anything. He was will-less now, but she resolved to make a last effort.

Alice Dancer stepped in, smiling.

"Oh Catherine," she said with irritation, smile fading. Finding a comb on the dresser, she sat beside her daughter and began combing her hair. "How can you let yourself look like this? Don't you want to look pretty?"

Catherine recoiled from her mother's touch, but it was firm and insistent. She could remember, in the mists of the past, times when her mother would brush her hair for long, calm minutes, talking softly to her about her beauty. Only then was her mother happy, only then did the strain of life melt from her, replaced by hope.

Now she could barely stand to glance at her mother's face. It had twisted into a sinister grin, gums showing above the even, white teeth, eyes glaring.

But in a sense it was like the old times. Mother was excited, pleased, hopeful again. She talked about what a fine boy Jeremy was. Any girl would be happy to get him.

"You *would* be happy, wouldn't you, Catherine?"

"He doesn't want me, Mother. He told me so."

"No, you don't understand him. He came for you when you were sick. Remember how happy that made you? He didn't know, Cathy. If he'd known, he would have stayed with you. He wouldn't have said those things. He didn't mean them. Now he knows. Now he'll come."

"Keep me here if you want, but please send him away."

"Don't say silly things. You're in love with him, aren't you?"

"Keep me here then," Catherine said. "But bring dirt. Fill the room with dirt."

Catherine never slept, but at intervals darkness eclipsed her, pushing her down into a faint. When she awoke there would be new wounds, small and livid.

She awoke in the dead of night. She had learned to gauge the hour from the vast surrounding shell of darkness. Opening her robe, she searched for the new wounds and counted them. It had become a ritual. Tying her robe, she went to the door and worked the knob. As always, it was locked. On the outside now was also a bolt, but trying the knob had become the second of a triangle of rituals. The third led her to the closet.

Several dresses hung with the wedding gown now, but they held no interest for Catherine. On the floor of the closet lay the blue cardboard box. Catherine tugged the carton to the bed.

Slowly, she laid out the letters and photographs,

cards in her solitaire. In the deep hours of the night, she fended off the sad loneliness of decay with these fragments of the past, as if each letter and snapshot were a bandage, a salve for every bare wound. Catherine knew that soon there would be more wounds than pictures and letters, but as she fished each card from the box, she groped to fill out the spaces between the images, the girl's feelings between the lines. There are children who come to America and forget their native tongue; later, when they hear it spoken, the sounds excite a nebulous recognition, a trembling at the edge of comprehension. This was how Catherine felt as she laid out the pictures: they were her forgotten language. They were the mountains and streams of a vanished country to which she could never return.

She lay back on her pillow and dreamed of the dance, the mellow swaying lamps and the thrumming music.

Her reverie was broken by a sound from downstairs. Slippered feet shuffled on bare wood. The front door opened.

Catherine froze, listening.

"It's Jeremy," she whispered.

She heard her mother exclaim joyfully, followed by her footfalls clattering up the steps.

The door to Catherine's room unlocked for the last time.

"He's here!" Alice Dancer exclaimed. Her face was flushed, like a teenager's whose own date had arrived. "Quickly!" Alice Dancer scooped Catherine's mementos from the bed and into the box. She paused to glance at her daughter with dismay. "Oh Catherine, *can't* you take better care of your appearance? Hurry now, get into bed." And the sickbed scene, tried and true, was set again.

Jeremy appeared at the door. Catherine's palm rose to her lips, stifling a gasp. Dark circles underlined Jeremy's brooding eyes. His hair was tousled, and his breath came in short, forced pants.

Alice Dancer curtsied. It was a mad and inappropriate gesture in her bathrobe, but it went unnoticed by Catherine or Jeremy. The mother slipped out, leaving the door slightly ajar.

"Get away from the door!" Jeremy thundered, not turning from Catherine. "Close it and get away! I'll know if you're out there listening!"

Muttered complaints about "rudeness" filtered in, but footsteps padded away down the hall.

Jeremy lowered his voice and began talking in the hushed, fervent monotones of the confessional:

"I meant to come before. I was on my way. I was on my way but there was a detour."

For an instant, Catherine's face lit up with joy as she realized he meant Anna.

"Good," she said. Then she searched his bowed face. "Did you bring a gun?" she asked.

"No. I thought—" An image flashed before his eyes: Catherine's brain blown back against the wall behind lost, grateful eyes. He could not bear it.

"I'll dig a grave," he heard himself say.

Catherine climbed out of bed. The room had been stripped. There was nothing in it, not even a chair.

"I'm afraid to be buried again, Jeremy. It . . . it was such a long journey, and I was stupid. I had no idea I would have to travel the way I did. At first I had no idea where I was."

She halted before the boarded window and told how she returned to the surface of the earth. She had awakened in her coffin. "It was dark, and I had forgotten darkness and how frightening it could be." A terrible smell had invaded her nostrils, of dust laid thick. The place was narrow, and she could not move. "Then I smelled a stronger smell, like rotten meat. I lay there for a long time, and I couldn't tell how long it was taking. Centuries, I thought."

A thick silent scream arched through Jeremy's brain.

"I worried that you'd be dead then, and I would

have come back for no reason. I think maybe it was months. I was so dry, like I was made of paper. My tongue was like a twig. My eyes were like kernels. But slowly, they changed. Finally, I was able to reach and touch the inside of the box. I was afraid maybe it would be steel, but when I tore out some of the lining, it wasn't. I didn't have anything to scrape with, no ring or anything, so I started with my teeth."

"Please, Catherine, please."

But Catherine continued.

"I scraped and scraped a circle. It took a long time. When the wood came out, a lot of dirt fell on my face, but I pushed it down to my feet until I could sit up through the hole in the box. I kept scooping it back and scooping it back. It went fast, that part, until I felt roots and I pushed up as hard as I could . . ."

She turned to Jeremy, who was shuddering with his face in his hands.

"I couldn't go back the same way, Jeremy. I couldn't feel the earth fall on my face and know I would have to wait in the dark again."

She paused.

"You know," she said, "that there's only one way she'll let me out of here with you."

That same night, at 2:35 A.M., Jeremy asked Mark Dancer for his daughter's hand. Alice Dancer cried "Yes!" and skipped from one end of the living room to the other, and back again.

What followed was like a hallucination for Jeremy. He and Catherine had planned an escape. "Fire," she had said, and fire was the word that filled Jeremy's brain. But Alice Dancer seized a Bible from the top of the mantel and produced an orange pamphlet from inside. "Dearly beloved!" she exulted.

Then Jeremy realized that Alice Dancer knew what he and Catherine were. There would be no blood tests, no offering of identification. Not even a quick trip to one of those states where the barriers to wedlock were few.

Catherine's mother would marry them herself.

In her room, Catherine took down the wedding gown and laid it on the bed. Her mother burst in like a thief and helped her dress. Catherine's wounds stained the white linen, and Alice Dancer grew agitated, wondering aloud what could be done. "It will be dark, Mother," Catherine reminded, and the mother took comfort in that.

A shoebox lay on the top shelf of the closet. Alice Dancer carried it to Catherine, bringing out white pumps.

But Catherine said, "No, Mother—bring me the pair of patchwork slippers."

"Oh yes," Alice Dancer enthused. "Something old!" For something blue, there was a sky-colored sash; for something borrowed, a lace handkerchief of Alice's.

Catherine descended the stairs, her mother's arm locked in hers. She craned to peer into the living room. It was empty. Jeremy and your father are waiting outside," Alice Dancer said. "At the copse by the water."

At that moment, Catherine decided where her body would be destroyed.

Night air. It was like the cemetery air Catherine had first emerged into: warm and sweet, scented with the bay. The stars glittered overhead. The moon was down and the lawns were dark, seething with shadows. Catherine picked up the trailing hem of her gown.

The copse was a black gathering of birches on a hill overlooking the water. At the top of the hill stood two silhouettes. They turned to watch Catherine coming.

Catherine wanted to hurry. The breeze and the chirping of crickets were like the softest of chains, and she knew they must be broken. The processional was a dream, and Catherine had dreamed it often, long ago, in the language now forgotten. She had dreamed of a church, and flowers, and the cluster of friends, champagne glasses held high.

The copse neared like a gallows. Jeremy's eyes grew clearer, baleful and uncertain. Catherine wanted to hurry, but her mother disciplined her into a stately march, as if to unheard music.

Catherine glanced at the boat house, a gloomy outline against the glimmering ripples of the bay. It stood by the hill like a small friend. Often Catherine had gazed out from the slit in her room, and watched her father come and go from the old wooden structure, and heard the roaring of the engines he maintained, and thought of gasoline the way a drunkard thinks of muscatel.

Her father was wearing a tie, awkwardly knotted. His face was a milky balloon smeared with a grin. Catherine wanted to embrace him and tell him everything would be all right, that she would stay with him if she could.

But she looked again at the boat house.

Jeremy became a person, not a statue, not a pair of eyes. Suddenly she was standing by his side. Her mother broke away and positioned herself in front of them, Bible in hand, the pamphlet open within.

"Follow me," Catherine whispered urgently.

She bolted down the slope. Behind her she heard shouts and feet thudding on turf. Jeremy pulled even, took her hand. Catherine felt herself weakening immediately; strengthless, she let herself be pulled.

The boat house loomed like a dark, unspoken destiny. Jeremy flung open the door and pitched Catherine in. She toppled to the floor and heard the door latch shut.

"The gasoline!" Catherine cried.

Jeremy was already searching. The boat house smelled of ancient damp. A hull hung from the ceiling.

"We can siphon it if there isn't a can," Jeremy said.

"Here's one!" Catherine cried, clanking out a five-gallon container.

From outside came banging, shouts.

Then: *"Dearly beloved, we are gathered here together to join this man and woman in bonds of holy matrimony . . ."*

Jeremy shook the can. It was nearly full. He unscrewed the top. He splashed the gasoline across the wide floorboards, onto the walls, over the workbench and the leaning oars.

Catherine seized the can from his grip. Holding it high, she poured it over her pale gown. The reek of fumes filled the air.

" . . . if there is any person present who knows any reason why these two should not be so joined . . ."

"Matches," Catherine said. Her calm suffused the barnlike space.

Jeremy rummaged the cluttered, gas-soaked surface of the workbench.

"Nothing!" he said. "Nothing!"

The fumes climbed into his brain. He watched Catherine lunge at a crank and begin winching the suspended hull down onto its ways. She climbed into the boat and searched the instrument panel for a light.

Jeremy climbed in with her. Placing Catherine in the stern, he sloshed the last of the fuel on the hull. He pulled wires from the outboard motor.

He took Catherine's hand and placed it on the toggle of the pull starter.

"Pull this," he said. "Pull it hard, and you'll get a spark. Can you do it?"

" . . . Jeremy, will you take this woman to be your lawfully wedded wife, to have and to hold, in sickness and in health, until death do you part?"

Catherine and Jeremy froze in the stern of the boat. Outside, in the silence, they could hear Mark Dancer cry: "I smell gasoline! Alice, they're pouring gas in there!"

Jeremy sat beside Catherine. He pulled her fingers from the toggle and grasped it.

"I will," he intoned. "And not even then."

Catherine shook her head.

"Jeremy," she said quietly. "Get out. Go out among the living. You don't belong here. You belong with her. I came here alone. I will go back alone. It's my journey to make. It always was. Stay, Jeremy, stay. As long as you can."

"You need me. You're afraid."

"Jeremy, I will remember. How you came back for me—"

"—and you came back for me."

"And you came back for me."

She pushed him. It was a childish shove. Jeremy stepped out of the boat. He walked unsteadily to the door of the boat house.

"No," Catherine said. "Don't look back."

He unlatched the door, steeled himself, and rushed into the fresh night air. Leaping toward Mark and Alice Dancer, he seized them and propelled them from the boat house. A hollow, thundering boom knocked him to the grass. Alice Dancer screamed. The lawn flickered with the ghostly light of the flames.

Groggily, Jeremy got to his feet and faced the fire. The heat scorched his face. The boat house was a single, towering flame licking up at the stars. A jet of fire shot from the open door.

Nearby, Mark Dancer was restraining his hysterical wife.

"We didn't finish!" she screamed.

With an inarticulate cry, she tore from her husband's grip and raced toward the burning boat house. At the threshold, she fell away, shielding her face.

"Catherine!" she shouted against the roar.

She plunged through the fiery door.

Mark Dancer held up his hands, his mouth gaping in horror.

From within came screams of agony. Jeremy hurtled

toward the boat house, but the flames were overwhelming. The building listed toward him with a
sickening creak.

Then Alice Dancer appeared at the doorway. She
was bent over, dragging something. She tumbled back,
beating at the flames in her hair and clothes. A lifeless,
charred hand flopped across the threshold.

Mark Dancer shot forward and pulled his wife away
from the boat house as it moaned, cracked, and
sagged. With a final heave, the building crashed forward, spewing a fountain of red embers.

"Into the water!" Jeremy shouted.

A final time, Alice Dancer pulled away. Screaming
and writhing, she aimed herself toward the bay and
leaped into it. Clouds of hissing smoke boiled up.

Mark Dancer splashed in up to his knees. He dove
into the water. Tearing off his shirt, Jeremy followed.
They dove again and again. They called; they flailed;
they swam.

Exhausted, Jeremy dragged himself to the shore. He
found Mark Dancer there, gasping and choking, a
crumpled form with blank, terrible eyes. The sight of
him bludgeoned Jeremy into despair.

He looked to the glowing, hellish ruins of the boat
house.

When he turned from sea to land, he saw the hill,
the copse of trees that was to have been the wedding
site. On it stood a bold silhouette, hair streaming in
the wind, skirts blown back, arms rigid, and fists
clenched.

"Anna!" Jeremy cried.

He climbed to his feet. His leg gave out and he fell.

"Anna! This was not for you to see!"

"But I saw," she said. "I did see. I saw the wedding
march. I saw. I saw the funeral pyre."

He had shot up the hill, limping and weaving. Now
he stood panting, wet, half clothed, arms half reaching
out.

Anna Ravine reached up and put an eerily steady hand on Jeremy's shoulder.

"Who was she?" Anna asked in a level voice. "Who are you?"

Tears flowed down Jeremy's anguished face to join the rivulets trickling from his hair.

"Who?" Anna asked again. Then, as if it meant something, she waved her arm at the bay, the smoldering boat house.

Jeremy drew himself up. "Does no one know me here?" he recited.

Now it was Anna biting back tears.

"Jeremy," she said. "There is one thing I need to know from you. Did you take her. Did you marry her. Did you say 'I do'?"

Far off, like a wail of sorrow from another world, or like a cry of warning, Jeremy heard a siren approaching.

"Yes," he said.

Anna turned slowly away.

❧ nineteen ❧

Nancy burst out the door. It swung back and forth behind her as she marched down the short length of hospital corridor to the waiting room. Her mother sat in the waiting room, rosary in hand, gazing with vacant tension out a window. A February snow was falling under gray skies.

"You have got to get him *out* of there!" Nancy said.

"What can I do?" Mary Ravine said. "He won't listen to me. He won't listen to anyone."

"Anyone but Anna!" Nancy threw herself down on the vinyl couch. "You don't understand, Mom. She's *fighting* the contractions."

"I know that, but why? I don't see why."

"It doesn't matter why! All that matters is they want to sedate her and Daddy won't let them! He's standing there like a big bulldog, snapping at anybody who tries to get close to Anna, with her giving out the orders. He's crazy, Mom! Can't he see that she's hysterical? It's a madhouse in there!"

"She was always good at influencing him," Mary Ravine said. "He always listened to her most."

"Has he been drinking?"

"A little. The worry, Nancy."

"A little. Oh my God. Two beers and he gets simpleminded. He's probably drunk. I mean he is in there literally threatening the orderlies. We'll have to bring him down with a tranquilizer dart or something. This is impossible! Can't you at least *try* to talk to him again? Or to Anna?"

"No one can talk to Anna now," Mary said solemnly.

Nancy fell silent, remembering how they had carried Anna out of the frigid woods earlier that night. She shuddered at the images—of Big Bill crashing through the underbrush, flashlight beam wavering among the dark trunks—of finding Anna in the snow, breath gusting, clutching at her stomach, crying "No, no, no!"—of her face tortured with a pain Nancy feared had cut too deep—

She sprang from the sofa.

"We've got to do *something!*" she said. "She can't fight the baby. It's got to be born!"

"She doesn't want it to be," said Mary.

"She's got no choice! She doesn't have to keep it. She can put it up for adoption. *We'll* take it, Brook and me. It's Jeremy's—"

"No one will take care of that baby but me," Mary said.

"This is useless," Nancy said. "Come on, you're coming with me. Will you try?"

An angry black orderly stood guard at the door of the delivery room.

"Has anything changed?" Nancy asked.

"I just hope he wears himself out," he said, "before that girl does herself some real harm. Go on in. It's a standoff."

The labor room was dim. At Anna's request, her father had cut all lights except for a bedside lamp. Anna writhed in the pool of light, white hospital gown and white sheets like the mound of snow Nancy had helped pull her from earlier that night. Big Bill sat beside Anna, holding her hand with a fierce expression. Bullet-headed, hairless and large, he looked like a demon. Two nurses, an obstetrician, and an orderly stood ranged at the dark wall near the door. Nancy and Mary joined them.

"The contractions are growing stronger," one of the nurses whispered, "but she's breathing against them. I think she's in transition already. Her legs are cramping. You can see them shaking. It must hurt like hell."

"My mother's going to try and talk to them," Nancy whispered in return.

"Here," said the second nurse, holding out a stainless-steel bowl. "Give her these ice chips to take to him. And this cloth. She's sweating like crazy. Have him feed her a few chips."

In the shadowy room, Mary pressed back against a piece of gleaming equipment that had been wheeled in from delivery. Her broad face was a mass of wrinkles, her short hair roughly combed. Nancy gave her the bowl and squeezed her hand, feeling a welling up of pity for her. This was the birth of her first grandchild.

"Mrs. Ravine?" The obstetrician, a young black woman, slid closer. "I think you should understand that this is not the end of the world. Your daughter's baby will be born no matter what she does, and I'm sure it will be just fine—"

Nancy caught the two nurses exchanging dubious glances.

"She's healthy, she could have the child at home," the obstetrician continued, "but she's suffering from what we call prepartum hysteria, and I think it would be best if we could sedate her for the actual delivery."

Mary took the bowl of ice and stepped to the twilight edge of the circle of light, her short, thick body moving heavily. She called to her husband.

"Bill. I brought some ice and a towel, Bill."

He squinted. "Mary?" he said in his harsh, New England–accented voice. "Tell them fellas to go away. We're okay in here. Anna and me are fine."

"She's hot, Bill. She needs this ice."

"Ice? We don't need no ice. You want ice, Anna?"

Anna's face on the pillow was white and beaded with sweat, her black eyebrows like streaks of charcoal over the wide-set, staring green eyes, her hair a tangle of stormy wisps.

"No," she rasped. "Make them go away, Daddy."

"I tried that already, honey. They won't go. Should we charge 'em?"

The contractions came and Anna said nothing through set teeth. Her eyes crushed shut. Her hand tore from Big Bill's and clutched at her mountainous stomach. Big Bill brushed away the hair that flailed across her brow.

"She *is* hot, ain't she?" he mused. "You *are* hot, Anna. We better get some a that ice. Come on with that ice, Mary."

Mary heaved a deep sigh and walked forward, the bowl held out like the serving dishes Nancy had seen her carry so many times. But as she entered the pool of light, she halted, half in shadow, like a planet whose face is always turned to the sun.

"Bill," she said. "The doctor says Anna's gonna die."

The obstetrician took a step. Nancy reached out and put a restraining hand on her arm.

"Bah, what's she know," Big Bill growled.

"She's a doctor, Bill," Mary said in a weary, familiar, explanatory voice. "She says if they don't put her under she's gonna rupture."

Nancy heard Anna say, "Don't believe them, Daddy." The words, desperate and weak, sent a chill through her.

"We don't believe any a that," Big Bill announced.

"It's true, Bill," Mary grew angry. "Are *you* a doctor? Is Anna a doctor? She's gonna have bleeding . . ."

She turned to the obstetrician, at a loss to continue the lie.

Nancy gripped the obstetrician's arm, pleading with

her eyes. The doctor nodded her dark head. She marched to Mary's side.

"You get back!" Big Bill said, pointing a stubby finger.

"It's true, Mr. Ravine," the obstetrician said. "What your wife says is true. Anna must be sedated at once. She's already hemorrhaging—" The doctor launched into a catalog of possible dangers while Anna clawed at the air, begging with her father not to listen.

But slowly, he did begin to listen. Nancy watched the transformation, wondering if the words were sinking in or if the drinks were merely wearing off. He fell still, blinking.

Finally, he lowered his face to Anna's.

"Did you hear what the doctor said, Anna? Did you hear? We got to take care of you, honey."

". . . don't believe . . . don't believe . . ."

The obstetrician gestured at the orderly. The orderly gathered Mary and Nancy, escorting them out the door.

The corridor was blindingly bright after the claustrophobic gloom of the labor room. The door shut behind them. Nancy crossed the fingers of both hands and held them up.

Mary sagged against the wall.

The guard orderly rushed to her side, and with Nancy's help ushered her to the waiting room.

As Mary Ravine drank from a paper cup, Nancy saw her father emerge from the labor room. He was alone. His large frame drooped. His face was dead. He gazed around as if lost in a featureless world.

Nancy went to him.

"They give her the needle," he said, feebly mimicking the procedure.

"Come on, Daddy. Let's sit and wait."

Nancy led him to the waiting area. As they sat silently with cigarette-smoking patients, she became aware of a tall, gangling man in a gray suit standing at the far end of the corridor, the white sky showing behind him through a window. He was talking secretively with one of the nurses from the labor room.

Armand questioned the nurse in rough, heavily accented English. Thanking her again, he broke off and headed for the stairway. Descending six bleak, concrete levels, he emerged into a large and empty waiting room. Part of a newly modernized but still-unopened section of the hospital, it looked like an airport departure gate. There was only one passenger, a slim, silver-haired gentleman who looked up anxiously. It was Jean Colombe.

Armand spoke in coarse Parisian: "They have sedated her."

Colombe questioned his driver closely, bursting into irritation over details he had failed to wring from the nurse. Then he fell back in his chair and poured himself another brandy from a bottle resting on a bare magazine table. Armand stood motionless, like a switched-off machine, his long face impassive, hands folded over his belt buckle.

Colombe drank, lit a cigarette, and rubbed his face, feeling stubble. He realized he had forgotten to shave. *I must look like hell,* he thought. *I feel like hell.*

"None of them have any idea I am here?" he asked for perhaps the eighth time.

Armand shook his head.

"And you, Armand, you have no idea, either?"

Armand remained impassive.

"Ah, you know," said Colombe. "But you do not approve."

"I think that you should be at the seaside resting," Armand said. "After your coronary—"

"Coronary! That was no coronary. My heart is sound."

The words were empty bravado, and Colombe knew it. He knew Armand knew it. Colombe felt ill from too much drink. He stubbed his cigarette out in a full ashtray. From too little sleep. Ill and filthy and . . . corrupted.

After the debacle in Martha's Vineyard, he had returned to Paris, advising himself that there was no point in being further concerned with Anna. That the world was full of young women, he knew only too well. He did not regret losing Anna. He only regretted making a fool of himself over her. That pitiful bribe! If he had schemed to appear in the worst possible light, he could have done no better. He had fulfilled all of Anna's most wretched expectations, lived up to her starkest accusations. For a moment, in that sad apartment, Anna had made him feel bared and cheap. And in retrospect he could not shake the disturbing thought that he had wanted nothing else. There was no cunning in his bribe, no hope that it would work. It had been a double act of cruelty, to Anna—and to himself.

Yes, there were young women in throngs. As the years accumulated, Colombe had come to appreciate the stages of their development and ripening. The world was always replenished with new supplies of them, growing from too-young girls en route to the fading of middle age.

Yet he himself had begun to fade. Not gradually, he realized, but all at once, as if a fifteen-minute sojourn in a small apartment in Martha's Vineyard had terminated his youth. The mirror no longer reflected a dashing, distinguished man in his midfifties (and looking, as everyone said, not a day over forty—except for the fine, silvered hair). Now it showed old age. Now it whispered death . . .

And death had nearly come. A stroke had felled Colombe in the act of sex. He toppled in bed, seized by gigantic pain, his field of vision filled with a terrified, naked girl.

The girl fled to a telephone. Faintly, he could hear her dialing, shouting for an ambulance. The sound grew more remote, and another girl entered Jean Colombe's bedroom.

She was small and thin, and she wore a wedding dress. With her came a reek of gasoline, a sharp sting of ashes. She drifted through the grandly molded door and to his bedside. She laid a cool, white hand on Colombe's bare chest, and the pain fled.

He had awakened in a hospital.

. . . Armand was right. He belonged at the seaside. The doctors counseled rest. But months passed, and he tired of inaction. A measure of health returned, but something more central and vital had vanished forever, he feared.

A great contempt grew in Colombe as he convalesced, and because he could not distract himself, he began to think. It was bad for him, because his thoughts returned again and again to a sad little apartment in Martha's Vineyard.

Until he himself returned to America, to find Anna.

He had found only wreckage.

Tossing back his glass of brandy, Colombe lit another cigarette.

"Armand," he said, "perhaps you should go back up. Here, drink this. No, do. Perhaps it will warm you, old friend. Its taste is bitter enough to me. Go up, now. There is no reason you should waste your time with an obsessed old man. And Armand! I must know everything, do you understand?"

The elevator carried Armand to the obstetrics floor. As the doors chugged open, he glimpsed his informant rushing down the corridor with a tray. He loped after her and caught her.

"I can't talk to you now!" she hissed.

"What is wrong?" Armand asked.

The nurse pulled away, Armand followed.

"She's—the doctor won't sedate her any more deeply. She's—it isn't taking. I can't understand it."

"Is there still trouble?"

"She tried to get off the delivery table," the nurse said in hot exasperation. "We're having to hold her down. She can't be conscious, though. She just can't."

The nurse accelerated to the waiting area. Armand hung back, watching the Ravines—sister and parents —rise anxiously.

Signaling her mother and father to wait, Nancy fell in beside the nurse. Freckled and red-haired, she reminded Nancy of Gwen.

"Is everything going all right?" she asked.

"Not really," the nurse said. "The doctor doesn't want to up the general anesthesia, and what we've given her hasn't put her out completely. She's struggling like a devil. We've got her arms strapped and two orderlies pinning her, but whatever it is that's gotten into that girl, it's cutting through the sedatives as the contractions get stronger."

"Can't you just—knock her out?"

"The *doctor*," the nurse said with mild contempt, "believes too much general anesthesia can cause collateral damage to the newborn. I think we ought to put her out and go for a cesarean, but no." The nurse halted at the door to the delivery room. Balancing the tray, she wiped her forehead with a sleeve and said: "You know, this can all be so easy sometimes—but it doesn't get much worse than this."

Nancy looked at the wall.

"What's she afraid of?" she asked. "What?"

"Afraid," the nurse said. "Afraid is too small a word. She's terrified. She's—you should hear her in there—my God, she seems to think she's carrying a monster. She rambles on about the dead, about the children of the dead. She's more than hysterical; she's at the edge."

"Can I come in?" Nancy asked.

"I don't think so," the nurse said. "We've got too many cooks in there already."

"She's my sister."

"Listen, I've got things to do. If you slip in in a minute or two, it's got nothing to do with me, okay? Take heart, now. We'll pull her through."

Nancy marked time outside the door. After a few minutes had passed, she edged it open and slid inside.

The sharp smells of ozone and antiseptic bit the lining of her nostrils. The delivery room was bright and crowded. Through a gap in shifting bodies, Nancy caught a glimpse of Anna under a central bank of operating lights. Her arms were immobilized by straps on the delivery table. Her legs were spread and cocked into stirrups. An orderly held each thigh and hip. Two nurses were present. The obstetrician, sweat coating her brown face, hovered over Anna, a dazed-looking medical student by her side. Beside the table, an anesthesiologist sat monitoring dials while a colleague conferred with him.

The bodies shifted again, and Anna was hidden. Nancy clung to the wall, bumping into an instrument table that gave off a loud rattle. No one seemed to notice.

"The cervix isn't dilating adequately," she heard. "I think we should cut. This has gone too far."

"Not yet," she heard the obstetrician say. "I won't do a section while she's convulsing like this."

"More general won't hurt her," the red-haired nurse put in.

"But it may the baby," the obstetrician said curtly.

Nancy listened, heart thumping, dimly aware that in the pressured tones of the discussion she could sense a routine gone out of control, a swerve into confusion from the ordered, standard procedures of delivery. Time stretched and twisted. Nancy fixed on the milling, white-coated bodies, the gleam of stainless steel, and the minor waves of shock that passed through the group when a thump or a moan announced particularly vivid resistance from the swollen, tortured, hidden body on the delivery table. Nancy bit her thumbnail until she tasted blood.

Finally the obstetrician said: "The end. Time for a spinal. Nurse, C-section."

Nancy heard a faint sigh of relief. The level of

tension seemed to drop several notches, and she herself was glad it would soon be over.

"Hold her. Bear down. Damn! All right, on her back again."

Instruments clattered. The red-haired nurse glanced through to Nancy and gestured her to leave. Nancy stayed put.

"Wait a second," she heard the obstetrician say. "Hold on . . . baby's crowning. Forceps."

Then, with a suddenness that shocked Nancy, a baby, wet and rubber-red, was held up by the legs. She couldn't see the whole child, but it was a girl. She waited for the newborn's wail.

None came.

Nancy pressed forward to the edge of the show, fingernails cutting into her palms. Suddenly a piercing shriek cut across the light-flooded delivery room. The obstetrician laughed.

"I don't think little darling likes it here," she said. She handed the baby to the red-haired nurse, who carried it to a plastic bassinet. Nancy surged toward the bassinet.

"She's just fine," the nurse said with a smile. "Nice little head of hair on her too. Black as silk."

Nancy craned over to gaze at the tiny, shut-eyed creature. *I want one*, she thought.

"They didn't have to cut?" she asked.

"No. I guess the spinal got things going. Just when we'd given up." She lowered her voice to a whisper. "That doctor is a hippy, if you ask me. This whole circus wasn't obstetrics, it was midwifery."

Nancy realized how exhausted she had become. She groped to a chair and sat down heavily. She felt faint and blissful at the same time.

The nurse said, "You'll be all right?"

Who cares if I'm all right? Nancy thought. She got up and tottered to Anna's side. The white-smocked bodies parted.

Anna's face was pale and drained. She stared with

glassy eyes, lying absolutely motionless, as if the life that had been pulled from her had drawn out her own vitality. Nancy glanced at the obstetrician. The woman's lips were set with tension. Nancy's heart sank.

"I'm sure she'll be fine," the obstetrician said.

Nancy understood: fine physically. She turned back to Anna and smiled down.

"You did great," she soothed. "You did just great." She wondered if Anna could hear or if she were beyond hearing. Beyond hearing forever.

"It's a girl, Anna. Did they tell you that? A beautiful, healthy baby girl, Anna."

Anna's face stirred. She gazed up with mute, pleading incomprehension.

The glass of water crashed to the floor. Mary Ravine snatched tissues from Anna's bedside and bent in a timeless gesture to stop the spreading flood.

"God, I'm clumsy!" Nancy apologized. All the time she kept her eyes on Anna. She gave no reaction to the noise. She sat motionless against her pillow, her arm still outstretched to receive the glass.

"Mary," Big Bill said. "Let the orderly come and do that."

Nancy paced to the opposite side of the room. Wrapping her arms around herself, she stared out the window at the parking lot. Sunshine fell brilliantly on newly fallen snow. A team of maintenance men were working around a jeep with snow plow attached. They seemed far away.

She tried not to look at Anna, to forget her for a few moments and compose herself. But it was as if she could still see her, reflected in the windowpane, a thing of wood or stone, with unblinking eyes.

When Nancy turned, she saw her father gently take hold of Anna's arm and replace it in her lap. Big Bill smiled.

"She moved, though," he said. "Did you see it? She

242

lifted her arm for the water. Good girl, Anna." He kissed her forehead.

Anna's sudden motion had scared the wits out of Nancy. The glass had slipped from her hand. She wished she could take Anna's gesture as a sign of hope, but it had been so rigid and automatic—like something out of a mental hospital. Not a sign of life, but a sign of derangement.

Nancy fled the room, trying to beat down the frayed, sleepless agitation that was boiling in her head.

In the hall she came upon the tall, gangling man again, conferring with the red-haired nurse. They fell silent as she stalked past.

Suddenly, Nancy spun and stepped between the nurse and the man.

"Who are you?" she asked angrily. "Why are you snooping around here?"

The nurse broke in: "This gentleman's wife is a patient here—"

"No she isn't," Nancy interrupted. "Who are you really?"

"My wife is having a baby," Armand said.

Nancy squinted at him. His accent was French. An idea popped into her mind, and she blurted it out.

"You're Jean Colombe," she said. "No. No, you can't be." Then it occurred to her—Brook had described him: "You're his driver, Arnold."

Armand ducked his head.

"Armand," he said.

The nurse walked away briskly.

"She's been feeding you information," Nancy said.

"Yes," said Armand.

"Is he still so interested?"

"He is interested in nothing else."

Nancy caught a sadness in Armand's eyes. She remembered Anna's, fixed and empty.

"Jean, is he here? Where?"

243

Armand pointed downward.

They rode the elevator together. It was crowded with morning traffic. Nancy had come to know the rhythm of the hospital. Three days of powerless, hopeless waiting had taught her.

Armand stepped out onto an empty floor. Nancy followed. In the center of a bare, modern waiting area sat a distinguished-looking man, slim as an arrow, impeccably tailored in a deep blue suit. But as Nancy drew closer, she could see Colombe was disheveled, badly shaven, his eyes lined with black circles, the suit rumpled. It was scarcely the man Anna had so often described.

Colombe shot to his feet, glaring at Armand. Armand shrugged.

"Mr. Colombe," Nancy said, putting out her hand. "It's good to meet you. I feel in your debt."

"In my debt, Miss Ravine? Whatever for? Will you sit down?"

"No, I can't. Do you really love her, Mr. Colombe?"

"If that question prefaces a request for me to leave, then the answer is no."

"But if it doesn't?"

"Miss Ravine, I have sat in this place for an eternity, gathering what news I could through Armand. Every hour it has been my only wish that Anna should recover. He has not seen her; you have. Can you tell me anything more hopeful than that infernal nurse has been able to provide?"

"No, I can't."

"You'll forgive me if I sit."

Nancy watched him light a cigarette. He held it in crabbed fingers. She perched at the edge of a chair opposite him. A bottle of brandy sat on the magazine table between.

"If you would like your twenty-five thousand dollars back," she said, "Brook can start repaying now."

A wash of agony passed over Colombe's face.

"Is this why you've come?" he asked. "As an emissary for him?"

"He's ashamed he accepted your money—"

Colombe got to his feet and began pacing, smoke trailing in the air.

"No more than—not one hundredth as much as I am to have offered it!" he cried. "You must feel a great contempt for me, Miss Ravine. You and your sister both."

"I think that right now Anna isn't feeling much at all."

"So this was the debt to which you referred?"

"No. Not the money. You drove Brook away from Anna and back to me. He was mine first." Nancy blushed at the childishness of this last statement.

Armand said, "Some good came of it, then."

"Armand tries ceaselessly to cheer me up," Colombe explained. "Thank you, Armand. Great good, I hope," he said to Nancy, "great good for you, great shame for me."

Nancy sat back in the chair. No, she thought, this was scarcely the man Anna had described, or even the well-dressed devil Brook had dealt with. She glanced around the barren room.

"Have you slept here?" she asked.

"In a manner of speaking. Don't pity me. But Armand will be glad to get back to a bed, won't you, Armand?"

"I will be glad when your mind is at peace," Armand replied in French.

"Then perhaps you shall never be glad. Be glad of a bed, Armand. It is surer."

"Can I have a cigarette?" Nancy said. "I think I need one."

Armand moved quickly to offer her one from the pack on the table. He lit it with his lighter and brought her an ashtray.

Nancy felt the nicotine rushing to her head. It was

strong tobacco and it made her dizzy. She balanced the cigarette carefully in the ashtray.

Not looking at him, she asked: "Will you come up with me, Mr. Colombe? Come and see Anna?"

"She despises me. So much that she taught me to despise myself."

"I hope so, Mr. Colombe. I hope . . . that she orders you out of her room."

Colombe's face drained.

"Monsieur," Armand said, rushing to his side.

"Leave me alone," Colombe said. Then to Nancy: "Very well, I understand. Very well, I will hope the same."

As the crowded elevator rose, it seemed to Nancy that Colombe was dying. Armand stood close by, watching him carefully, with barely masked concern. They emerged onto the obstetrics floor.

Colombe led the way, moving down the corridor as if he knew every tile and lamp, walking like a man determined to receive the guillotine with dignity.

Mary and Big Bill stood outside the room.

"Don't go in," Big Bill whispered. "She wants to be alone."

"How do you—" Nancy began.

"He doesn't," her mother said wearily.

"I know," Big Bill insisted. "I know what Anna wants. She don't have to talk. I can tell."

Her expression a blank wall of worry, Mary took her husband's arm and guided him gently to the waiting area.

"You see how it is," Nancy said, watching them go.

"I am sorry," said Colombe.

Nancy put her hand to the knob and pushed open the door.

"I'll leave you with her," she said.

As Colombe entered the sun-bright room alone, the door shut loudly behind him. He moved slowly, as if afraid to disturb the still air that surrounded Anna's bed. Her face, changed but familiar, sent a double ache through him. Nancy had told him what to expect, but he was unprepared for her stare.

She seemed to be gazing through him, through the walls of the room, through the hospital—through the world and into another world.

He pulled a chair to her bed and sat, hands folded tensely on his knees.

"Good morning, Anna. It's Jean. Jean Colombe. I have come to tell you something"—he hesitated—"and I will tell it even if you cannot hear. I know that I sicken you. But though I sicken you, I love you more than anyone living. I am empty and I am dead inside. It is just as you said. It is worse; now I know it and it is inescapable. The joy of life is over for me."

Colombe paused, waiting for a reaction.

"I have come," he continued, "to make an offer. I know you are thinking, 'This is the same Jean. Always negotiating, always buying and selling.' But this is my offer, Anna: I offer you everything.

"Whatever you want, you shall have. I will take in your daughter and raise her as my own. I will love her because she is a part of you. She will be my heir—"

Anna shuddered. Colombe broke off. He began to recall, in stark flashes, what Armand had reported: Anna's thrashing terror of childbirth, her struggles, her resistance. It dawned upon him that Anna had walled herself up as an attempt to flee reality. He wondered . . .

He leaped in.

"Or we can escape," he said urgently. "Anna, we can escape together. You can leave this hospital and these people. Your daughter. I can see to it that she receives the best of care, Anna. If you don't wish to—" He choked on the words. He had come to make an offering, to cleanse himself. Now he was holding out a deal which would permit Anna to bury her child, forget her own baby.

Still, Colombe sensed, with the powerful intuition of a born trader, that this was what Anna wanted most.

He could arrange it for her. She could never see the child again, yet be assured—as only liberal applications of wealth could assure—that the girl was well cared for.

It was poisonous. But he needed her.

"If you don't wish to see your daughter again," he said quietly, "I can make those arrangements. We can hide from this world, this past. Without me, you might be trapped. But I can give you freedom."

With a sudden, mechanical motion, Anna threw off her covers.

Colombe scraped his chair back. Hope welled up bitterly.

"I'll see to it that she is raised in a fine home," he said. "With loving guardians. Anna, come to me. I'll make it all possible."

Anna swung her feet off the bed and placed them flat on the floor. She seemed barely human, like a machine assembled from beautiful parts, awakened for the first time.

Colombe rose feverishly. He hunted out her robe, threw it over her shoulders. His desperate face bent close to her beautiful one.

"Will you come with me, Anna? Come with me now?"

Anna Ravine held out her hand.

PART THREE

five years after

❧ twenty ❧

Gwen threw herself into a chair, looking ridiculous and pretty in a long, near-Victorian gown of mauve linen. She twiddled her lace trim and watched Nancy Ravine staring anxiously at her own reflection in a full-length mirror.

On the verge of tears, Nancy clutched the sides of her head.

"It doesn't fit!" she moaned.

"It fits, Nancy," Gwen said.

"Look at this bodice!" Nancy plucked at her chest. "This? This fits?"

She filled the mirror, head to toe, in a single cascade of white.

"Oh why don't people just get married naked?" she asked.

"So do it," Gwen said. "Get married naked. Serve Budweiser in cans. Cut a Twinkie. Just don't turn crazy on me, please."

"You're supposed to be supportive!"

"All right, then," Gwen said. "I'll be supportive: it fits."

"No it doesn't!"

"It would if you'd breathe. I mean if you'd inhale and then exhale like a normal person, then it would fit."

"Mother!" Nancy called. "Mom!"

Mary Ravine streaked in—short, compact, dressed in a cloud of pink organdy, she hovered around her youngest like a wrestler about to engage. In her hand she held a threaded needle.

"Breathe," she said.

"That's what I told her," Gwen said.

"I *am* breathing," Nancy said.

"Let down your straps," Mary Ravine said.

Nancy did it and stood waiting, trembling in her brassiere. Her mother's hand flew quickly over the bodice, deepening a dart.

"Put it up," she said.

As if a miracle had happened, Nancy's face broke into a look of exultation. She embraced her mother fiercely.

"Now you're perfect," Mary said.

Nancy regarded herself in the mirror. She checked the bodice. She posed left profile, right. She hugged her mother again.

"You guys are great," Gwen said. Now it was her turn to clutch the sides of her head. "This wedding thing," she said.

"Is it raining?" Nancy asked with sudden tension. The ready room was windowless, tucked into a back corner of the old church.

"And who cares if it is raining?" Mary Ravine asked.

"It's raining," Nancy said with dumb resignation.

Gwen got up. "Do you expect God to regulate the weather," she asked, "which falls on farmers and lovers and everybody—"

Nancy held herself stoically.

"It's raining on my wedding day," she intoned.

"It's sprinkling!" Gwen said, stalking around and waving her hands in what could have been a little antirain dance.

Mary said, "Everyone wants everything perfect on their wedding day."

A rap rap rap sounded on the door.

"Come in," Nancy said.

A face shoved in, between doorknob and jamb.

"It stopped raining," a small girl piped.

"Come in, Toni, come in," Nancy said irritably.

The girl entered, carrying a bouquet and staring with amazement at Nancy's dress. A petal fell from one flower. Toni quickly stooped to pick it up, trying to fix it back onto its stem. She was a bony little creature just five years old, with fine brown hair, in a mauve linen gown that was a miniature of Gwen's.

"Perfect," Gwen said. "Picture perfect."

"Oh Gwen," Nancy said. "I'm nervous."

They were alone in the room. Gwen hovered at the door, ready to rush off and take her place at the altar with the other bridesmaids.

"What's to be nervous?" she said. "You walk down the aisle, you repeat what the minister says, you walk back up the aisle. Then everybody makes a fuss over you and you eat cake."

Nancy put a hand over her stomach. For a moment she went as white as her gown and her crown of baby's breath.

"Unsure?" Gwen asked. "Listen, I've got a motorcycle parked out back with the motor running . . ."

She drew closer and put a hand on Nancy's shoulder.

"After five years with him, Nancy, still unsure?"

Anger flared briefly in Nancy's eyes.

"He betrayed me once," she said simply.

"Gwen!" a voice called offstage.

"That's me," Gwen said. "Let it go, Nancy. He betrayed you and you forgave him, remember? You forgave."

Nancy shook her head quickly, gulping back a sudden rush of bitter tears.

"He betrayed me," she said. "I can never forget that."

Gwen gave a fast kiss, a squeeze of the hand.

"See you at the guillotine!" she called, and was gone.

For a while, it seemed a long while, Nancy waited alone in the room. A smell of church wafted through the open door. A certain kind of love had closed to her forever, Nancy thought, but she must forget that. Brook was at the altar for her. Not an icon, not a god, but Brook, Brook weak and strong.

Nancy Ravine heard the wedding march begin. She lifted the hem of her gown.

"Look serene," she whispered to herself.

Somebody gave Toni a push. She stumbled the first few steps and then recovered, pacing solemnly the way they had practiced. She held her bouquet tightly in a double fist, staring fixedly at the strip of white tissue that ran down the long, long aisle. She had never felt so alone and exposed, and besides that there was something in her shoe, probably a bug. She hummed along with the music to give her confidence.

Toni heard the chorus of sentimental ohhhs going up on either side, but not for a second did she consider that they might be for her. Nobody paid much attention to her usually. She wished she could stop and shake the bug out of her shoe. But when she glanced up from the floor, she saw oceans of people staring at her. Some of the women were dabbing at their eyes with handkerchiefs. Toni wondered if something was going wrong. It briefly occurred to her that someone had put a bug in everybody's shoe.

She got to the altar and took a false step to the right. Somebody hissed "Toni! This way!" and she stepped to the left to join the line of bridesmaids.

Aunt Nancy and Big Bill marched up, Big Bill looking huge and a little zany in his morning coat, Nancy's dress going swish, swish. The music stopped, but Toni kept humming. She heard gentle laughter, then somebody rapped her on the head and she fell quiet.

Then it was boring for a long time. Toni looked at the man on the cross and at the tall, colored windows. Gwen on one side kept nudging her to stop doing things: stop shifting from one foot to another, stop looking straight up at the ceiling, stop sniffing. Finally something happened: Brook bent down and kissed Nancy. Toni looked on with mild interest. The crowd murmured contentedly, like a cat. Toni heard Brook say, softly but distinctly, "I love you."

And that, she knew, was good.

"Come on!" a small boy in a small suit yelled, tugging at Toni's shoulder.

"You'll rip it!" she hissed. The receiving line in the church foyer had reached its end. The bridal party was stirring toward the grand exit to cars and the reception. But they had neglected to cue Toni, and so she stood forgotten by a column, tired from having to beam at people so much.

"But we found the way to the steeple!" the boy said.

"Oh yeah?" Toni glanced from side to side like an animal and ran off, with the boy leading.

They scurried onto the dais and behind the screen, through a low door, and around a corner. Toni found herself on a flight of the narrowest stairs she had ever seen. Childish voices called down from above. The boy's eyes flashed happily and he started up the steps.

Toni fell on her face. Undaunted, she collected herself, set her bouquet in a dusty window alcove, hiked her gown to forestall another stumble, and raced behind. From the children way ahead came sounds of joy and expectation. All Toni could think was, *I'm missing something*.

"Wait for me!"

Many steps up, as the staircase turned and spiraled, Antoinette Colombe collapsed in a sudden black exhaustion.

One chivalrous boy heard Toni's hard sigh and her fall and came running down to see to her.

"I saw such a beautiful woman," Toni said with a bleary smile, as if shaking off a fleeting dream.

"It's not much further," said the boy.

Toni surged to her feet. Face screwed up in determination, she launched herself up the stairs.

All at once, the musty old stairwell broke into a fresh, open space flooded with new sunlight. The planks were covered with bird spots, and in the cupola overhead Toni glimpsed birds fluttering among the bells, peering nervously at the intruders.

"Look!" cried the other children, two boys and a girl gathered at the railing.

Toni went to them, excited but infinitely careful of her dress, already hearing Aunt Nancy scold. She looked out.

"The whole world," she said in awe.

In fact it *was* the whole world, Toni's whole world: the whole—almost—of Martha's Vineyard. The town below, all white houses and shingle roofs, stretched to the docks. Beyond, to the west, the sun shone in a blue sky. In the eastern sky clouds sailed away, trailing ragged skirts and pouring down a mist of far-off rain onto the sea. The land lay gold that way, gold all ways, and it seemed to Toni that she could rule over the entire great island from her steeple.

She ran from rail to rail, taking in all the views, especially fascinated with the immediate town, so toylike and puny.

"They're coming out!" she said, pointing straight down.

On the church steps below came a white figure and a gray figure, around them a crowd.

"Let's spit on them," someone suggested.

Discussion followed, and the idea was rejected.

Toni watched as the New Bedford ferry crested in over the sea, toiling over its path, making for its temporary harbor. Toni liked the ferry, how it came and went and came again. She had often waited for Nancy or Brook on the dock, jumping up and down when they appeared on the gangplank, to be rewarded with a pat on the head or a light kiss on the cheek.

She watched the tiny passengers disembark. A cab left the dock, yellow and buglike. To her surprise, it crawled the streets and stopped just up the way from the church. Out got two men, little as dolls: a gray-haired man and a black-haired man. The younger one leaned on a cane.

❧ twenty-one ❧

Sometimes, in the dead of night, Anna Colombe would awaken between one pill and another. In the background, the long-acting sedatives flattened her anxieties to a distant, clanking hum. But still for fleeting moments she clutched at dim memories. Guilt sloshed back and forth like aquarium water. Anna would gaze around her extravagant bedroom, a room suffused with the perfume and moonlight of Provence. She would ask herself, *Why is this beautiful place so like a hell?*

Then the nurse stationed outside the door would come scurrying in with a fresh dose and a glass of water.

"Hush, madame, hush. It is only a nightmare."

And if Madame were more panicky than usual, or refused her pill, there was always the needle. How quiet Madame grew then, and the nurse could return to her chair and her book, and her musings on the torments of the very rich.

Morning. A brisk little whirlwind of cheerfulness descended on Anna in the form of a pretty maid with breakfast tray: croissants, café au lait in a bowl, a newly cut flower. The curtains flew open to reveal dazzling fall sunshine and a view down the hillside to the Mediterranean.

"Is it not a beautiful day?" the maid chirped in French.

"*Ils sont tous beaux,*" Anna said—they are all beautiful. Then suddenly: "Why do I have no mail? Why—" It was dawning on her; she switched to English. "Why, *never*, do I ever have any mail? There should be mail on this tray, shouldn't there?"

The nurse breezed in with a smile.

In the afternoon, Anna came in from poolside and wandered through the great, airy house. The walls were pastel stucco and the furnishings that costliest of rustic types, the true French Provincial. The effect everywhere was light, comforting, and understated. Anna wore a white maillot bathing suit, and had come in to escape the rays of midday. Even in her permanent daze she remembered the basic rules of beauty, and sun kills the skin's youth. She knew she was no longer beautiful. But still she remembered the rules of beauty.

She was no longer beautiful because—well, she had seen, especially in France, the most extraordinarily ugly women celebrated as sirens. And on a smaller scale, she met nearly every day, at the incessant entertainments Jean devised, financiers and aristocrats escorting women any other woman would recognize as plain.

Plain, if they were dead. But in life they glowed. An energy, a spirit—even such a simple one as that of lust and will—shone through them, transfiguring the ordinary flesh.

That light, Anna knew, had died in her.

At the living room, she veered right. The nurse was instantly beside her, catching Anna's elbow. Anna shrugged her off with an irritable "*laissez-moi!*"— leave me alone.

Crossing the living room, she dove down a hallway. For a moment she was lost: the hallway was like so many others. The halls of the shooting club came back from her childhood, the halls of the house in Tuscany. It was all a jumble. She laughed.

"I want to see Jean," she said carefully. "I know his office is here. Take me to it."

The nurse obliged cheerfully.

Jean was seated at a splendid Directoire desk. A computer terminal, sleek and modern, sat on it. Jean, gray and aristocratic, tapped at the keyboard.

"Am I in there?" Anna asked.

She drifted to the computer. She touched its casing. "I am, aren't I? I'm in there."

A little startled, Jean rose and embraced Anna, with that desperation that always took her by surprise.

"You are in here," he said, putting her hand on his chest.

Before dinner, Anna Colombe took a nap. It was almost always a good sleep, because she knew there was daylight on either side of it. Daylight was good because in daylight you did not have to turn inward for something to see. In daylight all the beauty Jean had bought was worth what he had paid.

And at night there were the pills.

But night was far away, and Anna directed the nurse to stay outside.

Anna had a lovely desk of her own, a piece of rolltop Americana in the south of France. And in it, hidden carefully, taped to the underside of one of the tiny drawers, was a card and a later clipping, both smuggled in by Armand.

The card was some months old now, the clipping not so old. The card invited Anna to the wedding of Miss Nancy Ravine to a Mr. Brook Halpern in Edgartown, Martha's Vineyard, in June. The clipping, from the society pages of the *New York Times,* told of same.

How furtively yet solemnly Armand had brought them, in a moment when the nurse was off. It seemed the old fellow had got religion or something; clearly he believed he was delivering the mail on behalf of some higher power.

So Anna, in her white bathing suit, sat looking at an old invitation.

That night, Anna dressed in floating silk—someone else did her shopping now—slid on heels, and went out into the garden to receive her guests.

It was Jean's conceit of the evening to have troubadour music in the walled garden. *Who are these people?* Anna wondered as she clicked across the terrace and down onto the walkways. The nurse stayed behind, on the lookout.

The caterers were busy. Anna knew all their faces, smiling over white uniforms, but the staff continued to produce novelty at the buffet.

"How do you do it, Anna?" a guest of arch sophistication asked.

"It's all in the machine," Anna said. "I don't do a thing."

The sounds of lute and mandolin danced through the air. There is no conversation so sure, so empty, as that of those who know "everyone." It makes a beautiful noise. Add the season, add the food, add that perfect parcel of ancient land where heretics and poets burned to scent the real estate with old romance —and get the sum of the world that Jean Colombe had made for his bride.

They were friendly faces. Some Anna knew from way back, and these took both her hands and told her with worried gladness, "How *good* you look!" Everyone had a compliment or a story for her, a piece of gossip. A few of the men, thin and cultured, could always coax a laugh out of her with their savage, telling wit. Everyone was beautifully dressed, in that relaxed, almost drooping fashion of those who do not need to posture. Champagne was always available on a proffered silver tray, but the passing rage—and more costly in France—was Jack Daniel's Tennessee Sour Mash.

Suddenly, Anna realized she had finished a first circuit—met everyone. For an instant she stood beneath a poplar tree by the ivy-covered wall. *How apart I am,* she thought peacefully. She tilted up her face.

Above, stars filled the awesome night sky. Quiet, twinkling, noble—the stars, Anna felt sure, were the very richest of them all.

She laughed aloud. Two unknown faces turned toward her, already politely amused. Anna waved a hand at the dome of heaven. "Wealthy," she said. "Every last one of them."

Actually, the couple seemed to get it. "They do have style," said the man, who looked like a round little king. "They keep the most outrageous hours and still look fresh," said the woman, a round and perfect match for her mate. "But too many of them for a proper aristocracy," the husband rejoined with a big grin.

"Some shine brighter than others," Anna said, gazing upward dizzily. "But they all shine. The sky must be a democracy."

That finished the evening's political discussion. *Where on earth is Jean?* Anna wondered. She gave a little bow to her two guests.

As she wound through the excellent mob, Anna heard a rising commotion. She was not too good anymore at figuring the direction of sounds, but this seemed to be coming from the buffet tables along the far wall.

On the buffet, a small girl was stamping her feet, brandishing an immense spoon, and yelling in English for her Uncle Bennie. The girl was blond and wore a blue pinafore, but as Anna cut through the crowd and caught sight of her, all she saw was a tiny Fury.

"Uncle *Ben-*nie!"

Uncle Bennie made his appearance. Uncle Bennie

was a man of just-fading youth, a little portly, with huge pale eyes and colorless hair.

"I don't understand," he said, hurrying toward the buffet. He addressed no one in particular. "I put her to bed with a Seconal and a tot of brandy. Maggie! Why aren't you napping like a good girl!"

Maggie hit her uncle on the head with the large spoon. He fell back, stricken.

The girl began crying for her parents, and the crowd—the way any crowd, even a good crowd, will sometimes do—began laughing. The girl kicked dishes of asparagus and baby aubergines off the table. The caterers shrieked and held their ears: "The vegetables!"

Then Anna came forward in her cloud of cream silk. She held out her arms, and for a moment she was beautiful again, ethereally beautiful.

The girl Maggie fell still, a scowl pasted on her face and the spoon held ready. Anna shook her mane of dark hair and soon was holding Maggie.

"Where are they?" Maggie asked.

"Shh. Shh," Anna whispered. "You're supposed to be asleep."

"But where *are* they?" Maggie wailed. "Uncle Bennie was supposed to take *care* of me!"

"Asleep," Anna said. "They're all asleep."

They spun together, Anna cradling the girl over her shoulder and crooning into her pink ear. But the last "asleep" came out in a sob.

Anna sank to the flagstones, embracing the girl.

"I'm sorry," she said.

But the child heard nothing, having drifted off to a weary, drugged sleep.

Jean Colombe strode into the clearing the crowd had made.

"Armand!" he shouted. "Who let a child in here! Who's responsible!"

Jean stalked around his wife and the dozing, close-held child. His face was pale, shot with red blotches.

Tall, thin—like something stretched taut—he circled his kneeling, sobbing, shattered wife.

"Who's responsible! Armand! You know that children are forbidden!"

One week later a messenger got through. That morning the staff drained the pool and cleaned it with long brushes and began refilling it with sparkling water. Pool and bathhouse were both in current mode —fine shades of gray, salmon, and cerulean with a faintly classical cast, pleasant and nouveau. From poolside the view included rugged mountains and pine forest.

Late afternoon, the caterers came like nomads and pitched their tents. The sun set gloriously. A cool breeze sighed in from the sea. A few lazy clouds hung, half silver half shadow, beside a giant moon. The lights threw up a mysterious, rippling aurora.

Around the light gathered another cloud of guests, inexorably gay. Even to the jaded, the house of that legendary, noble shark Colombe was an enchanting place, somehow reminiscent of a more enchanting time.

Jean circulated freely, keeping half an eye on his wife. He was convinced that Anna needed to be more closely monitored. Both a nurse and a guard now trailed her discreetly, dressed in evening clothes but still painfully obvious.

The incident of the previous week had subtly turned the tide of opinion against Anna. Jean Colombe was one of those few men who combine birth, wealth, looks, and native intelligence with will and personal genius. Many of the younger guests wondered at the wife he had chosen. At present Anna looked ghastly, a well-built woman with vacuous eyes, almost rigid with pharmaceuticals. "And not even a breeder," some would comment. The couple was childless, and from last week everyone knew that Anna suffered some fixation on the subject. When the observers, not necessarily malicious but earnestly curious, remembered that Jean had signed an unprecedentedly open marriage contract with Anna, they wondered what hidden persuasion this woman could work. It all bespoke awesome powers in the bedroom.

Somehow this unextraordinary person had become heiress to a kingdom. Not the boundaried kind, from the Rhine to the Atlantic, say. But the new kind, a network of interlocking corporate ownerships whose chief executives owed fealty to Jean Colombe.

That night, however, a messenger got through.

At the deepest of the ocean's depths, where sunlight never penetrates, the water is icy, black, and still. Life is sparse; only a few drifting sea creatures manage in the tremendous pressure. The creatures are translucent, finless, blind, and glowing. They pass months or years alone in the deep, between rare meetings with others of their own kind.

Anna drifted through the poolside crowd like one of these creatures. She was finally isolated, transparent, powerless, and blind. Sometimes, briefly, she seemed to glow, but it was a hopeless semaphore flickering in the deep. She let the glacial currents of the party tow her along, as inside her the sluggish currents of her veins carried their cargo of sedatives.

At one end the pool deck ended in a low wall. As Anna approached it, her bodyguard trotted closer, because over the edge was a sheer, short drop to a rugged slope of rock. Usually Anna enjoyed the view: the surrounding hills were bare and romantic. But tonight the hills did nothing for her. They seemed wispy and surreal. From far off she heard a whispering voice, and it was a long moment before she looked down and saw a man standing on the rocks below, half hidden by a scrub pine.

He was an old, sad-faced man, complexion stark white in the moonlight. There was a fear in his eyes as he nodded quickly to Anna, lifting a finger to his lips.

"Your daughter," he hissed.

The bodyguard came bullying up to the wall beside Anna. With invisible speed he drew out a revolver. The old man recoiled against a rock.

"Your daughter is sick!" he cried.

The bodyguard vaulted over the wall. Deftly, he collared the old man and struck him unconscious. Dangling the limp form like a puppet, the bodyguard held the man up.

Anna squinted down into the darkness. It was someone . . . someone from long ago. She felt herself being pulled from the wall, the nurse holding her arm and cooing into her ear, telling her to forget about this stupid incident and return to her guests.

But all Anna could hear was the tolling of a single word: *"Forget, forget."*

"Reveillez-vous, madame," came a harsh whisper. *"Reveillez-vous, je vous en prie."*

Anna surfaced from a dreamless dream of shifting orbs.

It was Armand by her bed, big and slab-faced, like a granite carving. Anna realized that weeks had passed since she had last seen Jean's man. She had dimly sensed a lessening of trust between Jean and Armand, after decades of loyalty. It only now occurred to her that when the time had come for a bodyguard, Armand had not been chosen.

Armand leaned forward anxiously, his heavy brows knitted.

"What is it?" Anna asked. She sat up achingly, her muscles sore from her long, dead sleep.

"Je viens de vous conduire a votre fille, si vous voudrez y aller."

Anna shook her head heavily.

"Say again. Say in English," she asked.

"I come to take you to your daughter, if you will go."

Suddenly Armand reached out and slapped Anna

crisply on the cheek, at the same time stifling her scream.

"You did not answer," he explained. "You only were staring for a long time."

He slowly removed his hand.

"How long?" Anna asked.

"Four minutes, five," said Armand. "I think you will go with me. I will help. You can stand?"

"Yes." Anna swung her legs from under the covers. She stood. "I remember . . . I remember a man, a dark-haired man, and a girl with pale, pale skin. Are these real memories, Armand, or did I dream them? Are you taking me to a dream? There is a daughter, isn't there? Alive, eating, and drinking."

"Be silent," Armand said. "Save your strength."

In the gloomy hallway, Anna said, "Where's the nurse—and bodyguard, where is he?"

"*Restez tranquille,*"—don't worry, Armand said. "Come, we will go out the terrace and through the east gate."

The house opened by gradations to the outside, a slow falling away of stuccoed walls to half-shuttered walls, to tiled rooms open at one end to the weather, then to portico and at last to terrace, where Jean Colombe ran gasping up to Anna, clutching his silk robe around him.

He glared at Armand.

"Old comrade," he said in French. "You are stealing from me." He glanced at Armand's waist, and Anna realized Armand was wearing a pistol in his belt.

"God forgive you, sir," said Armand. "I am ending an infamy."

"Anna," Jean said. "I know that you can't hear me, not really. That is my own doing, my own fault. If your daughter is dying, that is no fault of mine. I have sent funds, they have returned them. I have sent doctors—"

Anna, her head wobbling and trembling like an old

woman's, broke away from Armand and spat at Jean's feet.

On the plane out of Nice they had nothing to give her. Armand cursed his own stupidity; he had not planned.

Anna felt as if she were being wrung out and rolled on broken glass. The tendons inside her elbows and behind her knees were strung taut and tender. She shuddered in her seat, took the drink the stewardess offered. Armand held her arm, his face a mask of worry.

Anna looked out the window. The white light of the morning cloud-tops burned into her brain. She lowered the plastic shutter.

It was only the beginning.

On the ground at Kennedy the withdrawal symptoms grew savage. Airport security stopped Armand. They were concerned; he was fairly dragging an invalid. The woman belonged in a hospital. Could they help?

"No," Anna whispered to Armand. "He could track me there. He's expecting this. I know it. This—this is the long leash."

Armand did not understand all of Anna's English. But he watched as she pulled herself upright and began, in an exaggerated upper-class accent, to exclaim about nightlife, jet lag, and too much cognac on the plane. The security men departed.

Anna walked rigidly, without help, to the taxi stand outside the terminal. Armand waved a fifty-dollar bill and a cab jerked out of line for them.

In the backseat Anna said, "Oh Christ. Oh God," through clenched teeth.

Armand tried to comfort her. Autumn sunlight blazed through the taxi windows. Armand shut the Plexiglas partition between driver and passenger.

"*Il faut que nous aillions à l'hôpital,*" he muttered.

"No," Anna said. "Find a hotel somewhere. A bungalow. Something away from people."

For a while she fainted. When she woke up, she found that she had been wrong: she knew at last where they really kept hell. They kept it in a hotel room in a stunted harbor town in Massachusetts. A room with shuttered windows and none of the many nameless potions which her chemistry had come to depend on. Neurons long subdued began to fire violently at random: Anna convulsed, eyes bulging, pinned to her damp bed by the coiled arms of Armand.

❧ twenty-two ❧

At the eastern end of Martha's Vineyard, far from the towns, stood an old whaling captain's house. To the few neighbor children it had always seemed forbidding despite its whiteness, its spacious porches, its broad green lawns and shading trees. The children, perhaps, could sense the influence of the grave, with its broken spire, that dominated the backyard. It was the grave of the whaling captain's young wife, who died while he was off at sea in the year 1847.

Often Jeremy stared at the spire from the window of the study. Locally, the monument was a mystery: no one understood what the broken, tapering column of marble meant. But Jeremy understood too well.

It was a broken mainmast.

The house was not near the hospital, but that no longer mattered. The chief physician had said, the day before Toni came home, "She'll fluctuate, better and worse; sometimes much of one, other times much of the other." The doctor's voice trailed off, and in that trailing off Jeremy heard his daughter's own life leaking away. He cursed the doctor to his face and sent him away. He spent the night in the study of the huge house he had rented so exorbitantly. He drank and he looked out at the shadow the broken grave marker

270

cast in the moonlight, a black finger pointing toward him.

Someone was laughing at him.

Toni came home in a wheelchair. Jeremy lifted her up to the October sun.

"Spin me," Toni said. "Spin me."

An enormous parlor covered most of the first floor. Jeremy converted it to a huge, bright room for Toni. The various machines—oxygen, dialysis—rested in wooden cabinets. He banned flowers. Flowers were not for the living. He installed a projection television set with stereo sound. They watched *The Wizard of Oz* two dozen times. "If I on-ly had a brain," Toni sang.

Mark Dancer returned without Anna. "I gave the message," he said. One side of his face was a purple bruise.

A week passed. Then a month. Jeremy's dark eyes became caverns that brightened only for his daughter.

One day in November—the brightest, warmest November in living memory—a boy came to the door rattling a can for charity. Jeremy left Toni's bedside.

The boy stepped back on the porch, frightened.

"I came for the United Way, sir. For the needy."

Jeremy emptied his pockets and hurled bills and coins to the boards.

"Here!" he said. "And that is the last I give!"

In his heart Jeremy Penn had crossed out humanity. In the night he stalked the upper floors, a shadow behind the windows. In the late hours he raged against death; in the early hours before dawn he pleaded with it.

For a sign, the smallest sign, he would trade his own life. "I've cheated death," he said. "Now death cheats me."

But death, he knew, would make no trade. Cheated, he was pretending Jeremy to be worthless.

Yes, someone was laughing at Jeremy—pushing back his black cowl and opening his white, lipless mouth.

As for Toni, her eyes sparkled, because it had happened just like in the stories she had always told herself. In the end the father she had never known—wandering, mysterious, strong, and rich—had come back to her.

❧ twenty-three ❧

"No, wait here please, Armand," Anna said.

She stepped out of the car. All at once her autumn furs seemed too warm. Around the fine old house glowed an aura of eternal springtime that, oddly, made her shudder.

A woman in gingham answered the door. But uniform or no uniform, Anna knew a nurse when she saw one.

During the week, she had gathered stories to tell, introductions to make. They slipped through her.

"I," she said, "am the girl's mother."

From a window Anna saw Toni sitting on the lawn in yellow overalls and a sweater with crossed six-guns on it. She was introducing bears. She had always liked bears. Now she had dozens of them, so many that they constantly forgot each other's names, even as Toni herself seemed to forget more and more.

With a sure voice accustomed to instructing servants, Anna told the nurse in gingham to wait. She crossed the lawn and knelt beside the small girl.

"Hello, Toni."

Toni looked up, vaguely surprised. She saw a haggard woman, face drawn and pale, dark hair lackluster. A thin, featureless woman in a too-large fur coat.

"Hi," Toni said without enthusiasm. She went on walking bears at each other.

"Toni," Anna said. "Have you ever been told about your mother?"

Toni shook her head quickly. She glanced at Anna out of the corner of one eye.

"My mother is bad," she said.

With the suddenness of a charging animal, footsteps came rushing behind Anna. Before she could turn, a fierce hand jerked her to her feet.

She found herself suddenly facing Jeremy Penn. His face was hard and cold.

With a quick flash of guilt, he released Anna's arm. He stepped back, grasping and regrasping the handle of his cane. For a moment, as he gazed at her, his dark eyes saddened with pity.

"Golden, meet Ted," Toni was saying obliviously from her place on the grass.

"So you came," Jeremy said. "You came at last. For God's sake what kept you?"

There was anguish in his voice, but Anna failed to hear. She had waited for a torrent of recrimination, knowing she deserved it. Recrimination is what she heard.

"I had other appointments," she said coldly.

Nancy rushed down the stairs. Brook paced in front of the fireplace in a gray suit, brandy in hand.

"What is it?" he asked. "Get your fist out of your mouth."

"The things they're saying to each other!" Nancy sobbed.

The nurse strode in.

"Mr. Halpern," she said. "I think you'd better get Mr. Penn." She nodded through the doorway toward Toni's parlor suite.

When the nurse had left, Brook put his arms around Nancy.

"They hate each other," she said into his chest.

Nancy realized then, in Brook's arms, how kind and

safe her own world had become, remembered how he had asked her and asked her, "Will you marry me?"

"We've never talked that way," she said.

Brook smiled down at her, remembering otherwise.

"And never will," he said.

Breaking away, he took a last gulp of brandy.

"I'll get him," he said.

A cry sounded from the other room and Brook quickened his step.

A knock sounded on the door of the study. Anna and Jeremy fell silent.

"Yes?" Jeremy called.

"Jeremy," came Brook's voice. "You'd better come."

"I'll help," Anna said, trotting behind Jeremy as he strode, powerful and limping, to the study door.

Jeremy spun, raising his cane almost as if to strike.

"You can't help now, don't you see? The mountains won't move. Not faith, not hope"—he said them like curses—"not your last-minute maternal streak." He opened his palm in a gesture at the floor. "She's in hell down there. What you saw this afternoon, that was one of his jokes."

"His?" Anna shook her head in disbelief. It was as if he capitalized the word: *His*.

Jeremy turned to the wall.

"He lets her play sometimes, only to pull her back." He paused. "I forbid you to see her."

"Today I dreamed," Toni cried. "Today I dreamed."

She began to fret and toss, her face mottled red and white. The nurse prepared another injection, but Jeremy knew that the pain would climb through. He held the girl's hand.

The room was kept dim; light hurt Toni's eyes. At the edges of the big room, lamps burned low, throwing the nurse's shadow on the walls.

"I don't like the needle," Toni said in a fleeting moment of lucidity.

Jeremy held her arm straight while she cried out to be left alone. He stroked his daughter's forehead, slicking back the damp, loose hairline.

Anna stood paralyzed at the doorway.

Hours later the nurse lay dozing on a couch. Jeremy's chin hung to his chest. With an unconscious sigh, he slumped to one side, propped by his cane.

Anna crept closer to the bed. Her face was drawn and tense. One hand clawing back her hair, she stood over the sleeping form of her daughter.

Toni wore a pink tanktop. Her thin arms tightly embraced a pillow, her face pressed deep into its softness. The girl's eyelids were not so much closed as squeezed shut, as if to force sleep. Her small face was lined. Anna remembered reading once that man is different from the animals because he foresees his own death. She saw now that most children were animals; a child that could see her own death was a child no longer.

To be deprived of childhood seemed worse to Anna than to be deprived of life. All at once she understood the desperate attempts—Disneyland, toy sprees—that were lavished on dying children. Anything to maintain the illusion, anything to divert the wide, knowing, helpless eyes.

Anna sank into a chair on the other side of the bed from Jeremy. Her hands clenched together in her lap. The person in the bed was so little, so like her own self. For a long moment Anna's thoughts arched forward to the future: party dresses, boyfriends.

Toni stirred with an anxious moan. Her hands groped and folded the sheets. *They say,* Anna thought, *that for you there is no future.*

She could not believe, could not grasp it. So instead, it grasped her: she saw the coffin, small and white, saw the funeral gathering.

Again Toni stirred, with the same anxious restlessness, the same shallow sleep. Anna looked to the sleeping nurse. Maybe it was time for something, another painkiller.

All at once, Anna Ravine knew that she had failed. Life had taught her nothing, had made her selfish, ignorant, blind. Jean had never kept her prisoner: his whole wealth was founded on finer methods. He had given her what she wanted. He had struck a deal and she had signed on the dotted line.

On the other side of that dotted line, fenced out, had been a baby girl.

Now, if she could have torn her own heart out to fend the demon from that baby girl's body—

Anna fell by the bedside and buried her face in the bedclothes.

"Anything," she said. "I'll give anything."

Understanding came in a flash.

Anna gazed across the blankets at Jeremy asleep in his chair, black hair tousled over his pale face.

"Anything," she said.

An hour later, Toni awakened with an anxious moan. Her eyelids popped open, startled and a little insane.

"Hush. Hush," Anna said.

The girl turned and twisted, staring, seeing nothing, her small hands clutching the edge of her blanket.

Anna began to sing a lullaby, but it was useless. Toni whimpered, and the whimpers soon grew to cries, and the cries to screams.

Jeremy started out of his sleep. The nurse was up and on her feet like a seasoned soldier.

Toni screamed.

Anna stood up and knew that she had no understanding. There was only the inescapable, final Thing.

Dawn began to show at the windows, but it was only a reminder of a sleepless night, the beginning of a fall day when the sun would shine on orange leaves and irreparable pain.

Anna sat crumpled in a big chair, her hands over her face like someone stunned by a bright flash, her feet tucked beneath her.

She stirred and moaned. Twilight was enough to wreck her desperate sleep. Anxiety welled, throwing off the mantle of dreams.

Anna felt herself being lifted, just as, thousands of years past, her father would lift her from a doze in front of the TV set and carry her to bed. Far off, she heard the scurry of curtains closing, and darkness came again. From a great distance she felt someone standing and gazing down at her. A hand caressed her face, then pulled away as if burned.

"She's calling for you," a voice said.

"Who?"

The voice grew stern.

"Toni."

Anna was instantly active, grabbing at all sides for robe, clothes, anything.

Jeremy stilled her with his hand.

"She had a dream," he said. "She dreamed . . . she dreamed a woman came from the land of the dead and healed her. But that woman will never come, will she?"

Anna began to speak about hope. Jeremy put a finger to her lips.

"Where were you, friend?" he whispered. He gave a fast nod. "Come on," he said. "Let's go to her. You should be introduced while she can still know you. Where are your shoes?"

Jeremy knelt to search for them under the couch, and found none. Then he caught sight of a pair poking out where he had already groped. He wondered if he were growing delirious.

Touching her bare skin, Jeremy took one of Anna's small feet in his hand and fit on the shoe. It was more of a slipper, smooth and strangely warm.

Abruptly, Anna reached down and stayed Jeremy's arm before he could fit the second one.

Into her haggard face, life and beauty began to return. She took the slipper from him and held it up to the grainy light of the morning.

It was patchwork.

The sun gleamed and glanced on the diamonds of blue and green and yellow and red satin.

Bending down with monumental slowness, Anna softly pulled the patchwork slipper over her other foot.

Jeremy looked up at her, searching to understand.

SDG

AN ODYSSEY
INTO THE
OCCULT

Peter Straub
___Ghost Story 60106/$4.50
___Julia 49564/$3.95
___If You Could See Me Now 62423/$4.50

Harold Lee Friedman
___Crib 52365/$3.50
___Don't Tell Mommy 47257/$3.50

Ken Eulo
___The Ghost of Veronica Gray 54303/$3.95

Andrew Neiderman
___Imp 50786/$3.50
___Night Howl 60634/$3.50

Judi Miller
___Save The Last Dance for Me 83650/$2.75
___Hush Little Baby 43182/$2.95